A POUND OF FLESH, SORTA

Science Traveler Series

Book 7

A POUND OF FLESH, SORTA

Science Traveler Series

Book 7

J. L. Greger

Bug Press

New Mexico

A Pound of Flesh, Sorta

Bug Press
An imprint of IngramSpark
Bernalillo, New Mexico 87004
http://www.jlgreger.com

ISBN (paperback): 9780960028566
ISBN (EPUB): 9780960028573
Library of Congress Catalogue Number: 2020904567

DEDICATION

To the real Bug—my faithful and loving companion.

To the fictional Shylock for demanding a "pound of flesh" in the *Merchant of Venice*.

ACKNOWLEDGMENTS

I want to thank John Byram showing patience with me as he edited this manuscript. I also want to thank Barbara Hodges for designing the cover.

I appreciate the staff at the Albuquerque Wastewater Facility and the FBI Field Office in Albuquerque for allowing me to tour their facilities and answering my strange questions.

CHAPTER 1: Sara Almquist on Wednesday

Sara Almquist looked at the white parcel in front of her door. A brown UPS delivery van careened around the corner away from her home. This was typical when the doorbell rang at this time of day. She never reached the door before the delivery guy was climbing into his truck. Today she was either a little slower than usual or he was a little faster.

The box was clearly marked with her name and address. She didn't remember ordering anything recently, but she sometimes forgot orders. Maybe Eric Sanders had sent her a surprise package. Red "PERISHABLE" stamps were on the top and sides of the package. She guessed it must be food. Bug, her black and white Japanese Chin, was smelling the carton intently and waving his plumed tail. He seldom gave boxes left at the door a second sniff. It must be special.

She carried the package, about the size of six shoe boxes, to the counter in her kitchen. It was odd that the label listed the shipper as "New Mexico Industries," but didn't show a return address. She didn't know a company with that name. She pulled a utility knife from her tool drawer and slit the silver duct tape connecting the two flaps of the box. A Styrofoam carton was tightly wedged inside. Sanders had sent her something fragile or that needed to be kept cold—maybe it was tropical flowers or gourmet cheeses?

She cut the tape around the lid, lifted the lid, took out two blue gel freeze packs, and screamed. The shock passed quickly, and her innate curiosity and scientific training took over.

A firm-looking ivory mass with streaks of pink and ridges lay in the box. It was probably the tissue of a large animal. It was not squishy like brains or squiggly tubes like intestines. It looked sorta like the tripe sold in rural meat markets, but this blob had big linear ridges, not a honeycomb of ridges. It was most likely the stomach of an animal. Several red, almost black, spots dotted the creases between the ridges.

She wasn't going to touch it. It might be laced with a poison. This wasn't a gift from a friend. Someone was angry with her.

Four months ago, Sara had helped local police and the FBI identify the butcher at a *carnicería* in nearby Mercado as the killer of homeless veterans who interfered with his drug business in Albuquerque. It had been a complicated case and her friend Eric Sanders, then assigned by the State Department to the embassy in Cuba, had tracked an assassin hired by the drug syndicate from Havana to Miami to Albuquerque. Now the butcher, his wife, drug kingpins from Miami, and a number of former members of the Albuquerque Police Department awaited trial for murder and drug trafficking. They would be tried in federal court under the Racketeer Influenced and Corrupt Organizations Act, better known as the "RICO" Act. Sara would be a key witness for the prosecution.

The mass didn't look like it would explode or emit dangerous gasses, but it was covered with plastic film. As a scientist, she'd seen many disgusting samples over the years. As Sara put the ice packs and the lid back on the carton, she thought she heard a ticking noise. Her imagination was probably working overtime, but she saw no reason to tempt fate. She carried the carton out of her house and placed it in her driveway. If it exploded, the house wouldn't suffer too much damage. She didn't think the package was big enough to contain a lot of explosives, but it wouldn't take much with the right ones.

Rather than call 9-1-1, Sara punched the button for Mercado Police Chief Gil Andrews. She had his cell phone number on speed dial because they had worked together on several cases during the last couple of years. "Gil? I have an emergency. Just received a package of… tripe or something like it. Anyway, it's ticking."

"What do you mean 'tripe?' Ticking?"

"The carton is in my driveway so it won't blow up my house."

After a few quick questions, he said, "Call Ulysses. He'll want his lab crew to see your new mess, but my bomb squad and I are on our way."

Sara suspected he was right. Her car had been blown up in the FBI parking lot during the investigation of the Albuquerque drug trade four months ago. Neither Gil nor Ulysses Howe, the special agent in charge of the Albuquerque office of the FBI, thought she panicked easily. Ulysses would consider the package a serious threat. Even so, Ulysses was often difficult to reach, but his assistant, Kit, was not. She used her speed dial. "Hi, Kit. I have an emergency. Just received a ticking package. Gil is on his way."

"Ulysses is in a meeting, but I'll interrupt. He'll be thankful this bomb isn't in our own parking lot. That incident generated a lot of snickers nationally in FBI circles." Kit giggled. "Hang on..."

Sara had scooped up Bug before Kit spoke again. "I talked to Ulysses. Don't be brave. Get out of your house. Wait at the corner. Bye."

In less than two minutes, a fire truck with sirens blaring stopped next to Sara at the entrance to her street. A second fire truck whizzed past Sara's house to the nearest fire hydrant.

A fireman jumped from the first truck and pointed to the box in Sara's driveway. "Is that it?" He snickered. "Pretty small."

Sara reddened. "I know. Maybe we don't need to bother the neighbors. They're tired of police stakeouts and emergencies at my house."

A neighbor ambled out of the house to look at the package.

"Too late." The fireman sighed. "We'll go to your nearest neighbors and advise them to close their front doors and stay away from their windows. An explosion could throw shards of glass."

A police van swung onto the street. Two officers jumped from the car and immediately donned bomb protection gear. While the woman unloaded gear onto a trolley, the man approached Sara. "We're the bomb squad—Bob and Barb. Gil is right behind us. You and Gil can watch us and listen in to our comments with this." He handed her a device that looked like a smart phone with an oversized screen and speaker. "Might be wise for you and your dog to stand behind the fire truck. First, we'll assess the situation. If it's a complicated explosive, an FBI bomb squad will take over. They're on their way here and will be watching us on the video feed." Bob put on a protective helmet and closed the visor.

Bob and Barb waddled with their trolley stacked high with equipment toward the package. It looked small, and Sara thought slightly ridiculous in her driveway. The two set up tripods and focused cameras on the package.

Another marked police car roared in. Gil ran toward Sara and Bug who stood behind the fire truck. He nodded at her and grabbed the screen, so Sara could hold Bug. The normally placid dog whimpered appreciatively.

Soon pictures of the box appeared on the screen. Bob and two firemen tinkered with the cameras while Barb pulled a stethoscope from one of her pails. She moved the stethoscope across the package. Her voice sounded artificially high. "It's definitely ticking!"

Gil gasped. "Damn. I'd hoped this time you panicked needlessly."

Sara described the package to Gil as Bob and Barb discussed details with the FBI bomb squad.

Bob swept another gadget over the top and sides of the carton. "Cold. Bomb could respond to time or temperature. Better keep it cold." Barb put shields around the package.

As Bob removed the lid, Sara said, "I already removed the lid and blue ice packs once."

"Good." Bob threw the ice packs into an open plastic evidence bag held by Barb and stared at the ivory mass. "What is this gunk?"

Sara said, "Might be tripe—cow's stomach—but it doesn't look quite right."

Gil studied the image on the phone. "Certainly possible. Can you probe it without tearing the plastic covering?"

"Ugh." Barb probed the mass with a rod. "Tough. The probe can't penetrate it easily." She tapped the black plastic tray underneath the blob with her probe. "Appears to be on a tray like butchers use to sell hamburger. Oops."

The view on the screen wasn't clear. Sara thought either Barb had torn the food wrap, or it had become detached from the black tray. After consulting with the FBI bomb squad, Barb used tweezers to tug the food wrap off the ivory blob. She dangled it for a couple of seconds for all to see before she dropped it into an evidence bag held by Bob. "The device is underneath. Still ticking."

A bass voice boomed from the speaker. "Bob and Barb, try to lift the mass and tray without pulling any wires or triggering the device."

Bob used tongs to lift one and then another corner of the mass. "No sign of wires here." He lifted more. "No attachment to the mass. Can't see any wires attached to the black tray, but they could be attached underneath. Should we keep going?"

The bass voice was softer this time. "We're ten minutes away. Keep going. This device appears primitive but could be deceptive. When you put the mass into a clean plastic container, put a counterweight on the tray. Try a pound one in your toolbox."

Bob sorted through his toolbox and pulled out a metal cube with a handle. Barb opened a plastic container. When she nodded, he slid the cube onto the tray as she pulled the mass off and slopped it into the container.

A sigh came from the phone. "So far, so good."

Barb sealed the clear container with a lid and handed it to a fireman who darted back to the police van, as he'd done for the other filled evidence bags and containers. Bob started to lift the edge of the tray a bit. A bit more. "No wires."

Barb grabbed the tray with tongs and inserted it into a plastic bag. Again, the fireman collected the specimen bag.

Everyone studied the remaining contents in the box in silence.

"What's in the clear plastic bag?" said the bass voice.

Bob poked it with tongs. "Looks like an alarm clock. Old metal one. Ticking. I'm afraid to move it. Might set off the bomb. Two plastic containers on either side."

Barb focused a light on the clear lids on the two shallow containers, which looked like they came from a deli. The pink, red, and gray swirled contents didn't look like deli products, or at least not fresh ones.

"What should I move first?" Bob slid a sensor across the lid of one container. "Cold. Probably ice packs below. Our training never prepared us for this."

"We've never seen one like this either. If a wire was inserted through the cheap plastic of those containers, the plastic would crack and the container leak. Doubt they're wired. Move one of them. Try not to remove the lid."

Bob grasped the lips on the container and the lid with tongs. The container didn't move. He tried again. No movement. He pinched the lips of the container and lid with pliers. A small cracking noise. "The plastic on the lid split. So far, no wires."

The bass voice boomed. "Don't use pliers. Use two tweezers and be prepared to dump it into a larger container."

Barb opened a large plastic container. Bob slipped tweezers over the edge of the plastic lip of the deli container in two places. As he lifted, Barb moved the larger container underneath. The small container cracked. Grayish-pink, lumpy slime dripped down.

"Crazy. Sorta looks like rat gut." Sara paused. "Can't be sure."

Bob let the stringy mass, the deli container, and split lid fall into the large container. Barb sealed the lid of the larger container.

The FBI bomb squad all talked at once. Finally, one clear voice said, "Put the last container in a separate sealed container. Now for the clock."

Barb used tweezers to untwist the metal tie holding the bag shut. Bob pulled the clock from the bag. "'Seth Thomas' and 'alarm' are written on the face. Clock reads two-thirty. Weird."

Sara looked at her watch. It was two-forty in the afternoon. "Is the alarm set?"

"Don't know. The alarm hand is pointed to three." Bob turned over the clock. "This will get dicey. No visible screws on the back. Think it's an old wind up."

Barb said, "We don't know how to stop the ticking or the alarm."

The bass voice sounded relaxed. "I think there's a lever on the side, push down. Should stop the alarm from ringing."

Barb pushed the lever down. "Now what? It's still ticking."

"Doubt it will explode, so put the clock back in the bag. Insert it into another evidence bag. We'll take it apart and swab for DNA and prints when we get there. What's left?"

Bob poked among the four blue items on the bottom of the Styrofoam container. "Cold packs. No wires. It's a hoax."

The bomb squad packed up their equipment in silence.

Gil hummed "Rhinestone Cowboy." He always reverted to Glen Campbell songs when he was thinking about something important. Sara knew this was his way of announcing he didn't want to be disturbed, but she was embarrassed and didn't want to face the crowd any longer. "Sorry for the false alarm. Please stop by the house before you leave."

Bug snorted when she put him on the ground, and he trotted rapidly to their house without stopping to sniff every bush as he usually did. Sara thought even Bug was embarrassed.

As she walked, Sara wondered whether this package was a practical joke or a threat. The contents of the package were disgusting but not dangerous, as far as she could tell. A district attorney would consider this hoax laughable and treat it as a misdemeanor, not a real threat.

Who would do this? Her neighbors teased her about the commotion she brought to the neighborhood, but they wouldn't waste their time on this prank. Maybe someone awaiting trial did it? She doubted the butcher, his wife, or members the drug cartel sent the package. They weren't afraid to kill those who annoyed them. Police officers, fired for graft, might have come up with this hoax while drunk. They'd know this joke wouldn't lead to serious charges. However, Sara thought this was too complex of prank for them.

Wait—the ivory blob had several dark spots. Suddenly she remembered slides from a pathology course she'd taken in graduate school. The dark spots could be ulcers. Was someone trying to alert her to an epidemiology problem—a human health hazard? Was it totally unrelated to the upcoming trials?

She walked over to the bomb crew. "I think a veterinary pathologist should look at this tripe, or whatever it is. If I'm guessing right, the animal was sick."

Bob's eyes narrowed.

"I'll bring bags of ice out, so you can keep the blob and the guts cool. It's better for the pathologist that way. This may be an important clue."

"For what?"

CHAPTER 2: Sara

Gil slid onto a stool at the large island in Sara's kitchen. He sneezed and wiped his nose with a red bandana. "You made the bomb crew nervous when you brought out a bag of ice. Hell, you made me and Ulysses nervous, too."

Sara looked up from her computer screen. "Sorry." She pushed the screen toward him. "The first sample—the big ivory blob—looks like an abomasum, the fourth stomach of a ruminant. I can't tell whether it came from a cow, sheep, or goat because the blob was only a section of it, I think." She showed him another photo. "It doesn't have the honeycomb pattern of the reticulum or rumen."

"Use English. Not science mumbo jumbo."

"You have a farm background and know a cow, or any ruminant, has four so-called stomachs. Technically, the cleaned tripe used as human food is the reticulum of a cow."

Gil looked like he'd sneeze but didn't. "Good stuff if the cook is good. My wife always gets her tripe at the *carnicería* near my office. Well, until it closed because I arrested the butcher and his wife for murder— what was it—four months ago. Of course, then the FBI took the case under RICO laws because the butcher ruled a large drug network. One of his henchmen could be threatening you to keep you from testifying at the trial."

"Thought about it. I'd be dead now if they sent a gift. Besides, butchers don't have the abomasums of cows lying around, unless they dress whole animals. Most don't. They get sides of beef and selected salable organs from…"

"So, who sent the tripe?"

"Wait—I'm not through. A USDA meat inspector must be present when livestock are killed for commercial sale as human food. At least if the meat might be sold out of state. Most butchers get their meat from slaughterhouses large enough to keep an inspector on the premises full-time. Do you know who supplied our local *carnicería*? Did the FBI identify them as part of the butcher's drug ring?"

"Don't know. Is this really relevant?"

"I saw dark red spots on the blob. Probably ulcers. Means the animal was sick. A USDA meat inspector rejects meat from the carcasses of sick animals and has the carcasses destroyed."

"Sara, I know you'll get to the point eventually. Can you hurry? My allergies are killing me. I didn't sleep well last night. Hay fever. I'm grouchy today."

Sara snickered but didn't speed her delivery. "I doubt the tripe came from our drug-lord butcher, his cohorts, or even his supplier. Perhaps someone sent me the sample, so I'd investigate, or get someone else to investigate, the cause of the ulcers? Maybe they were so excited they forgot to send their name and additional info."

Gil shook his head. "No one gets that excited about a cow's ulcers. Ulysses has contacted the New Mexico Department of Agriculture for help. I figure it will be months before he gets a report."

His phone pinged. "What's this? Text message from Ulysses. A pathologist in Veterinary Diagnostic Services in the New Mexico Department of Agriculture has agreed to look at the tripe and gunk in the deli containers, immediately."

"Guess whoever sent the package got what he wanted—an expert to examine the tissues." Sara bit her lip. "Maybe the sender wanted to hide his identity to avoid retribution from an employer, like the slaughterhouse owner, maybe?"

"Do you realize how many 'maybes' you've said? Besides, a slaughterhouse owner doesn't keep the guts of rats around. The ticking clock makes it look like a teenage prank."

Sara stared at Gil. "We both know this package was too elaborate to be a prank."

"The sender isn't psychologically normal, at least not when he or she created this package." He cleared his throat. "You're not going to like what I say next. Ulysses agrees with me. You should be in protective custody until we learn more about the sender of this weird package."

"But…"

"The federal prosecutor considers you a valuable asset until the trials of the butcher, his wife, and other leaders in the drug cartel are over. From past experience, we know this house isn't the easiest place to guard *even* when Sanders was here. By the way, where *is* your wayward boyfriend?"

"You know he's a workaholic. After he was shot during the arrest of the drug cartel members, he didn't recuperate well. Then, he was tense because he got so many calls from staff in the embassy in Cuba and the State Department in Washington."

Gil coughed and covered his mouth with the red bandana handkerchief. "More likely he had a guilty conscience."

Sara suspected the handkerchief hid a smirk. Gil and Sanders worked well together on the drug cartel case. However, they seemed to like goading each other. She wasn't sure why. "Okay, there was a six-ton pink elephant in the room. We never argued. What could I say? He knew he'd betrayed my trust when he had an affair with Maria." She pursed her lips. "However, the other women on his staff claimed she'd played him like a fiddle. I suspect that's what bothered him the most. She outsmarted him and used him to obtain embassy secrets for the drug cartel. I doubt he'll stray again."

Gil didn't even hide his smile with the bandana. "Mainly because everyone laughed at him, including his boss, the assistant secretary of state. A master spook sleeping with the enemy."

"Officially, he's not a spook. He supervises sensitive data collection by the government."

Gil's phone rang and he left her kitchen before he replied. When he returned, he said, "Have you talked to Sanders since he left your care here?"

"Yes, this morning. Almost every morning. He's leading a team fixing the security at the U.S. embassy in Cuba and orienting a new temporary chargé d'affaires. He would have had the temporary title if he hadn't shown poor judgment with Maria." Sara frowned. "At least that's what he says."

"Then you won't be upset to learn Ulysses called Sanders to tell him about your package." He sighed. "As usual, you two are in sync. Sanders doubted anyone from the current drug cartel case would threaten you with tripe. He suggested someone had read about your exploits in the newspaper and wanted to pique your interest in a new case."

Sara smiled. She knew her man. "So, will you or the FBI monitor the situation, but not isolate me in a safe house?" When Gil didn't reply immediately, she continued, "I was thinking. The tripe and rat guts, or whatever they are, seem like the types of hints one of the homeless vets would give me."

"Yep, one of the guys with a history in the psych unit at the VA Medical Center in Albuquerque. Especially the squirrelly ones who gave us the clues to find the killers of their friends."

"They're not squirrelly. They just view the world differently."

"Like I said—strange."

Sara sniffed. "I was thinking. The FBI assigned Carbonne to remain in Albuquerque and explore the details of the drug cartel connections, rather than return to the U.S. embassy in Havana with Sanders. I bet he'd be willing to talk to the homeless vets. He gained the trust of a lot of them when he was undercover on the drug cartel case. I think he's still in contact with a couple of them."

Gil sneezed violently. "We—you, Sanders, Ulysses, and I—have worked together too much. Ulysses already assigned Carbonne to do some basic legwork."

His cell phone pinged. "I've been summoned." He studied the next message. "Strange—it's a message from a pathologist at the state ag lab." He blinked, "You are to report to her office. Do you know why?"

Sara looked at the name and smiled.

CHAPTER 3: Sara

Sara thought Lydia Griegos looked about the same as the last time she saw her five years before at a public health conference—slender and elegant with her long gray hair tied back. She was the archetypal Hispanic lady of the Southwest. "Lydia, glad you agreed to examine the samples. Since you asked me to bring Bug, I assume there was something contagious in them."

Lydia shoved a rolling chair at Sara and motioned toward a small table. "I knew it would be interesting if you were involved, and I haven't had a chance to talk to you in ages. I saw more of you before you moved to New Mexico."

"Don't go to many conferences anymore. Officially I'm semi-retired and only consult on a couple of projects for USAID and the State Department."

Lydia slid into her chair. "Few scientists, let alone semi-retired ones, are involved in such high-profile projects. According to the *Albuquerque Journal,* you were a key figure in tracking a drug ring stretching from Cuba to Miami to here."

Sara felt heat rise up her neck. She wished her name appeared less in the newspaper because she didn't like to remember the ordeal. Maybe she was also superstitious. She didn't want to tangle again with any remnants of the drug cartel headed by the butcher and his wife. She preferred her privacy and hated when people she hardly knew recognized her in stores and asked questions. However, Lydia had a right to be curious. "Had no choice."

"That's not what Ulysses Howe said when he called my boss and insisted a veterinary pathologist look ASAP at the contents of the package left at your house."

Sara wasn't going to chit-chat about the butcher and his drug ring before she testified in court. "Can I let Bug out of this kennel?" Sara pointed to a rolling pet carrier. "As a pet therapy dog, he's used to walking around a hospital and not being dragged in a kennel."

Sara unzipped the case. Bug snorted and stepped out with his head high and his tail swaying elegantly. He walked toward Lydia's outstretched hand, sniffed, strutted back to Sara, and curled up at her feet.

Lydia smiled. "The famous Bug. More self-assured than even your graduate students. I was always impressed by your students at conferences—poised and prepared. You appear to train dogs well, too."

"He's my baby." Sara rubbed Bug's ears. "Enough chit-chat. I'm afraid the samples you received were in bad shape. The bomb squad was intent on preventing an explosion, not on preserving biological samples." She grimaced. "And I was too addled to keep the samples on ice at all times. Not a well-managed crime scene. I'm afraid bacteria on one surface could have cross-contaminated others. Then too, the FBI had to check for fingerprints and swab for human DNA on the containers."

Lydia pulled a page from her desk and rolled her chair the three feet to the small table. "The samples weren't in the best condition, and the FBI bomb squad were indignant at having to deliver what they called 'guts' here. However, I have preliminary information. As you guessed, the gray and pink mass in the small deli container was the guts of a rodent, but the sample's from a prairie dog and not a rat."

Sara choked. "Oh dear. I've heard reports of plague in prairie dogs in the Southwest from time to time over the last forty years."

Lydia shoved the page toward her. "The initial screening found bacteria which looked like safety pins under the microscope. That's *Yersinia pestis*—the bacteria that cause the plague. Of course, more tests will be done."

"So, do I need to start an antibiotic regime? I didn't poke the rat— I guess the prairie dog—guts but I touched the plastic on the tripe. The sender of the package could have cross-contaminated the samples. How about Bug? He sniffed the outer container, and I touched him.”

“It’s definitely antibiotics for both of you. You’re not apt to develop bubonic plaque. It’s usually transmitted by infected fleas, but sometimes hunters and meat processors who handle the carcasses of infected animals become ill.” She pulled two vials of pills from the cabinet behind her. “The FBI wanted me to give you the antibiotics. They felt a panic might ensue if you went to your physician or an urgent care clinic and told your story. They don’t want leaks of information until we finish our tests, but we’ve already notified the Centers for Disease Control.”

“How about the bomb crew and the others who processed the package at my house?”

Lydia looked surprised. “Weren’t you told? The bomb crews, fire fighters, police, and FBI at the site were all summoned here. The diagnostic labs for the New Mexico Department of Health and for the Department of Agriculture share this building. A physician in the Department of Health is lecturing your cohorts now on the plague and dispersing antibiotics. Ulysses Howe suggested you and I brainstorm a bit alone before he joined us.”

Sara read the labels on both vials. “Standard procedures.”

Lydia’s brow wrinkled. “Yes. Now for more ‘standard procedures.’ The New Mexico Department of Agriculture hasn’t received reports of prairie dog die-offs from plague in the last year. As we speak, others are talking to their counterparts in the departments of health and agriculture in nearby states and at the Centers for Disease Control.”

“Anyone talk to the New Mexico Department of Game and Fish or the National Park Service? Rangers might have seen something odd or at least should be on the lookout for new developments.”

Lydia rolled her chair back to her desk and checked her computer. “They’re on the contact list.” She turned back to Sara. “There were ice crystals in the prairie dog’s gut. It had been frozen. So, the time of death can’t be determined.”

"Has the FBI pressured you to identify the location of the prairie dog die-off because then they'll know where to look for the sender of the package?"

Lydia nodded. "I told them we'd find the sender within six days. The Centers for Disease Control will put out an alert today to physicians in the Southwest to look for patients with symptoms of the plague. However, the FBI agents want answers faster."

"Fair enough, but haven't they checked with UPS? Where did the package originate? The label said the shipper was—let me think—'New Mexico Industries.'"

Lydia returned to her computer and typed rapidly as Sara spoke. "I don't know. I wasn't prepared for so many questions."

There was a knock on the door. A tall, fit man with cropped, graying curly black hair appeared.

Sara stood and shook his hand. "Glad to see you Ulysses. How did I rate *you*, not one of your agents?"

He chuckled. "You're too much of a challenge for most agents. I'm used to how you think." He turned to Lydia. "Your emails didn't surprise me. Sara is challenging. By the way Sara, an agent has already contacted UPS."

Lydia pushed another chair toward him. "I've known her longer than you. I know her style."

"Okay. I'll live up to my reputation." Sara straightened in her chair. "I'm convinced the package came from a concerned citizen, not someone in the drug cartel. However, it might be wise to check on the slaughterhouse that supplied meat to the *carnicería* in Mercado. It could have been part of the drug ring's operations."

Lydia looked at her lap.

Ulysses sighed. "You are scary in your deductions sometimes." He shook his head. "We found the owner of that meat packing plant to be a helpful source of information on drug movements by the butcher in Mercado. Well, after we offered him immunity from prosecution a couple of months ago. Of course, you shouldn't mention what I said before the trial. We'll talk to him about your package because we can't rule out the possibility that your package was an act of intimidation by the drug cartel."

Sara turned to Lydia. "Have you had a chance to test the sample that looked like tripe?"

Lydia smiled. "I'm prepared for that question. You were right, mainly. The ivory mass was a section from the abomasum, the real or so-called 'fourth stomach' of a sheep, not a cow. The dark spots were ulcers."

"How are a prairie dog's gut and a sheep's stomach connected?"

"We're puzzled, too." Lydia turned to her computer screen and began to peruse his email. "I asked a microbiologist to swab the sheep abomasum's interior surface and examine it microscopically. Contamination from the prairie dog's gut is possible. However, to be thorough it seemed like a logical starting point. I thought I might have a response by now." She frowned. "You know the potential appearance of plague automatically becomes a high priority issue in this lab, even if the FBI isn't involved."

"I didn't know sheep could get the plague.

Ulysses chuckled and patted Sara's back. "Glad to know you have limits."

"Technically all mammals, which can be infested with fleas, are susceptible to the plague. However, stomach ulcers are not a symptom of the plague." Lydia's gaze returned to her computer screen after a soft ping. "Good—a new email from the microbiologist."

Sara thought she saw a slide preparation on the screen.

"He found safety pin-shaped bacteria in the tissue. The prep isn't a good one." Lydia rolled her chair back to the table. "Now the real work begins. The lab has to determine whether the bacteria are there because of contamination or because the sheep had a *Yersinia* infection. We also have to examine the ulcers carefully and check with our colleagues worldwide for odd symptoms of *Yersinia* infections in sheep."

Sara tapped her fingers on the table. "How did the sender make the connection between the prairie dog and the sheep?"

Lydia shrugged. "A rancher or farmer may have found dead prairie dogs in a field where his sheep were grazing. If he had seen a prairie dog die-off from plague even twenty years ago, he might have guessed the cause. Perhaps his sheep had acted lethargic or ill lately."

Sara leaned forward engrossed in thought. "Don't you have maps of the locations of previous die-offs? Most ranchers and farmers remain in an area their whole lives." She turned to Ulysses. "Might help you focus your search."

Ulysses was already poking at his laptop. "My thoughts, too."

Sara continued, "I was raised on a farm in the Midwest. No sheep. But they always seemed pretty lethargic to me. How would a rancher recognize lethargy in sheep?"

Lydia shrugged again. "I don't have a farm background, but this animal—judging by the ulcers—may have had diarrhea or blood in its feces. Several ulcers had perforated the gut. Anyway, the farmer or rancher who slaughtered the animal noticed the ulcers in the stomach."

"Wow, he or she was astute."

"More than you realize. The second deli container was filed with lymph glands from the sheep. One of the symptoms of the plague is enlarged lymph nodes with so-called buboes. They're being prepared for analyses now."

Sara's head was whirling. "Maybe this wasn't a farmer or rancher. My dad butchered a steer every winter for family use. As a teen, I watched parts of the butchering process as I packaged the meat and stowed it in the freezer. But I wouldn't know how to locate and surgically remove the lymph glands from an animal. Dad might have in a steer. I don't know. The sender was awfully knowledgeable. Perhaps he or she was a vet tech or even a veterinarian who regularly worked with large animals."

Lydia nodded. Ulysses didn't even look up. He was pecking intently at his laptop.

Sara continued. "Maybe we're looking at this the wrong way. An alternate scenario is someone working in a slaughterhouse noted the ulcers and investigated the sheep's farm or ranch of origin. If so, the sender probably didn't know about the plague, but he or she had butchered animals and recognized the sheep as a sick animal. Then he or she found the dead prairie dog."

Ulysses kept pecking at his laptop. "Lots of potential leads."

Sara grimaced. She didn't want to sound paranoid and admit her next thought, but Ulysses already thought she was a bit odd. "This could be the result of a laboratory experiment. Homeland Security experts have suggested several times plague could be an effective bioterror tool."

Ulysses's dark complexion turned gray. "Damn."

CHAPTER 4: Eric Sanders

Ulysses had called around two. Sanders had expected Sara to call him, but on second thought, that wasn't Sara's style. She wouldn't bother him unless she needed him. She knew the last four months had been hell for him. However, he was concerned and couldn't concentrate on his work. He kept thinking about how he'd gotten involved with Sara.

He'd collected and analyzed data worldwide for the State Department, often through USAID, and improved security in many U.S. embassies and consulates over the last twenty-five years, but he'd always been fascinated by Cuba. Maybe because it was a banned area for so many years. After Castro's rise to power, the U.S embassy had operated as an Interest Section under the auspices of the Swiss embassy for more than forty years. He'd jumped at the chance to do reconnaissance in Cuba when the U.S. began to normalize relations.

One of his ideas had been to expand scientific exchanges between the U.S and Cuba, as his predecessors had done in China forty years earlier. He quickly identified the right scientist—an epidemiologist who had a broad knowledge of scientific issues, had worked well with Bolivian officials and citizens to find practical solutions to their problems, and was observant—too observant. She'd learned a lot of useful details on the movement of cocaine from Bolivia and was almost killed. The woman was Sara.

He'd taken her to Havana with him for meetings with Cuban scientists. Unfortunately, he'd fallen for her in the process. Sara wasn't his usual type. She was a good woman. Attractive, even pretty, but not provocative. Smart. Honest, too frank, but folksy. She assumed good relationships were based on trust, mutual interests and beliefs, and monogamy. She didn't embarrass him with a nickname, like his former girlfriends did, but called him "Sanders" as he preferred.

His boss, a woman assistant secretary of state, had even commented, "It's about time you finally found a mature woman who is a partner not a decoration." His boss was right. He'd dated mostly young, fiery socialites since his divorce twenty years ago.

Sara had refused to be a vagabond who followed him to assignments. She worked part-time via computer on analyses and planning for USAID, lived in Albuquerque, and visited Washington, D.C., once or twice a month. Even so, she'd been drawn into the line of fire again four months ago as he and his staff traced the movement of drugs from Cuba to Miami and eventually to Albuquerque.

He'd been wounded during the capture of the butcher, whom the press had dubbed the "Butcher Don." Afterwards, he'd recuperated in Albuquerque for a month. Then he'd returned to the U.S. embassy in Havana to fix its leaky security and to lead the orientation of the new chargé d'affaires. He knew he would have been appointed the temporary chargé d'affaires but for his mistake—a dalliance with an inexperienced economic attaché in the embassy in Havana. He learned too late she had strong ties to drug gangs in Miami. To apologize to Sara, he'd proposed a vacation in India to see the romantic Taj Mahal. However, he'd postponed the trip twice as he grappled with problems in the embassy in Havana. Strangely, Sara hadn't complained.

His work at the Cuban embassy was complete now. His new assignment would primarily be at a desk in Washington. This was not what he wanted. He enjoyed field work.

Sara surprised him and called him at four. She was energized. She was also upset because she didn't want to go to a safe house.

He encouraged her to accept Ulysses's offer for two nights of protection until basic data had been collected on her strange package. He was surprised by Sara's resistance. She was seldom temperamental. Gil must have been ham-handed again. But he couldn't really blame him. Gil had rescued Sara twice from armed intruders in her home, and he probably didn't want to push his—or her—luck.

She'd ended their short conversation by saying, "Okay, but I wouldn't be closeted over a strange package if the prosecutor wasn't so worried about the trial for the Butcher Don and his colleagues in the drug gangs."

He agreed with her. Although the package signaled a potentially significant public health threat, it didn't seem to be linked to crime families in New Mexico. Unless Ulysses hadn't admitted all the details to Sara. He'd check tomorrow but wouldn't trouble Sara with that thought now.

When he called her at six-thirty her time in the evening, or eight-thirty his time, she and Bug were settled safely somewhere in the Albuquerque area. She was cautious and didn't say where. As expected, she'd adjusted graciously to her confinement. She'd made spaghetti for the staff protecting her. The guards were lucky. Sara's marinara sauce was outstanding.

However, cooking hadn't distracted Sara much. She spouted data on the plague in the rural areas of northern New Mexico and Arizona during the last twenty years. She was in her element as an epidemiologist. He hadn't realized cases of bubonic plague were reported almost every year among residents of the tribal lands of the Four Corners about two hundred miles west of Albuquerque.

He would have rather discussed his plan for a trip to India than learn about the plague, but he was patient.

Then she launched into another topic. He found the information she'd gained chatting with Paul Carbonne more interesting. Ulysses had assigned Carbonne to investigate Sara's package, probably because Carbonne had worked with Sara and Gil to identify the Butcher Don as a murderer and drug czar. Sara had called Carbonne as soon as agents took her to the safe house.

She reported Carbonne's findings quickly and with little commentary. He had checked UPS records and visited the UPS Store on Central Avenue where the package had been logged in shortly before closing on Tuesday. The scrawny man on the UPS surveillance tape who delivered the package had long, gray hair that hid much of his face. He wore a knit cap, sunglasses, old khakis, and a gray T-shirt. He paid in cash for next-day delivery of a product he described as "frozen meat from a family farm."

The clerk had stated the man looked like the picture on his driver's license. After questioning the clerk, Carbonne had concluded the man was tanned, perhaps a Native American, and older and shorter than the twenty-one-year-old clerk. The clerk thought the man was disoriented and didn't respond immediately when addressed by the name on the driver's license—Dan Steele. Carbonne thought the clerk was confused, too, and an almost useless witness.

When Carbonne had checked with the Division of Motor Vehicles and the Albuquerque police, he learned Dan Steele had reported his driver's license and wallet stolen Wednesday morning after spending the previous night at bars on Central Avenue. The picture on file of Dan Steele at the Division of Motor Vehicles was of a muscular man with bushy gray hair.

Carbonne had hypothesized to Sara that the messenger who delivered the package to the UPS Store might be one of the many homeless veterans who wandered the so-called International District in Albuquerque between Central Avenue and the VA Medical Center on Gibson Boulevard. The real sender of the package had probably given the veteran enough money to guarantee the messenger would drink himself senseless and thus be unable to identify the sender.

Sara sighed. "So, Carbonne decided he'd go undercover for a couple of days and wander around the various halfway houses, soup kitchens, and other haunts for homeless around the city. I wonder why he bothers. It may have worked before when he got evidence against the Butcher Don, but now they all know he's not a homeless veteran."

Sanders murmured, "I suspect they talk more because they forget he's an FBI agent for a moment." He didn't wait for Sara to launch into another topic. "I've been thinking. I promised to take you to India. Maybe now would be a good time to go. Diwali, the Hindu festival of lights, is in October this year."

"But…"

"Ulysses, Lydia Griegos, and Carbonne can manage the investigation of your package. This case is not going to develop rapidly. The trial for the Butcher Don isn't scheduled until late November or December. And both Gil and Ulysses are concerned about your safety. They'd be relieved to have you out of their jurisdiction."

"I guess you're right. Is your work at the embassy in Havana almost done?"

"As much as I can do. We think we've stopped the leaks and generally refined our security procedures. A medical team couldn't identify the cause of the neurological problems among the embassy staff. You know, more than twenty people reported symptoms. Our medical experts thought the Cubans tried some new directional technology to cause brain injuries, but we can't prove it. Then yesterday a Canadian team proposed the symptoms might be due to a pesticide the Cubans used to control the Zika virus. The Cubans, of course, denied everything." Pause. "Let's get back to a more pleasant topic. I've checked on flights to India."

"Good, but…."

He wasn't going to let her distract him. "Seats are still available for this weekend and all of the next two weeks. Bug can stay with his usual sitter here."

Sara cleared her throat. "One little problem. The Indian government, really all governments, don't allow international travel by people for six days after they're exposed to the plague."

He wondered whether there was a hidden message to her comment. Maybe she didn't want to go to India? That was doubtful because she liked exotic travel. Maybe she didn't want to spend time with him?

Sara broke the awkward silence. "If you're available this weekend, I'd prefer to spend some quiet time with you here.

CHAPTER 5: Sara on Thursday

Sara heard the angst in Sanders's voice and wondered how to explain her thoughts to him, when she couldn't justify them to herself. She'd had several opportunities to attend conferences or consult in India over the years. She'd avoided them because India frightened her, even though she knew her fears weren't logical.

She vividly remembered a friend's story about awakening one morning in southern India and finding the back pocket of his jeans slit and his wallet stolen while he slept. She'd been an impressionable student then. She'd since traveled to more dangerous locations but had never foolishly camped along the roadside like her friend.

She also knew five scientists who had acquired polio, uncontrollable eye infections that blinded them in one eye, or malaria during long-term assignments in India in the 1980s. This excuse wasn't valid now. India had eradicated polio. Malaria was a worse problem in parts of Southeast Asia, where she'd traveled, than in India. She and Sanders wouldn't be in rural areas of India and would stay in four-star hotels and eat no street food.

The real reason was subtler. She'd often been struck by how hundreds of people were killed in stampedes or in clashes between Muslims and Hindus in India. These incidents had bothered her because they seldom rated more than two inches of column in the *Washington Post* or *New York Times,* and the stories never appeared in papers like the *Albuquerque Journal.* Similar incidents in the U.S. or Europe would have made headlines. The bottom line seemed to be: Life was cheap in India. Realistically, she knew this lack of newspaper coverage reflected more about the limited interest of Americans in foreign cultures than anything about India.

Sara picked up Bug and cuddled him. She'd always thought her best feature wasn't her intelligence, as Sanders thought, but her ability to do what had to be done, no matter her fears. If she avoided situations that frightened her, she'd lose her best trait and her self-identity.

However, she'd been fascinated by the PBS Masterpiece Theater series, *The Jewel in the Crown*, when it first aired in 1984. Since then, she'd read quite a bit about the British Raj in India, Gandhi, and the separation of India and Pakistan. These cultural and religious clashes fascinated her and seemed relevant to the U.S. now.

She decided to explain her hang-ups to Sanders when he arrived in two days. He'd understand.

***

Sara saw a long article on the second page of the *Albuquerque Journal* as she chugged her first diet cola of the morning. The DA had accepted pleas from two Albuquerque police officers late yesterday. They were among those officers identified as working for the Butcher Don and his drug cartel by Lieutenant Jack Daniels. Although the Butcher Don and his close associates would be tried in a federal district court under RICO laws, the state district attorney's office based in Albuquerque was handling many of the corruption charges against the Albuquerque Police Department.

The article made Jack Daniels look like a hero. Sara knew better. He was an old-timer with a log, not a chip, on his shoulder. She'd annoyed Jack early in the investigation of the disappearance of homeless veterans four months ago. After Jack was indicted for abetting the murders of these homeless veterans and trying to kill her, he gained a place in the U.S. Federal Witness Protection Program. Sara had been angry. If anyone deserved to be in prison it was Jack. Ulysses had agreed, but Jack Daniels's notes on his fellow officers were phenomenal.

The story about these two officers was pathetic. The two women officers had been injured in a work-related accident ten years ago and had been assigned to manage the large Albuquerque police evidence room, a two-story warehouse. Their lawyer asserted the women had been harassed constantly by their fellow officers. Several male officers called this evidence room the "Gimp Girls' Garage." Sara wondered whether Jack had coined the term. She knew firsthand he didn't like women with any authority and had a foul mouth.

The two women had also annoyed many in the APD because they not only posted reminders all over the evidence room but also nagged everyone about two basic rules: No food or drink. Wear plastic gloves always.

Jack's story—actually the DA's story—and their lawyer's story diverged at this point. Jack claimed the two women had found an ingenious way to destroy evidence as ordered by the drug cartel. They dribbled chunks of frosting and donut crumbs in and on the paper bags holding documents and organic matter. Then they released rats in the evidence room. According to the news story, pest exterminators had been called repeatedly to this warehouse because so much evidence was found in shreds. Jack had supplied a photo of one of the women dropping a piece of a donut into an evidence bag and a shot of the other pulling a rat from a box. The DA said their sabotage had caused at least twenty cases against drug dealers to be dismissed.

The women's lawyer asserted they were innocent. The photos were posed shots meant to be funny. The women had willingly allowed the DA to examine all their financial records. They had received no payments from anyone associated with the drug cartel. However, one had a son who had been arrested twice for selling drugs.

The DA must have felt sorry for the women, had too many other cases, or not trusted Jack. Maybe all three. He settled the women's cases as misdemeanors with small fines and no jail time, but they lost their pensions.

Sara wondered how Jack got the photos. She suspected Jack had known for years he would eventually be charged with collusion with the drug cartel, and he'd collected evidence against many of his fellow officers as get-out-of-jail cards.

On the same page, Sara found a two-inch item, "Man Killed in Work Accident." An employee at a meat packing plant had become entangled in the chains suspending a steer's carcass while removing the hide from the steer on Monday. An unnamed Occupational Health and Safety Administration official was quoted as saying, "Slaughterhouse employees have some of the most dangerous jobs in the U.S. because of the relentless rate at which meat is processed in most plants."

Sara reread the article twice not because she liked the macabre but because the packing plant was in Grants and processed meat from the Four Corners region, the most likely location of a prairie dog die-off. She dialed Carbonne's number. "Can you talk now?"

"Be quick."

"Did you see the article in the *Albuquerque Journal* about the death of a meat packing plant employee in Grants? It might be related to my package. Not many people could dissect the lymph glands out of a sheep or recognize abnormalities in the stomachs of livestock. Meat packers, especially those handling the carcass initially, would have those skills. The death might not be an accident."

"Call Kit, Ulysses's aide, in an hour."

CHAPTER 6: FBI Special Agent Ulysses Howe

Even though Ulysses hoped the package of offal that Sara had received was only a public health complaint, he'd taken control of the case for three reasons. The first reason was obvious. Sara was a high-profile witness for a big RICO case. Threats against her had to be taken seriously.

Second, he thought it likely that the samples came from tribal lands after he listened to the discussion between Lydia Griegos and Sara. Although many novels had been written about tribal police, the FBI had ultimate police authority on the pueblos. His staff contacted the leaders of seven pueblos in the area of previous prairie dog die-offs in northern New Mexico and Arizona. All appreciated the heads-up and agreed to be on the lookout for prairie dog die-offs on their lands and illnesses in their livestock.

The third reason made his stomach churn. He'd not been honest with Sara yesterday. He and several agents had been in frequent contact with the owner of the meat processing plant that had supplied sides of beef and lamb to the Butcher Don, ever since the Don's arrest. The agents had given the owner a code name—"Pigeon"—after he quickly admitted he'd overheard rumors that thousands of kilos of drugs had been shipped with sides of beef and lamb across state borders. However, he insisted he'd not been involved and knew no names. The FBI upped the pressure on him. After a month, Pigeon had cracked. He'd fingered the managers and owners of competing plants in Roswell, Las Cruces, and Albuquerque as facilitating drug shipments and had allowed the FBI to set up further sting operations from his plant to learn more about how the movements of meat and drugs were intertwined, not only in New Mexico but also in Colorado and Texas.

Pigeon had also negotiated with federal officials to go into the witness protection program with a strange stipulation. He would only enter it after he sold his meat packing business. However, no one savvy about meat packing wanted to invest in plants in the Southwest until the trial against the Butcher Don was over and all appeals were exhausted.

Ulysses valued Pigeon because FBI agents had found workers at the thirty-seven meat packing plants in New Mexico to be a silent group. They were more loyal to—more likely fearful of—their employers than members of any other organization, including the drug gangs. Many of the employees were barely literate. Quite a few had entered the U.S. illegally. Few could find other good-paying jobs near their homes. Most didn't want to relocate or seek vocational training. Agents suspected many accidents in meat plant were reprisals. A loss of a finger or a hand could be a form of discipline or an act of retaliation. Pigeon was the only owner of meat packing plant willing to talk to the FBI.

Ulysses felt his stomach begin to churn when Carbonne called. He instantly knew Sara was right. He needed to investigate the death of the employee killed in the plant in Grants. However, no one would talk if he sent several agents. He needed to send one individual, preferably with knowledge of the case already, to go undercover into the plant.

Carbonne was a city boy. He would not fade into the milieu of a meat processing plant. Lydia Griegos was too timid and too refined to mingle well with the plant's employees. Sara's farm background, knowledge of science, and ability to be one of the boys would make her a perfect undercover observer, but it was too risky for her at this time. Mercado Police Chief Gil Andrews would mix well with the employees but might be recognized. He'd been a police officer at various locations in New Mexico for almost thirty years. Most of his other agents in the Albuquerque office would be quickly recognized in Grants. It was sad, but two or three murders a month occurred somewhere on the lands of Native Americans in New Mexico. His agents spent a lot of time in Grants.

His calls to OSHA and the Office of the Inspector General of USDA were productive. An OSHA official agreed to convince the family of the man killed that the burial of his mangled body should be delayed until experts could assess more completely how to prevent future accidents. Murder wouldn't be mentioned. The OSHA official also agreed to send a list of all employees who were at the meat packing plant in Grants on the day of the accident.

The Office of the Inspector General of USDA had several special agents who investigated questionable accidents and fraud in meat packing plants. One had just finished an undercover investigation in Amarillo. The Inspector General agreed to send him to Albuquerque to meet with Ulysses.

Kit bounced into his office. "Don't make another call. I've found some info you aren't going to like."

Ulysses reached for the bottle of antacids in his upper desk drawer. "Okay."

"I read the APD report—the one Dan Steele filed about his stolen driver's license and cash. It was incomplete, as usual. So, I called the detective in charge of the case in APD. Guess what? The cell phone number that Dan Steele gave them is out of service." He shrugged. "I tried to get in here between your calls, but you were too quick."

Ulysses sighed. "What did you do?"

"I put in a request to our—the FBI's—National Crime Information Center and the National Instant Criminal Background System."

"Bottom line?" Ulysses wished Kit wouldn't try to keep the suspense up by withholding key pieces of information.

"Obviously not much yet, but I'm sure more is coming."

"Why?"

"They placed a two-day delay on their response. He must have a criminal or a drug record." Kit didn't turn to leave.

Ulysses knew he should stop taking quick-acting antacids, accept he had a chronic condition, and get a supply of long-acting ones. Or retire. "What else?"

Kit bit his lip and hung his head, the way he always did when he'd made a mistake. "I told the detective that he should have followed up more on Dan Steele because he might not be the innocent victim of a pickpocket. The detective slammed the phone down after he cursed at me."

"Can't you ever talk to me before you act? APD detectives are touchy enough now without annoying them intentionally. You know many of them think we used Jack Daniels unnecessarily to expose their dirty laundry."

Kit seemed to deflate before Ulysses's eyes.

Ulysses felt sorry for him. Kit's life as an openly gay man in the macho environment of law enforcement wasn't easy. "Of course, APD should be thankful we helped them clean up their corruption. I'm just testy today. The OSHA official who investigated the accident at the meat packing plant in Grants will send you a list of employees working at the plant on the day of the accident. Run the standard background checks on them. When a Frank McCoy from USDA calls, put him through immediately."

"Why?"

"He's the answer to a problem. Don't mention his name to anyone."

Kit nostrils flared in annoyance. "There's *never* been a leak from my desk." He turned to go and then turned again. "I forgot. The marshals guarding Sara wonder whether they could leave her in an office here today. They've got more urgent requests. She's willing. They also don't want Carbonne to visit her in the safe house because he's well known among the homeless and apt to be spotted."

"They must like this safe house and want to reuse it. Hmm... better keep her busy. Give her the names of the plant employees and their background checks when they come in. She might be able to identify useful patterns. Also, give her everything from Lydia Griegos. Most of the agents don't like to sort through dense lab reports for useful details."

Kit smirked. "I already put her on payroll again to make her legit. Easy. She has a high-level security clearance because of her part-time employment at USAID."

"Good. But I don't want either Carbonne or Sara to know about Frank McCoy until I'm ready. They're both good—too good—at solving riddles."

CHAPTER 7: Sara

Bug pranced toward Ulysses's office in the FBI building. He strutted almost as confidently as he did at University and VA Hospitals, where he did weekly pet therapy visits. As soon as Bug saw Kit, he lunged to the side of Kit's desk. Sara released the leash so Bug could twirl on his hind legs.

"Bug remembered me." Kit immediately began to rummage through a lower desk drawer for a bag of dog treats while Bug sat patiently and eyed him like prey.

"Of course—you gave him treats." Sara slid into the chair in front of Kit's desk. "The marshals said you would have a job for me."

Kit scanned his computer screen. "Somewhere…."

"Don't worry. I brought along plenty to work on from my USAID projects in Bolivia and Cuba. And even a novel, in case I get bored. I can come back later if you tell me where Bug and I can settle today."

"Just wait…." Kit handed a slip of paper to Sara. "The code will give you access to this room and a laptop." He tinkered with his computer. "Carbonne plans to stop by around noon with updates and lunch." He sighed and pulled three pages off his printer. "We need background checks on all the plant employees on this list. Sorry I didn't get it done. Then you can start your voodoo."

Sara scanned the list. "Does this list of employees at the meat packing plant include the USDA meat inspector? I don't think he's an employee of the plant per se, but they can't operate if an inspector isn't present."

He flared. "How would I know? I'm not a farm boy."

Sara wondered why Kit seemed so grouchy—no, stressed. "Don't worry. This will keep me busy."

"One more job. APD screwed up again. They didn't get a working phone number for Dan Steele. See if you can find one for him. Seems he was at the VA Hospital before he hit the bars on Central on Tuesday and lost his wallet. I requested basic info and got a two-day hold from the National Instant Criminal Background System."

"Oh, he might not be a random victim of a pickpocket."

Kit smiled. "That's what I thought."

"HIPPA regulations will prevent me from getting into his medical records without a court order, but I'll try to get enough data so we can get a warrant for them." Sara stood.

Bug began to twirl again. As Kit reached for the bag, she said, "Don't. He won't eat his dog food if he gets any more treats today. Little scamp."

***

Carbonne had changed since the last time she'd seen him four months ago. He no longer shaved his head and face. He looked like a wild man. His scalp was covered with black curly hair and his face with a thick beard. She must have stared too long.

"It's easier to get info when you look like a bum." He slid a large pizza onto the table in the small room assigned to Sara. "Figured Bug and I would like the sausage, and you'd like the mushrooms."

Sara placed soda, paper plates, and napkins on the table. "I've got basic facts on Dan Steele. He completed one year in the environmental sciences major at New Mexico State University. Low grades. After his tour of duty in Iraq, he worked at a meat packing plant and then at state parks in Carlsbad and Elephant Butte Lake. The record is spotty. He works now at the Ice Cave and Bandera Volcano near Grants but has a partial medical disability."

"You've been busy." Carbonne pulled a piece of sausage off his slice of pizza and flipped it to Bug. Then he folded the thin slice and stuffed it into his mouth. "Looks like…" He talked with his mouth full. "…you and I followed similar leads this morning. Figured we needed to talk." He grabbed another slice. "Haven't eaten since yesterday. No time. The guys on the street give more coherent answers in the morning."

Sara noted Bug had eaten the piece of sausage and put another piece of sausage on a napkin in front of him. She also noticed Carbonne had gone so deep undercover that Bug now ate more politely than the detective. "Why don't we eat a couple of slices before we talk."

Carbonne wolfed down several slices, tossing pieces of sausage to Bug. Sara enjoyed the pizza at a slower rate and accepted that Bug wouldn't eat much of his nutritionally balanced dog food today.

"A couple of guys sitting on the picnic benches by Building Two—the old gymnasium on the VA campus—recognized the picture of Dan Steele on his driver's license. Took them a while, but those guys are often hesitant." He chewed his fourth slice of pizza slowly. "Said he comes to the psych clinic in Building One most months."

"Kit told me already. That's why I checked his military records."

Carbonne nodded. "Pattern always the same. Comes to the clinic, stops by Building Two, and finds a couple of veterans. They eat at the Frontier Restaurant on Central and drift through bars until he gets back to his room in one of the seedy motels—remnants from the days of the old Highway 66—on Central. No funny business. A lonely guy who likes to talk about his problems—bad dreams and flashbacks—with other old soldiers."

"So, he's probably getting treatment for post-traumatic stress disorder or some other psych condition at the VA." Sara took a sip of her diet soda. "It all fits. Individuals who have been hospitalized for mental illness can't buy a gun. Most federal and New Mexico park rangers have law enforcement activities. Thus, he couldn't get a permanent position as a federal or state park ranger."

"How'd he get his current job at the ice caves?"

"It's a privately owned tourist attraction. His interest in parks, and presumably wildlife, makes him a logical sender of the package I got—at least the guts of the prairie dog." Sara fed Bug a piece of sausage. "Oh, I forgot one point. The manager of the meat packing plant in Grants also has the last name of Steele."

Carbonne stopped chewing. "What?"

"I haven't checked his background yet. Also, I haven't delved into the background of the man killed in the plant—Melvin Melendez. Most likely he's a poor immigrant with few options. I doubt I'll find anything of interest to you, but I like to be thorough. Just in case."

"Hmm. The pickpocket who took Dan Steele driver's license may have targeted him for a reason."

"Any leads on the guy who delivered my mystery box to UPS?"

"Nothing. Too many scrawny men with long stringy gray hair among the homeless." He finished his fifth piece of pizza. "Let's see if Kit has new details."

***

Sara opened the door to Kit's office. The big-shouldered man talking to Kit reminded Sara of her father. His skin wasn't really tanned; it was burned. The skin on his lower face and hands were a brownish-red shade, but his forehead was quite pale. He must have worn a wide-brimmed hat when he worked in the sun. Her father had been a farmer. She guessed this man was a farmer or rancher, too. The man's plaid, long-sleeve cowboy shirt seemed to confirm her guess. However, his tight jeans definitely didn't remind her of her father.

"Oh dear. You and Carbonne… better wait outside." Kit motioned for Sara to close the door.

Sara turned to Carbonne. "He looks like he stepped off a ranch in eastern New Mexico or west Texas. I wonder whether he's in costume or always dresses that way."

"Costume. Kit didn't want us to see the dude"

"Why the secrecy?"

Carbonne scratched his chin. "Damn beard itches. Don't know why anyone keeps a beard in summer."

Sara was surprised. It wasn't like Carbonne to be tactful. "I think we're thinking alike. Ulysses came to the same conclusion we did over lunch. You're not the right agent to investigate the death of the employee at the meat packing plant in Grants."

"You think?" He chuckled. "But I'm unbeatable on the streets of a city. Grants with its population of less than ten thousand is a mere town. Course, it does have plenty of alcoholic bums." He scratched his chin more.

Kit opened the door. The stranger was gone. He must have entered Ulysses's office through the door connecting Kit's and Ulysses's offices.

Carbonne barged ahead. "You need to get warrants for the medical records of Dan Steele and all the veterans who are employees at the plant."

Kit nodded. "I scanned Sara's email already. I'm sure the court will grant us access to Dan Steele's records. I doubt you've got enough on the others."

Sara paused before responding, clearly lost in thought. "Don't worry. I'll contact OSHA and get reports on previous accidents at the plant. I can build a case that injured workers had reasons to be angry at the management of the plant but were afraid to report them directly. It should be easy to get medical reports on injured individuals."

"Great…." Before Kit could say more, the office phone rang. He turned ashen as he listened. "I think the right agent for this case is in my office now—Agent Paul Carbonne. I'll put my phone on speaker mode."

"Hi, I'm Selena at the Albuquerque Wastewater Utility on Second Street. The man cleaning the grating in our wastewater input found a hand."

Carbonne slid into a chair. "Just a hand?"

"Yes. I called the Albuquerque police. They said your lab could ID it faster than theirs. Can you come get it? It's creeping us out."

"Are you sure it's not the paw of a dog or a wild animal?"

"Dogs don't have long fingers and a thumb. Neither do coyotes or bears."

"Any rings, tattoos, birthmarks?" Carbonne tapped notes onto his phone.

"Do you realize how bad it looks after being pushed through our sewer system? Black and green gunk over most of it. I can't tell you whether it's a man's or a woman's hand or even the skin color."

Someone in the background yelled, "Tell them it looks worse than the hand we found two years ago in our filters."

CHAPTER 8: Sanders

Sanders had not been totally honest with Sara. Yes, he'd handled multiple security problems at the U.S. embassy in Havana on Monday, but he'd left on Tuesday, his last day as a ranking official in the State Department mission to Cuba. He'd spent the rest of the day briefing the woman selected to be the interim chargé d'affaires in Cuba. She wouldn't make the same mistakes as her predecessor.

Sara assumed he was in Havana on Wednesday; he hadn't corrected her. Perhaps because he wanted to forget how he'd spent the day. Federal officials had spent hours trying to convince him to talk to Maria.

Federal prosecutors had charged her with racketeering and the premeditated murder of two law enforcement officers as she tried to eliminate Sara and him as witnesses against the Butcher Don in New Mexico. State Department and Justice Department officials threatened to charge her with espionage. Her lawyers claimed she was employed by private businessmen, not the Cuban government. The officials countered that she consciously endangered the welfare of the U.S. She had told them both, "It doesn't matter. Dead is dead."

Then a federal prosecutor told her that he could reduce her sentence to prison time, not execution, if she cooperated. She countered, "If I cooperate with you, they will find me and kill me even in isolation in a maximum-security prison."

Sanders listened to his boss and six other federal officials on Wednesday. All ended their comments the same way: "You have to talk to Maria. After all, you were her lover." He was tired of being reminded of his foolishness. Maybe they were jealous. She *was* beautiful.

On Thursday, he was briefed more, wired, and sent to see Maria in prison. The warden led him to the antechamber of a so-called private interview room. In some ways this "private" interview room was more public than the usual caged area used by multiple prisoners and their guests, because cameras were strategically located around the room. The warden proudly noted the cameras were not visible in the room because of the strategic placement of woodwork, shelves, and mirrors. Sanders knew the camouflage had failed as he watched Maria strut about the room. She stopped and winked at five of the six cameras in the room before she sat down. Thus, he felt foolish before he started the interview.

At first, Maria refused to talk. Finally, she said, "Why didn't they send in one of my real lovers, not someone I was paid to seduce?" She languorously caressed her neck and then her upper left arm with her right hand. Her fingernails were no longer polished in her usual eggplant shade, but her nails appeared to be shaped and shiny. Her movements were still graceful and seductive.

He wondered why she bothered to manicure her nails. Was she trying to seduce her guards or her visitors? Prison records indicated her only visitors were five lawyers, whose fees were paid by her wealthy family in the Miami area. FBI agents now believed several, if not most, of her relatives were involved in the movement of drugs from South and Central America to the U.S. The past chargé d'affaires should have checked her background more thoroughly before he hired her to be the economic attaché at the embassy in Havana.

"I worked hard to get your attention. You were so old and pathetically earnest about your work and your *Sara.*"

He knew those listening were snickering. He focused on the key questions that prosecutors wanted answered. They had told him to scare her. He doubted he could. "You were earnest about your work too. The Cuban government has arrested the couple who supervised your work on the island."

Her lips quivered a bit.

"I've misspoken. We know they weren't your supervisors, merely your local contacts. You were lucky; you were arrested in the U.S. The

Cubans are harsh on drug dealers." He showed her a picture of one of her past colleagues in what looked like a pig sty.

She glanced at the picture before she studied the ceiling and stroked her neck. "The paint on this ceiling is cracked."

"I assume your attorneys informed you that two of your family members and four of your friends in Miami were charged with racketeering. Four in New Mexico, including the so-called Butcher Don, are awaiting trial for racketeering, murder, or both."

She looked bored, pulled at her prison shirt, and rubbed the cleavage between her full breasts.

"Despite all the arrests, we don't have your real boss—the person who ordered the hit on me. I suspect the attempts on Sara were ordered to draw me out."

She drew her finger across her lips. "You *do* have a big ego."

He could almost hear the laughs in the anteroom. "Perhaps, but I told them you wouldn't answer my questions unless I made you a good offer. Here's the deal. Prison officials and the U.S. Marshals can alter your identity. Basically, switch your identity with someone else in isolation at the maximum-security prison in Colorado. You'd be safe under a new name."

She stopped stroking herself. "Won't work. Too many involved."

He suspected that she was right. He'd have to ad lib. "True. If you agree, only three high-ranking officials will be aware of the deal. My notes on this visit will be destroyed. Your lawyers won't be told. We suspect their roles are more to keep you silent and report on you than to protect you."

She sucked in her breath.

He guessed his last comment had reinforced her fear, but it would take more to earn her trust. "It can work."

She curled a few strands of hair around her fingers. "How do I agree?"

He'd never realized before that she never stopped flirting. "Give me the name of the person who ordered the hit on me. We also want the name of the person who supervised the Butcher Don."

She sniffed her hair.

He decided to ad lib more. Sara suspected a few individuals in the meat packing industry were involved in the drug trade, but he didn't want to mention Sara's name. "The FBI is focusing on men with deep covers in the meat packing industry."

Her eyes widened slightly.

This was the first time today she'd shown any real emotion. Sara was on to something. "You remember Carbonne. He believes…."

She sniffed and stared at the ceiling. "Tell him his drunk veteran routine doesn't fool anyone."

He wondered how she knew about Carbonne's disguise. He hadn't used the bum persona in Cuba. Either her guards or lawyers had given her data. "You might as well benefit by confirming our suspicions and save yourself."

Maria tossed her long hair. "You'd better treat Sara well. You won't have her long. She's seen too much again."

He gasped involuntarily. "Save yourself and accept my offer."

She buzzed the guard and announced, "I want to leave."

He was relieved the interview was over and quickly went to the FBI van parked in the lot outside the front entrance of the prison. "We need to review everything said to her in past interviews. I think she reported details we used to entice her to talk to her outside contacts and has endangered Sara, Carbonne, and others."

A man's voice boomed from a speaker. Sanders recognized the voice of the lead FBI agent on the case in Washington. "I already have asked for a detailed analysis of all interviews with her since her arrest. We've recorded all her conversations with us after she arrived in Washington. We'll recheck her guards' backgrounds."

Sanders heard Ulysses's bass. "Can't say the same for New Mexico. We'll do our best." Pause. "Better yet. I'll send transcripts of all our conversations with Maria before she was transferred to you in Washington. Then you can do the analyses. Sara, Carbonne, and our analysts can't handle more today. I think Sara's time is better spent investigating the characters in the meat packing industry."

Sanders responded, "I thought I might be the only one who noticed how Maria responded to my comment on the meat packing industry." He paused. "Her threats on Sara were serious. I'm worried."

"So am I." Ulysses continued, "I need more support from Washington, pronto. Hmm… Don't know how to say this. Sanders—why didn't you suspect Maria from day one? No one turns it on like she does without a reason."

Sanders heard several snickers on the line. The men in the van snorted. He feared Maria was right. He was too old to notice her at first. No, he wasn't that old; he was too busy.

CHAPTER 9: Sara

Sara didn't have to wait long to learn more about the mystery man in Kit's office. Ulysses summoned her about an hour after Carbonne had left to the water processing plant.

The sun-burnt cowboy stood when she entered Ulysses's office. "You, ma'am, must be Dr. Sara Almquist. I'm Frank McCoy, special agent with the Office of the Inspector General of USDA." He nodded to Ulysses and then winked at Sara. "He tells me you may be my best resource here. An epidemiologist and a farm girl, but too valuable a witness to go into the field with me. He didn't tell me you were so attractive."

Ulysses waved for Sara to join them at a small table. "Glib lines don't work on her. She's heard them all." He sighed. "I tried to fill Frank in on all our loose ends. Then I decided he should talk to you. He will enter the plant in Grants as a USDA certified meat inspector. The regular inspector claimed he was sick two hours before the accident, and the plant manager almost had to stop the processing line until a temporary inspector arrived. We…"

"That explains it." Sara bounced a bit in her chair. "I've spent the last twenty minutes trying to figure out why the USDA meat inspector—Hank Diaz—wasn't on the OSHA list of those in the plant at the time of the accident."

Ulysses winked at Frank. "I told you she's good."

Frank coughed. "My boss in the Inspector General's Office of USDA thought it was an odd coincidence, too. My first assignment is to introduce myself to Hank Diaz and get him to give me a tour of the plant.

Any background you give me on him could be useful. He's not apt to be talkative."

Sara nodded. "You might also talk to the part-time inspector who was present at the accident and the plant manager."

"On my list."

Ulysses drummed the table and peered at Sara. "I'm afraid to ask, but do we have a reason to believe your UPS package and the accident are linked?"

Sara suppressed a smile. "The plant manager is Caleb Steele. I think he's related to Dan Steele. Dan is the man who delivered my package to UPS. Well at least, his name was on the ID flashed at the UPS Store. They both attended high school in Grants. Dan is two years older than Caleb."

Both men straightened in their chairs. Ulysses drummed the table again. "Anything else?"

"We requested a court order for Dan Steele's medical records. It looks like he has a partial medical disability for a psychological reason because of his time in Iraq, but I'm guessing."

Frank leaned back. "Once I show up in Grants, I have to assume I'll be watched. Any suggestions on how to contact you two and pass evidence?"

Ulysses nodded. "Carbonne can roll into Grants as a drunk. There's a dozen low-end hotels and bars on I-40 going into Grants."

Sara bit her lip. "This may be corny, but there are great tourist sites in the Grants area: El Morro National Monument, El Malpais National Monument, and the Ice Cave and Bandera Volcano. As a newcomer to the area…" She looked at Frank. "…you might logically visit these sites. Anyone from the FBI in Albuquerque could zip out on I-40 to them."

Frank nodded. "Might work."

Sara continued to chew her lip. "Couple of slight problems. Dan Steele is employed at the Bandera Volcano tourist site. Whoever sent my package knew a bit about wildlife ecology and might be a park ranger."

Sara heard Kit shout, "No!" even though the door to his office was closed.

Carbonne burst through the doorway from Kit's to Ulysses's office. "Glad I went to the Wastewater Utility or we would have lost half the evidence. Do you know how bad the input water stinks in hot weather?"

Sara, Ulysses, and Frank nodded because a stench emanated from Carbonne.

"The hand was wrapped in—you could say was grasping—long gray fibers. They would have pitched the gray mass."

Ulysses pulled a handkerchief from his pocket and wiped his nose. "I'm afraid to ask. What were the fibers?"

"Bet my paycheck, the strands of a damn wig. Told the lab crew to analyze it carefully."

"Why?"

"The man photographed at the UPS Store with Dan Steele's ID had long gray hair and wore a knit cap. Only crazies or those hiding their identity wear a knit cap in summer here. Damn! Should have known it was a wig in the photo. Damn! The guy must have known the UPS Store had camera surveillance. Means all my work was a waste. I asked all the residents of the streets and at the VA about a man with long gray hair."

He plopped in a chair at the table and dropped a bag at his feet. "I wanted to leave my wet shoes with Kit. He made a fuss."

Sara knew Carbonne deserved a hug, but he smelled—how could she describe it?—like raw sewage. She forced herself to pat him on the shoulder. "Not totally wasted. You got info on Dan Steele from your street buddies."

Carbonne snorted.

"Did the tape from the UPS Store include an image of the unknown man's face?"

He scratched his beard. "I asked the lab to blow up the images of his face as soon as I confiscated the tape." He sniffed his hand. "Damn!"

Ulysses shook his head.

Carbonne glared at Ulysses. "You think I enjoy being a slob? You're wrong. This beard holds odors. The whole sewage plant smells some in summer but the input building is unbelievable. They have the screens and filters for the input water in a building so the stink doesn't waft through the neighborhood. The net result is: We retrieved the hand in a hot humid building, which stunk like a dirty swamp. Fill me in fast, so I can clean up."

Ulysses put his handkerchief in his pocket. "You didn't say—was the lab able to produce a usable picture of the man's face?"

"Not really. Gaunt. Not Dan Steele. Wrinkled, so over forty or has been on the streets awhile. Problem is a twenty-year-old can look fifty after a year of drugs, alcohol, and street life." Carbonne reached out to shake Frank's hand. "You the one going undercover into the plant in Grants?"

Frank turned to Ulysses. "I've got a problem if this place is leaky. Is your assistant talkative?"

Before Ulysses could answer, Carbonne said, "No, Sara and I figured it out when we spied you earlier in Kit's office." He shrugged. "Guess Sara didn't admit it. What's your cover?"

"I'm the temporary USDA certified meat inspector. We've been talking about how I'll contact you and Sara. She thought as a newcomer to the area I could visit tourist sites, and you could roam the street as a drunk."

"One problem. Lot of street guys from Grants come here in winter. I might be recognized as FBI."

Sara studied Carbonne. "Would anyone of the street crowd recognize you if you cleaned up?"

Ulysses guffawed. "Not sure *I* would. Let's plot our course. Sara, your plans?"

"I'll check out the Dan Steele and the employees in the plant, especially Caleb Steele, in reports of the police, park service, VA, OSHA, and USDA and in newspaper files. Grants is a small town. I'm apt to find family connections and other useful tidbits. For example, the accident could be retaliation for an event that happened several years ago. Maybe not related to drugs."

Frank frowned for only a second and then returned to his relaxed attitude. "By USDA reports, I assume you mean inspection reports of meat packing plants. Do you realize FSIS, that's the Food Safety and Inspection Service, has repeatedly found code violations at New Mexico meat packing plants? They've improved but are hardly models of good practices. You're apt to see hundreds of health- and safety-related violations at plants in New Mexico in the FSIS records during the last ten years. I'll have the Inspector General talk to FSIS officials. I think they can screen their data for you and speed up the process."

Ulysses stopped pecking at his laptop. "Don't forget, Sara, your highest priority is to translate scientific data into English for the rest of us." He turned to Carbonne. "Kit can only get so much from the APD."

"You want to me to milk their underbelly, including the slime bag, for info?"

Ulysses looked down at his laptop. "You and Sara have a special dislike for Jack Daniels, but he does know many secrets about this state."

"You saw his best side because he knew you could get him into witness protection. You know he hates me. Pick someone else."

"Can't. He'll fool them."

"Okay." Carbonne grimaced. "On a more positive note. The agents who routinely work the pueblo lands in western New Mexico might give Frank helpful info about key characters in the Grants area. He should meet them."

"Agreed." Ulysses covered his nose with a tissue.

"I'm through until I clean up." Carbonne rushed toward the door. "Maybe Frank and I could stop by the safe house tonight to update Sara and give her guards a break."

Ulysses smirked. "You'd do anything to get one of Sara's home cooked meals. She might be too busy. And you can't be in your usual disguise. You know the guys at the safe house think you're too recognizable by the street people. Sara, are you willing?"

Sara looked at her watch. "Won't be great. I'll send a shopping list to my guards." She saw Ulysses arch his eyebrows. "Don't worry I won't go over the per diem." She turned to Carbonne, "Sorry it won't be lasagna. I don't have the time, and I made spaghetti last night. So, the menu will be just Midwest farm cooking."

CHAPTER 10: Unknown Man and Sara

He followed the white Honda Civic when it pulled out of the Luecking Place exit of the FBI building at six-thirty. It was a car often used by Carbonne. The car stopped at Main Events Entertainment, and an unknown man jumped into the car. He kept his distance as the white car snaked through back streets until it reached the Smith's supermarket at the corner of Tramway Road and Montgomery Boulevard.

Two men, dressed in dark slacks and light-colored dress shirts without ties, entered the grocery store. One man was tall, muscular, and clean-cut. The other was average height with his dark hair slicked back into a tiny ponytail at the nape of his neck and without a beard. The men were an odd pair.

They reappeared ten minutes later with a small bag of groceries and walked rapidly across the parking lot and east on Montgomery for a block before they turned onto a side street in the nice homes of the Foothills area of Albuquerque. Neither paid much attention to the joggers racing by them but instead appeared to be in rapt conversation. They rang the bell at an ivory stucco home with a red tile roof on Hilltop Place and were immediately admitted by a man, or at least a tall individual in slacks, who remained in the shadows.

Not much to report to the boss. He didn't recognize either man.

***

Sara did a double take when Carbonne walked into the kitchen. She'd never seen him dressed up. He even walked differently than when he was in his street garb. Frank also seemed different without his Western gear. "You look like two guys ready for a night on the town. Dinner may be a disappointment."

Carbonne grinned. "Ulysses suggested we alter our appearance in case we were followed. He didn't want us to lead anyone to the safe house or blow our aliases." He held up one foot. "I even wore my heeled leather boots." He turned to the lead U.S. Marshal on duty. "I thought I was tailed when I left Main Events Entertainment by a blue Ford Fiesta, but after the third turn on back streets I didn't see it. Might want to be on the lookout for it."

"I rode shotgun the whole way. I agree with Carbonne. We lost him." Frank put the bag on the counter. "We brought a bag of croissants and a pan of brownies. Corny, but the leftovers will be popular tomorrow. No wine. Carbonne told me about previous attacks on you. He thought we needed to stay alert. I sure hope this is a quiet night."

The lead marshal had already served himself and was eating in the kitchen. "We all do. She only survived the last attacks because of Gil Andrews, her local police chief, and her boyfriend Sanders. Both are experienced marksmen and tacticians. I've got one marshal on guard at the front and one walking the periphery of the house while I eat and sit in on your conversation. We rotate every half hour."

"Time to eat." Sara noticed Carbonne looking at the bowl of scalloped potatoes with ham and carrots suspiciously.

"It's good. Lots of cheese, big chunks of ham, and green chilis." She pointed to the guard. "Look—he's ready for seconds."

The guard looked up from his plate. "Really is, and what she calls a Waldorf salad with apples, celery, raisins, and nuts is great. I also like the way she keeps cut up carrots, radishes, and celery in the refrigerator for snacks."

Carbonne sighed. "Only problem with Sara's cooking is that it's nutritious. My system isn't used to so many fruits and vegetables."

As Carbonne spooned the main dish onto his plate, Frank said, "Looks like the type of meal my first wife served."

"Oops." Sara sighed. "I can't grill outside at the safe house. There're limits…."

Frank laughed. "You read my comment wrong. I liked her cooking, but she didn't like my hours."

***

After the initial chit-chat, Sara announced, "Talked to Lydia. Good news from her point of view. Not so good from ours."

"Damn." Carbonne took a second serving of the main dish. "Not what I grew up eating, but it's good. Remember as you explain Lydia's info that this city boy doesn't understand agriculture or science."

"There were *Yersinia pestis*, that is plague bacteria, on the surface of sheep's abomasum."

Carbonne snorted.

She tried again and said, "The ivory mass in the package I received is a sheep's abomasum, the fourth stomach of a sheep. Lydia thinks the bacteria on its surface were contamination from the prairie dog guts because the sheep lymph glands, the contents of one of the plastic containers, did not have the swellings characteristic of plague. So, she doubts the sheep was infected with *Yersinia pestis*. No doubt the prairie dog died of a *Yersinia* infection. But Lydia ordered more tests."

Frank rocked his chair on its back legs.

"I can guess what you're thinking. I asked Lydia to do DNA analyses to see if the abomasum came from the same sheep as the lymph nodes. If it did, I think we have a problem. I don't see how someone could secretly collect the abomasum and lymph nodes from the same animal in a modern processing plant and then get them out of the plant. Suggests to me the sheep was home butchered, and our two cases are unrelated."

Frank brought his chair down with a thump. "Don't jump to conclusions. Might take the cooperation of several individuals. However, all major parts of the carcass are tagged with a bar code assigned to the animal before slaughter in a good plant. That way, the USDA inspector can pull all the tissues of an animal if infections are found in one tissue."

"Oh, I hadn't realized USDA had such good computer tracking systems in place."

"We've made real progress. Unfortunately, the bar codes don't leave the plant. We can't trace meat in the marketplace to its source yet."

Carbonne looked back and forth between Sara and Frank. "Hey guys, I'm still here."

Sara looked at Carbonne. "I thought I could prove my package and the accidents couldn't be related. I was wrong. The two problems could be related."

"Typical lab mumbo-jumbo."

"Not really, but tissues may have been cross-contaminated. We know the sheep was a sick animal. Several of the ulcers perforated the stomach lining. Lydia explained multiple potential reasons for these ulcers—viruses, cancer, and stress."

Carbonne stood up and began to pace. "Can't she ID the bacteria in the gunk sent to you?"

Sara continued, "Not really because there's a lot of bacteria in an animal's gut. And *Yersinia* bacterium from the prairie dog could have contaminated other samples in my package."

"Sorry I asked. English, please."

"Here's the bottom line. Lydia thinks an animal with this amount of ulceration would have had bloody diarrhea. The USDA inspector should not have allowed it to be butchered for meat consumed by humans."

Frank sighed. "I've got to get to know the USDA meat inspector and his substitute at the plant in Grants, pronto. I've also got to learn how this plant handles its 4D meat."

Sara blinked. "You're beyond me. What's '4D meat?'"

"Meat from sick and dying animals. It's considered unfit for human consumption. Many manufacturers of pet food won't use it, but some do. Dog racing tracks use it."

"Yuck." She picked up Bug who'd been at her feet. "Don't listen, baby." She turned back to Frank. "I don't think there are legal dog tracks in New Mexico, but there is illegal dog fighting here. One veterinarian warned me I must never leave Bug in my car, even if it was locked and cold outside. Bug is the type of dog they like to use as bait for fighting dogs."

"This discussion would keep most people from eating." Carbonne walked to the counter and brought the brownies to the table. "However, I was raised in a rough Philly neighborhood. I knew Sara was a science nerd." He peered at Frank. "Guess you are, too. Have some dessert before Sara entertains us with more gore."

Sara chewed a large square of brownie with fudge icing before she spoke. "This was a good choice of dessert, guys. Remember I speculated about Dan Steele this afternoon? Kit did his magic. The judge gave us access to Steele's VA medical records. Dan Steele listed his next of kin as his sibling: Caleb Steele, the manager of the plant."

"And?"

"As suspected, Dan Steele was institutionalized for severe PTSD after he attacked men in turbans on two occasions. They think he is no threat to others now, if he takes his medications."

Carbonne didn't stop chewing his brownie. "Anything else?"

"I thought I did pretty well considering my time constraints. The potatoes had to cook for over an hour. What did you two guys get?"

Frank spoke first. "The agents working the Indian lands are great sources of information. My boss will send all our background data on full-time and part-time USDA meat inspectors in New Mexico to you tomorrow."

Carbonne frowned. "Talked to Jack Daniels. Don't care what Ulysses thinks. Jack's still trolling for info even in witness protection. Funny. What good is it to him now?"

Frank stopped chewing his brownie. "Did you learn anything?"

"Owners of several meat packing plants in New Mexico are beholden to the gangs. They get kickbacks for allowing drugs to be shipped inside carcasses. Already knew that. Ulysses has a talkative one under his thumb. As usual, Jack gave me nothing specific. Never does until he wants a favor." Carbonne stared at Sara for a moment. "Asked if you had any received any surprise packages lately."

CHAPTER 11: Sara on Friday

"Wasn't Carbonne tailed by a blue Ford Fiesta last night? There's one on the right on Calle de Terra," said the male guard as the unmarked car passed the intersection with the small side street. "Maybe we can corner it if our other car comes down Manitoba."

Sara swayed in the back seat as the woman marshal swerved right and then left. The male guard summoned Albuquerque police vehicles.

The blue car sped up.

Sara doubted the driver of the bright blue Fiesta would have sped up if he didn't feel guilty. Of course, Sanders said she drove like an old woman. Everyone drove faster than she did. She saw an all-wheel drive SUV, the second unmarked vehicle of the U.S. Marshal Service, pull into the next intersection. The blue car had nowhere to go.

A police siren wailed. She didn't think the police substation near the safe house had enough personnel to respond quickly to requests, and the APD was generally overextended. Apparently, she was wrong, or the U.S. Marshal service had alerted the police to be ready before she'd left the safe house.

She held her breath as the blue car slowed slightly and ran over the curb to get past the SUV in the intersection. Somehow, the car skidded to a stop miraculously on the sidewalk without hitting a light post, turning over, or hitting the newly arrived marked APD car.

A second marked police car with lights flashing and siren blaring whizzed past. An officer jumped out of each police vehicle. They ran toward the blue car and yelled, "Get out with your hands up." Slowly the door opened. A young man in black jeans and a black T-shirt clambered out.

The police frisked him. The voice of the marshal, who'd driven the SUV, blared from the male guard's phone. "I got this under control. Go!"

Sara petted Bug and relaxed as the woman marshal did a U-turn and then turned onto a major street.

They drove for two blocks in heavy traffic. The male guard mumbled, "Odd. Turn off without signaling."

They went two blocks.

"Go into defensive mode. I'll notify the FBI headquarters. We need backup." The male guard continued, "An old black Camaro is following us. Picked us up one block after we left the blue Fiesta. The Camaro has kept three cars behind us consistently in heavy traffic."

Sara checked her seat belt and the one on Bug's seat. She slunk down in the seat a bit as the woman marshal turned and turned again. Each time the male guard said, "Still there."

The words—old black Camaro, old black Camaro—rang in her head. Suddenly she remembered. "It's Jack Daniels in the Camaro."

The two marshals ignored her.

"Jack used a souped-up black Camaro to tail Sanders during the investigation of the Butcher Don. You won't lose him."

They continued to turn corners and report on the phone to someone.

"Please check on Jack Daniels's location. He's in witness protection."

The male guard glanced at Sara. "Can't be Jack."

Sara couldn't hear his full conversation on the phone, but she heard him mention "Jack Daniels." Nothing more she could do but pray and try to keep from vomiting. She was nauseated from the constant jerks as the car lurched around one corner after another. Bug must have been car sick, too, because he moaned softly.

The male guard said, "Order from Ulysses. Get on a major street and head for the FBI building. He guesses Jack is either messing with Sara's mind or setting us up for attack by another vehicle we haven't noticed. He's sent out vehicles to try to nab the Camaro."

Sara plunked down in the chair in Kit's office. "Does Ulysses have time to see me?"

Kit frowned. "He's not in a good mood."

"Neither am I. Can I assume they weren't able to find the black Camaro?" She knew it wasn't an appropriate question but she asked anyway. "Who's in there now? Carbonne?"

"Lots of people. Carbonne is late."

Carbonne, in his bum alias, rushed in. He looked at Sara. "You look all right. Should have known last night the bastard Jack Daniels was involved. How did you know?"

"Sanders thought Jack Daniels was the best tracker he'd seen after Jack used an old black Camaro to tail him. Not surprising. Jack excels at sneakiness. But I don't understand. Why would he want to spook me?"

Carbonne knocked on the door. "I'm late." He looked back at Sara before he opened the door. "Jack doesn't do much on his own initiative. Someone's paying him."

Kit and Sara worked in tandem to trace the backgrounds of the plant employees in various data sets. After an hour, Sara said, "Can you break into their meeting? We need permission to alert Frank. If he left here just before I arrived, he'll be around Potters Place now."

J. L. Greger

CHAPTER 12: FBI Special Agent Ulysses Howe

Ulysses looked at the motley crew in his office. The chief representative from the U.S. Marshal's Office was playing with his phone and avoiding eye contact with the others in the room. Ulysses thought the marshal should be ashamed.

Marshals had last seen Jack Daniels last night at nine when he complained of a headache and supposedly went to bed. This morning at seven, a marshal knocked on Jack's door because Jack was scheduled to meet at eight with the prosecutor for the Butcher Don case. The marshals found no one in the room. Jack Daniels could be anywhere. Those marshals had contacted Ulysses for help minutes before Sara's guards had called to report they were being followed by a black Camaro.

The male and female guards who had driven Sara to the FBI building were incensed by their colleague's lame excuses. The prosecutor and another staff member in the U.S. Attorney's Office for the District of New Mexico looked smugly back and forth between the marshals.

The chief marshal sighed. "Let's keep this in perspective. Jack Daniels has disappeared several times. He always returns with a bag of donuts."

The prosecutor lost his usual reserve and cursed. Luckily, Carbonne rushed into the office before the marshal replied. Instead, they all choked as they stared wide-eyed at him.

"Sorry, I'm in my homeless veteran persona. Have the marshals located another safe house for Sara?"

Before anyone could reply to Carbonne, the prosecutor said, "Why don't we put Sara and Jack, minus any cars, in the new safe location.

We'd save money on guards. Sara has the best track record of any of us for extracting data from Jack."

Carbonne slouched into a chair. "Bad idea. Sara would strangle the prick."

That broke the ice. The group settled into an honest discussion. Jack Daniels had them over a barrel. The federal prosecutor admitted he had a recurring nightmare. "In my dream, a defense attorney during the RICO trial proves that a key point in Jack's testimony is false. That's why I insisted the FBI check and recheck all his comments and monitor Sara closely. She could still save most, but definitely not all, of our RICO charges against the Butcher Don and his cohorts if we lost Jack."

"Well then," said the chief marshal. "Is it worth the money to provide witness protection to Jack before the trial and potentially for years afterwards? Why not warehouse him in a local jail?"

Ulysses raised three fingers. "Three reasons. One, that would be murder. Jack couldn't survive a day in an Albuquerque jail because he's incriminated so many members of the APD. He'd fare no better in most jails and prisons in the state, except the jail in the small town of Mercado. Chief Gil Andrews runs a tight ship, but his jail isn't equipped to handle a prisoner for more than a couple of days. Two, we'd put a bull's-eye on Sara. I prefer to let the gangs focus on Jack. Three, we have to find him before we can house him again."

The chief marshal shook his head. "We can't find him without the help of the Albuquerque police. They know him."

Ulysses rolled his eyes. "My recollections are the APD had trouble locating Jack, even when he worked for them, on a number of occasions. They might be less help than you think. And we have to consider the possibility that his disappearance is not voluntary. Rogue members of APD or the drug cabal may have located Jack and disposed of him already."

The prosecutor shook his head. "I hate to do this, but I'll call the APD chief now and ask for his cooperation." He and his assistant went to the corner and began to whisper into their phones.

Ulysses was thankful when Kit knocked on the door and poked his head into the office. "Sorry to interrupt, but read your email from Sara now, please." He closed the door.

Ulysses apologized to those in his office and scanned his computer screen for an email from Sara. She and Kit had uncovered, amazingly quickly, all sorts of leads. Sara had labeled the report honestly, not as leads but as "Quirks of the Personnel at the Meat Packing Plant." He smiled at her sense of humor and focused on the starred item.

Sara reported that twenty of the fifty employees at the plant in Grants had police records for petty misdemeanors and another five for major misdemeanors. Two employees were felons, but none were on parole. All but two of the misdemeanors involved alcohol and/or domestic violence. Ulysses wasn't surprised. Alcohol abuse and domestic violence were major problems in many low-income communities, including the Native American ones in New Mexico. However, few of the employees lived on tribal lands; most had addresses in Grants. The exceptions were five employees who lived in Potters Place, a census designated location, which was really an unincorporated area on the Acoma Pueblo.

Sara's starred point was:

> *These five are probably related and have no police records. They haven't filed any injury reports with OSHA. One has worked at the plant for twenty years; the others from five to ten years. Perhaps, Frank should interview the employees living in Potters Place before he enters the plant. He's in the area now. We need your permission to give him an order.*

He wanted to read more, but this wasn't the time. He excused himself and poked his head into Kit's office. "This is the first time either of you two asked permission. Call Frank. Don't make it an order, just a suggestion. He may not want to stop in Potters Place because he may have to reveal his true identity. In any case, he'll find your new information useful."

He returned to his desk and apologized to the group again for the interruption, even though he thought it had been a blessing. No one's face was now flushed with annoyance. He looked at Carbonne. "You may want to scan the data Sara and Kit compiled on the Grants plant. Pigeon's plant deserves a similar analysis."

Carbonne waved his hand. "Are you suggesting the plant in Grants and Sara's weird package are related to Jack's antics or the Butcher Don case? I doubt it."

Ulysses drummed the table with his fingers, debating what to say. "It's too early to be sure."

The group wrapped up their discussion with three decisions. One, when found, Jack Daniels would be required to wear a monitoring device, would have no access to a car, and would be moved out of New Mexico until the trial. They felt they had to honor the prosecutor's promise of witness protection unless they proved he'd committed a major new felony. Two, Sara couldn't return to her home and required continued protection. Three, the prosecutor would record depositions with both Sara and Jack in case protection activities were unsuccessful.

Afterward, Ulysses didn't have the stomach to tell Sara about the tenuousness of her safety. He saw Sara had sent another email with a lengthier report. She was always productive but now she was working at a manic pace. Was it to distract herself from thinking about who would attack her next? He could think of nothing useful to say to Sara.

He returned to studying her report. The first three points in this extended report might be useful but were not surprising.

First, twenty of the employees at the plant were registered gun owners. Sara feared that many others owned unregistered guns because a number had committed felonies or misdemeanors, which prevented legal gun ownership.

Second, thirty of the fifty employees at the plant were veterans. Dan Steele was not the only person from Grants who regularly visited the VA in Albuquerque.

Third, the plant didn't appear to have nepotism rules. Thirty of the employees had one of four last names: Chino, Martinez, Diaz, and Lewis. Sara guessed interfamily or clan feuds might be related to the accidents in the plant.

Ulysses drummed his fingers on the table. Perhaps he should redirect Sara's efforts. The accident at the plant probably didn't relate to Sara. Her mysterious package of biohazardous materials was probably a plea for help and not a threat. However, she was being stalked. The most likely source of funds to mount a stalking program with several cars was a drug cartel. Probably the one headed by the Butcher Don. He sighed. That was an awful lot of "probablies."

Agent Roy Everhart called with more bad news. He'd arranged to meet Pigeon for breakfast at a café in Albuquerque. Pigeon didn't show. Everhart called Pigeon's plant and his home in Las Vegas, New Mexico. Nothing.

Everhart's story took a surprising twist when he contacted the U.S. Marshals. Pigeon had decided on Monday night he and his family must enter a witness protection program immediately. Up to then, Pigeon had been adamant that he wouldn't leave his home until the plant sold. The marshals questioned him for hours, but Pigeon wouldn't explain his sudden decision. They had moved him to a safe house in Belen on Tuesday.

Ulysses was annoyed. No, he was steamed. The marshals who had been in his office should have mentioned this development. Furthermore, he couldn't believe the Marshal Service had allowed Pigeon to choose the location of the safe house. Ulysses calmed down enough to realize that their question to Pigeon was not unreasonable. They had asked him where he had the fewest contacts and named five areas in New Mexico along I-25—Santa Fe, Albuquerque, Mercado, Los Lunas, and Belen. Pigeon had immediately insisted Belen was the only safe place for his family for the three or four nights before they were moved out of state.

Ulysses calmed down enough to hear Everhart's good news. The marshals reluctantly agreed agents could meet with Pigeon and his family at eleven today for one last time before the marshals whisked them out of state.

Ulysses had interviewed Pigeon several times. "You need to get honest answers on what spooked the family. You won't get them from Pigeon. Carbonne might because he has firsthand knowledge of most of the characters in the upcoming trial. He's also had a crash course on meat packing plants during the last day from a veteran USDA meat inspector."

"I'm not a beginner," complained Everhart.

Ulysses knew Everhart and Carbonne were at opposite ends of the spectrum in their approach to investigations and life in general. "Yes, but Pigeon is a great con artist. He won't be able to play to both you at once because of your different styles."

"Okay, I guess…."

Ulysses didn't want to hear Everhart's excuses. "I think you might also force Pigeon to be honest if you knew more about his business. Kit and Sara profiled the meat packing plant in Grants. I'll email their report to you. Get similar data on Pigeon's plant and use the facts as you interview him. If nothing else, you'll be better able to spot inconsistencies in his story."

"You act like you don't trust Pigeon at all. He *is* a witness for the prosecution."

Ulysses saw no reason to state the obvious. "Another idea. You said the son was in tears when he came home from school on Monday. Talk to his son's teacher before the interview with Pigeon. See if anything strange happened at school on Monday. Take a woman agent along for the interview, too. Separate the son and wife from the husband."

Fifteen minutes later, Kit knocked on his door and entered. "Carbonne wants you to read the medical examiner's report, not just the first paragraph as you usually do, and call him ASAP." He slammed the door shut when he left.

Ulysses sighed. He wondered what had annoyed Kit, but he had no time to explore the newest office spat, whatever it was. He scanned the report.

Carbonne had been right. The gray strands in the clenched fist were made of the polyester used to make artificial wigs. Any DNA in skin or sweat on the wig would have been washed off in the sewer and no analyses were recommended. However, the medical examiner had requested DNA analyses of the hand because he assumed eventually the rest of the body or parts of it would be found. The most potentially useful point in the report was that both the ring and little fingers were missing from the hand.

CHAPTER 13: USDA Inspector Frank McCoy

The drive after he left the traffic of Albuquerque on I-40 was boring. Mesas, distant hills, and olive green and golden pastures seemed to be baking under an almost cloudless sky. The most interesting part of the drive to him was the way the railroad snaked along I-40. Actually, the road followed the railway, which predated I-40 and its predecessor Route 66. He guessed that much of the frontage road by I-40 was the old Highway 66.

In one sense, he was glad the drive was boring. He needed to think.

The agents at the Albuquerque office of the FBI were typical white males with a couple of Hispanics, Blacks, Native Americans, and women sprinkled in. He'd found all the agents to be helpful and capable. However, a couple seemed to have little sympathy, maybe "respect" was a better word, for rural Native American and Hispanic communities. Accordingly, he doubted these agents ever got the complete cooperation of officials or citizens in those communities. Several agents also groused about the slob Carbonne. Frank agreed Carbonne was a character out of sync with many of the agents. However, Frank knew he wouldn't want to be grilled by Carbonne. He, like Ulysses, was too good at analyzing suspects psychologically.

Frank liked Ulysses, an extremely well-educated black man. But Ulysses was tired of the heavy crime load in New Mexico and the spats among his staff. Several agents had hinted his retirement was imminent. In general, he recognized the FBI crew based in Albuquerque couldn't effectively handle a new crisis.

Frank was less sure how he felt about Sara. The quick answer was he pitied her. She was trapped in a dangerous situation at least until the big trial was over. He also admired her. Who wouldn't? Smart, self-reliant, quietly attractive. She reminded him of his first wife and the mother of his daughter, except Sara didn't appear to be annoyed that her boyfriend was often absent. Maybe she was too absorbed in sleuthing?

He doubted Ulysses's crew would analyze him as he had them. That was good. He hadn't been totally honest with them. The Inspector General of USDA had let Ulysses think his call had initiated Frank's investigation of the plant in Grants. Frank had not corrected this misconception because FBI agents liked to think they were in charge. He also hadn't bothered to tell them that he'd completed his assignment in Amarillo for USDA last Friday and taken the weekend and three vacation days to visit old friends in New Mexico and Texas.

The Inspector General of USDA, like Sara, doubted it was a coincidence that Hank Diaz became violently ill two hours before the accident. Meat inspectors knew their backups were required to report to a plant within two hours after being called. Diaz worked for another hour and forty minutes waiting for Elijah Wood, the backup inspector. Diaz either was not sick or was scared. Frank believed both were true.

The second concern was Elijah Wood had called his boss in the USDA meat inspection service the day after the accident and threatened to quit. The official got Elijah to agree to remain as a backup inspector and to not talk about his plans until another backup inspector arrived.

Frank had let Ulysses and Sara think he would first talk to Hank Diaz and the plant manager Caleb Steele. He had instead made an appointment to talk to Elijah Wood at the El Malpais Ranger Station.

Sara's call jolted his thinking. The Native Americans living in Potters Place and working at the plant might have a unique perspective. Two of them and Caleb Steele were the only employees who had worked at the plant ten or more years. After listening to her suggestions, he said, "Forget the cloak and dagger stuff. I'll go to the office of the mayor for Acoma and explain I'm the new backup USDA meat inspector in the area. I'll ask if he's heard rumors about plague in the area."

Sara chuckled. "Good idea, but there's no mayor at Acoma. I think you'll have to talk to tribal council members because the governor is too busy."

After the call, he turned off I-40 and stopped at Sky City Casino and Hotel. The woman at the information desk proudly told him the Acoma Pueblo was built on an isolated mesa and was the oldest continually inhabited community in the U.S. She claimed her family still maintained a home on the plateau and at least one family member slept there every night. This week her cousin was living in the house.

Frank didn't say the houses on the historic mesa sounded more like hotels or family vacation houses than homes. Instead he asked her whether she'd heard about a prairie dog die-off in the area.

She blanched and said, "Not again." She quickly directed him to the administrative office of the tribal council. He was surprised to learn none of the pueblo offices were on the isolated mesa.

He didn't feel like rushing back out into the baking heat and wandered into the casino's gift shop to look at the ceramics made by Acoma potters. The thin walled pots with geometric designs in black and white with occasional orange accents didn't appeal to him, but they sure had fascinated his first wife. Then he roamed the casino. It was a typical New Mexico one, less showy than those in Las Vegas, Nevada. He lost a few dollars on craps before he headed south on Pueblo Road.

***

The dark-haired, middle-aged man closed the door to his office as soon as Frank asked whether anyone on the pueblo had noticed a die-off of prairie dogs. "Rumors of the plague aren't good for business at the casino." The council member returned to his chair and asked Frank for proof of his employment as a USDA meat inspector. When he was satisfied, he said, "One of our ditch bosses hinted that there might be a prairie dog die-off on one of the mesas." He added quickly. "Not in an area frequented by tourists."

Frank tried to not sound annoyed. "Why wasn't it reported it to the New Mexico Department of Agriculture?"

"Might have been. I don't know." He sent Frank to the office of the environmental officer.

***

The environmental officer listened as Frank explained his background and his concern as a meat inspector about the spread of *Yersinia* bacteria from prairie dogs to sheep and cattle grazing in the area of a die-off. The environmental officer chuckled as he closed the door to his office. "I wonder which council member you scared. Describe him."

Frank did.

"Yes, he's a nervous man. Here's the story. The prairie dog die-off is on land not owned by members of our pueblo. I don't know what our ditch boss was doing there about a week ago."

"What's a ditch boss?"

"You're not from around here. Water is life here and those who supervise our access to irrigation water are called ditch bosses."

Frank figured he was about to get the typical bureaucratic answer to his next question. "Did you report the siting?"

"Of course, to the Cooperative Extension Service for this county, Cibola County, in Grants."

Frank nodded. "What did the extension agent do?" He feared he was about to be sent to another office.

"After a few days, I realized the agent was managing 4-H exhibits at the State Fair in Albuquerque. I emailed the New Mexico Department of Agriculture but got no response." He frowned. "They must have received my message because you're here, but they should have sent someone out to collect samples by now."

Frank saw no reason to tell the environmental officer about Sara's package. Obviously, communication among government offices was a problem in New Mexico and that was nothing new. "Here's where to send reports of prairie dog die-offs in the future."

He watched as the environmental officer typed an email to Lydia Griegos. "I'm curious. I've read Tony Hillerman's books on law enforcement on the pueblos in the Southwest. Do tribal police get involved in environmental issues like prairie dog die-offs?"

The environmental officer looked up from his computer screen. "Sometimes." He sent the email. "The tribal police had their hands full last week. A drunken party resulted in the death of a five-year-old boy. All present denied shooting the boy and two guys had similar guns. Then too, our police chief was the boy's uncle." He shook his head. "After a lot of hard work, the FBI proved a bullet bounced off a metal button and hit the boy in the head. I guess I should have notified them, but...."

"They had bigger problems. I understand. I just want to understand how things are handled here." He waited for the environmental officer to offer more insights.

Finally, the environmental officer coughed. "I never thought to notify our current USDA meat inspector, Hank Diaz. He would have told me not to bother him."

"How about if you don't tell him that I stopped by?"

The environmental officer nodded. "No problem. I never see him. Diaz's a secretive man. Might help if you talked to the Lewises before you talk to Diaz. Five of them work in the plant. The wives of two of the men work at the nearby Haak'u Learning Center down the road. One's a teacher's aide in the Head Start program; the other runs the food service. I'll call and tell them you're coming."

CHAPTER 14: Sara

"All you're good for is to create work for others. Things will change when Ulysses retires." A muscular, blond man in a suit slammed the door to Kit's office and strutted down the hall, without acknowledging Sara and Bug as they returned from a walk.

She'd seen the agent before. He always addressed her as "ma'am" if others were present but ignored her if others weren't around. She knew nothing else about him except his slacks always looked uncomfortably tight and he was rumored to be a good marksman.

Kit was ashen but silent as she and Bug positioned themselves for another work session at the side table in Kit's office.

"Don't let one arrogant agent upset you."

"I didn't know Ulysses was retiring."

"Maybe he isn't, but the young Turk is hopeful." She noted tears in Kit's eyes. "Why did he stop by?"

"Long story. Ulysses told him to read our report on the plant in Grants before he interviewed the owner of the plant in Las Vegas who supplied meat to the Butcher Don. Evidently, the agent expected me to do the profile. I emailed him the list of sites we used. He stopped by to…"

"Blow off some steam?" Sara suspected field agents expected staff members would do most of their paperwork. "If he gave us the names of the plant employees, we could do it quickly." She thought a few seconds. "Might get the list of employees five or six months ago, before the Butcher Don was arrested, and now. Any changes in personnel might be interesting. Hell, request their employment lists for the last twenty years, like we did for the plant in Grants."

Kit cocked his head and frowned. "I'm forwarding two medical examiner's reports to you. Ulysses has seen the first one already. Read them while I try to please macho man."

Sara opened a short report from the medical examiner on the hand found in the sewer. She looked for points that agents might miss and emailed Ulysses:

> *The little finger was removed years ago. The ring finger was probably removed just before the victim was killed. The murderer was a sadist and/or wanted something from the victim.*

The medical examiner's second email was labeled as "Autopsy of a Meat Packing Plant Accident Victim—Melvin Melendez." She swallowed hard before she opened it because she knew the report was apt to be gruesome.

OSHA officials reported the man's arms had been caught in the hooks and chains attached to a beef carcass, and he been drawn up as the hide was yanked off the dangling carcass. Other workers claimed they were unaware of his predicament at first and continued to use their circular saws to cut the skin from the underlying tissue. The sworn statements of the three other employees involved in the de-hiding process were consistent. They all claimed they hadn't heard the man's screams. When they did, they couldn't get the line turned off for another minute. An OSHA official noted the noise level in this area of the plant was excruciating and the men all used earplugs.

The medical report was worse than she imagined—more graphic than the OSHA report. She could hardly look at the photos. Most of the bones in the arms and right hand were broken. The tendons attaching the arms at the shoulders were torn. Broken ribs had pierced the lungs. Sara wanted to gag. The man had died like medieval prisoners tortured on the rack.

She closed her eyes. Something was missing. *What was it?* She forced herself to reread the report. The medical examiner didn't mention any injuries on the left hand. She emailed the medical examiner.

Her thoughts were interrupted by Kit. He was alternately screeching and whimpering as he searched databases for data on the employees of the meat packing plant owned by the man called Pigeon by the FBI.

Two thoughts flashed through her mind: First, what was her FBI label? She hoped it wasn't "Know-It-All" or anything too demeaning. Second, Everhart won the battle. Kit was compiling a profile on the meat packing plant in Las Vegas.

Then visions of the autopsy report returned. She wished she'd had this autopsy report when she made her request to the district judge for warrants to see the medical records of all employees injured in the Grants meat packing plant over the last ten years. Those photos would make anyone forget the right to privacy of employees.

"I could use...." Kit glanced at her. His mouth flew open. "You look... gray, no *green*."

"The medical examiner's report...."

"Don't tell me. Why don't you get some fresh air?"

Sara nodded and led Bug out. After she and Bug had circled the outer perimeter of the FBI building twice, she focused her thoughts. Kit was a drama queen. It was hard to concentrate in his office but it was easier to coordinate data searches. But Kit didn't need her help to prepare the basic profile of Pigeon's plant. She could work more efficiently in the quiet of her own cubicle.

***

Sara had barely settled in her cubicle when she heard Bug snoring. He'd lain in his bed in Kit's office but never slept. In their cubicle, he'd fallen asleep at once. She felt calmer too.

Her phone rang. It was the medical examiner. "Got your email. Either I never received the left hand, or it was so minced that I didn't recognize it. The latter is likely. I should have searched harder for it, but we've been swamped with bodies this week."

Sara told him of her suspicion that the so-called accident might have been a murder.

The medical examiner sighed. "I can't prove the accident in the plant in Grants was murder, but that's a logical explanation of this bizarre incident. However, I might be able to help you get the medical records for victims of other so-called accidents at the plant in Grants. I'll ship my report off to the district judge immediately. By the way, we're golfing buddies, and he has a weak stomach."

"Thanks."

He hung up.

Sara closed her eyes. Maybe things would work out. But would they work out fast enough to save Bug and her?

The phone rang again. "Sara?"

She almost cried when she heard Sanders's voice. "A lot has happened since I talked to you last night. Jack Daniels followed our car from the safe house this morning. They've got to move me."

Sanders's voice remained smooth and low. "Did they catch the bastard?"

"No. They think he's reporting to the drug cartel now. I'm trying to keep busy because I don't want to think about where I'll spend the night."

Sanders said nothing.

She wished he would try to soothe her, but he never spouted false platitudes. "My problem is I'm running in circles—gathering clues that don't add up. Maybe because they're unrelated to my package or to the case against the Butcher Don, but I can't ignore them. They found a human hand in the sewer. It was missing two fingers."

Sanders coughed. "Don't describe it more."

"I've just read the autopsy of another man missing a hand. He was the guy killed in the supposed accident at the meat packing plant in Grants. I doubt the accident victim's hand was the one found in the sewer, but they haven't run the DNA analyses yet."

Sanders coughed again. "I've been away from you too long. I can barely follow this gruesome scenario of severed hands. Maybe you need to get away from the mayhem in New Mexico or at least focus on a topic besides meat packing plants."

"How? Bug and I are virtually prisoners in the building. The grounds and parking lots around this building bore even him."

"You'll think of something. My boss…"

Sara wished for more sympathy but guessed he wanted to distract her from her own problems.

"My boss reached an agreement with the previous chargé d'affaires at the embassy."

Sanders seldom referred to his boss by name or her title and was often vague during his phone conversations. She suspected he was afraid his calls were monitored. She didn't want to know by whom. "Any surprises in the agreement?"

"Not really. His wife is now at an undisclosed drug treatment center and won't face charges. He was fired from the State Department, five years short of full retirement."

His voice had lost its mellowness. He was peeved. She knew Sanders thought the previous chargé d' affaires to Cuba had endangered the lives of embassy staff and allowed several Miami-based businessmen and women to escape indictments for drug trafficking. Thus, although the federal trial of the Butcher Don in Albuquerque was an important blow to the drug cartel, its significance was diminished because of what Sanders usually called the "ineptness" of the chargé d'affaires. Sara thought there was more to Sanders's annoyance. He believed if the chargé d'affaires had listened to his advice, he would have captured Maria in Cuba and prevented the shoot-out in Albuquerque. In other words, if the chargé d'affaires had listened to Sanders, his affair with Maria would not have become public knowledge.

She knew he disliked questions on Maria, but she asked anyway. "How about Maria?"

"Maria won't be charged with espionage. She'll be tried in Albuquerque for racketeering, the murder of two law enforcement officers, and the attempted murder of you and me. She'll be kept in isolation in Washington until the trial."

"I feel better knowing the woman who pointed a gun at me isn't here in Albuquerque."

Sanders coughed. "Let's get back to your current situation. Why don't I talk to Ulysses? I've got an idea for a replacement safe house."

"Will I like it?"

"I'll get back to you this afternoon. By the way, you should be getting a delivery from Pappadeaux Seafood Kitchen soon. I ordered all your favorites."

"What? They don't deliver. Did you use GrubHub?"

"Better. I used Carbonne. Seems he needed to shop for a toy for a seven-year-old boy. He was glad to pick up the food if I ordered enough for him, although he resisted picking up a hamburger for Bug at McDonalds."

Sara was pleased. Sanders had remembered Bug didn't like seafood. She felt tears welling up in her eyes. She guessed she'd be less weepy if she got more sleep. It was hard to sleep with a guard outside your door.

"Sorry, I can't share it with you. You and Bug deserve a treat."

"Thanks, honey." Sara concluded the call as Carbonne, in a cleaned-up mode, entered her office with Kit trailing him.

Carbonne unpacked the bags containing gumbo, fried calamari, lobster and shrimp salad, and lots of fresh, crispy French bread and butter. "Sanders ordered enough food for at least four people. I invited Kit."

Kit sighed as he flounced onto a chair. "I didn't think I'd make the deadline Everhart gave me." He sighed and lifted the cover off a large Styrofoam container. "My, these calamari look good."

"Help yourself. I've got to feed Bug first."

Sara with Bug at her feet rummaged through the McDonald's bag, carefully applied ketchup to a small hamburger, and put a scrap of it in Bug's bowl. The dog watched her but didn't leap to the food. She wished he wasn't a picky eater. She sighed, took a bite of the burger, and gave him the bit of the burger from her mouth. "You know Bug, the rest of the world doesn't understand I'm your poison tester." The dog eagerly tasted the piece and wolfed down the rest of the pieces in his bowl.

Carbonne slurped gumbo and glanced at Bug. "Sometimes I feel sorry for Sanders. He can't compete with Bug for your attention."

Sara seemed to ignore his comments as she selected a golden fried ring of calamari. "Don't. He's not unhappy."

Carbonne studied Sara. "He likes challenges."

Sara checked on Bug and grabbed another piece of calamari. "Sanders made an odd comment. Why did you want to buy a toy for a seven-year-old boy? I thought your nephew was a baby."

Carbonne didn't look up. "Don't know how you and Sanders share so much info."

She figured he'd politely told her to mind her own business and turned to Kit who had loaded his plate with calamari and French bread. "Was Everhart pleased with your profile of Pigeon's meat packing plant?"

"Doubt he'll read it." Kit popped another calamari ring into his mouth.

"But I will. I think I might get ideas if I compare the accident reports at the two plants." Sara opened a second bowl of gumbo. "Kit— would you like some of my gumbo?"

Kit shook his head. "I like the calamari better." He stopped chewing. "Actually, I didn't read the report on Pigeon's plant. I just cut and pasted material. No time."

Carbonne finished his gumbo and opened a box of lobster salad. "Sara, no one writes reports like you do. Your little comments are more valuable than the actual info. They make me think."

"What do you expect from an old prof?"

He tasted the salad. "Their citrus dressing makes this lobster salad great. It's a shame not to sit and enjoy this food, but I've got to go. Ulysses wants me to go along with Everhart when he talks to Pigeon and his family. Ulysses says my different perspective will encourage Pigeon to talk. What he means is my lack of style may irritate Pigeon enough to blurt the truth occasionally. I also want to ask Pigeon's son Noah a couple of questions. He's old enough to notice things, and I'm sure Everhart won't bother to talk to a child."

When they left, she scanned her emails. She couldn't believe her eyes. There was an email from the district court. Fast decisions were usually bad news. She opened the email anyway.

She reread the document twice. In essence, the judge agreed the medical records of individuals who were identified as injured at the plant in Grants in OSHA reports over the last twenty years could be examined by the FBI. She emailed a thank you to the medical examiner.

CHAPTER 15: USDA Inspector Frank McCoy

The woman who greeted him at the door of the kitchen of the learning center appeared to be in her forties with her black hair tied in a knot at the back of her head. As he introduced himself, she adjusted the ties to her white bib apron, which were looped in front over her ample middle.

"What do you know about the prairie dog die-off near Potters Place? As a USDA meat inspector, I'm concerned livestock may have been exposed to the plague."

"Why me? All of us on the pueblo know about the die-off."

"It's news to USDA."

Her face remained blank. She didn't even blink.

"Those handling diseased carcasses could become sick. Has your husband or relatives developed coughs or respiratory problems in the last few days?"

"No. They're careful." She looked down. "How did you learn about the die-off?"

He decided he had to be provocative to get real answers from this unflappable woman. "The New Mexico Department of Agriculture received a package." He stared at her.

She kept her head down.

"It came by an indirect route."

She was smiling when she looked up. "Good. If you have more questions, the men will get home by two-thirty. They work from five to two in summer and fall. I don't know much about the plant."

He noticed her cadence. Her voice tended to go up at the end of each sentence, instead of down as was typical of most Americans. That lilt was common among Native American women in the Southwest. He wondered why he'd bothered to think about that detail when her smile was the most interesting part of the conversation. He bet she knew something about Sara's package.

He changed the focus of his questions to see if she'd become more talkative. "Do any of the women in your family work at the plant? I know it's hard to find jobs around Acoma."

"No." She looked at him almost defiantly. "Too dangerous." In a softer tone, "And it stinks." She stood straighter. "My daughter is a police officer."

"In Albuquerque."

"No, she's honest."

The woman was savvy and might open up to him if he played this right. "Good for her. I'm not from around here but I've heard about the problems in the Albuquerque Police Department. USDA sent me here because the meat inspector at the plant in Grants asked to be transferred. He claimed family problems."

For the first time, she looked surprised. "Hank Diaz wants to leave?"

"No, Elijah Wood. I guess he's the backup inspector. That's what I'd be."

"Too bad."

"Do you know Elijah Wood?"

She nodded.

He'd remembered a detail Sara had supplied. "I didn't think the members of the Acoma Pueblo would know someone from the Zuni Pueblo?"

She looked at her wristwatch. "Men will be home soon. They like Elijah. Will be surprised. Must finish cleaning up and get home." She gave him a passive stare.

He decided to use another of Sara's tidbits and see what the woman said. "Did your family call Elijah Wood to the livestock pen outside the plant shortly before the accident?"

She blinked. "Ask them." She turned rapidly.

He'd guessed right. He fumbled in his back pocket and pulled out a card—the type he used when working undercover as a meat inspector. He scribbled on it. "I'll leave my card on the table."

She was already removing dishes from the dishwasher and ignored him.

"I also added the email and phone number of Sara Almquist. She'd like to know why she received a strange package from the Acoma area."

A plastic tray clattered to the floor, but the woman didn't reply.

***

Her sister-in-law, the teaching aide was even less responsive to his questions as she stood like a statue at the door of a playroom, but she had more of an excuse. Two tykes, about three years of age, played tag behind her.

Again, he tried to be provocative. "Do you worry about your husband's safety at the plant?"

"No, his brother and sons are there."

"Will I be in danger? What should I do to protect myself at the plant?"

Her dark eyes softened. "Avoid Hank Diaz."

One of the tots let out a high-pitched, blood-curdling scream as she fell while running after the boy. He remembered those high-pitched shrieks as being his daughter's most annoying habit, until she became a teenager. He saw the child stand up. She was okay, but she screamed again and again until the aide walked toward her.

The aide scooped the child up and glanced at him. "The boss is grouchy but okay." She rocked the child in one arm, pushed Frank out of the doorway, and closed the door.

He decided to skip talking to their husbands. He'd confirmed his suspicions.

He scanned his emails and opened a message from Sara. It was obvious Sara was an academic who had lived by "publish or perish." She knew how to turn out terse reports fast and how to show off the best tidbits. Her comments to him were titled "Highlights of OSHA Reports."

Thirty employees at the plant in Grants filed accident reports with OSHA during the last ten years. The number is below the national norm for accidents at meat packing plants. I doubt this plant is better run than most. The management must discourage reporting of accidents.

So far, I've only done the follow up on a couple of accidents. Elijah Wood and Melvin Melendez, the man killed in the latest accident, both filed accident reports with OSHA during the last year. Elijah sought medical treatment for his broken arm from the Indian Health Service. Melvin was treated for his dislocated shoulder at the VA Hospital.

Sara added a footnote to her report.

Elijah might have a lot to say. I've attached his address, email address, and phone number.

Sara was analytical but intuitive. A dangerous combination. He wanted to have a long conversation with Sara and not just on this case. Her boyfriend was a fool not to spend more time with her. He looked at his watch. No time for long conversations now.

He filed a report with his boss at USDA and Sara and a shorter version to Carbonne. Then he punched buttons on his phone and waited. Elijah answered as he was about to leave a message. Elijah claimed he had a part-time custodial job at a ranger station for El Malpais. Frank didn't remember any mention of another job in Elijah's USDA employment records. His voice tone and the way he faltered on words were odd. Frank guessed Elijah spoke Spanish more often than English. Still, he had spoken English while in college. A B.S. was the minimum requirement for a USDA meat inspector. But it was more. Elijah's voice wavered up and down as if he was nervous, almost hysterically nervous.

Despite his problems in understanding Elijah, he eventually got organized directions from him. He was to turn south on State Road 117 and go on until he saw the first building on the left—the ranger station.

Frank enjoyed the drive at first. The landscape became more starkly gray and brown as he drove. The pines, which punctuated the landscape, seemed stunted. He thought they were piñons. He passed only two cars. Not exactly a hostile environment but not friendly either.

J. L. Greger

A large gravel truck approached him. He hadn't realized private groups could quarry for gravel on national conservation land. He looked in his rearview mirror and saw another dump truck. The quarry must be nearby. A pickup truck pulled out of a tiny spur road in front of him. It stopped. The driver jumped out and ran back up the spur road.

Frank slammed on his breaks. He couldn't pass the pickup truck because the gravel truck coming toward him had sped up. He looked in his rearview mirror. The other dump truck was also dangerously close. The ditch by the side of the road was rocky. He couldn't tell how deep, but it was his best choice.

His car tilted. He stabilized it partially. The ditch was steeper than he expected. He fought with the wheel, but the car flipped and flipped again.

CHAPTER 16: Sara

As Sara finished scanning Kit's report, she heard Bug's contented snort. She wanted to curl up and take a nap, too. *No rest for the wicked.* Funny how her parents' old expressions popped into her mind sometimes. She had a brainstorm, made a quick call, and pulled out the leftover lobster salad from a tiny refrigerator in the corner of her cubicle.

Ulysses was all smiles as Sara and Bug entered his office, especially when he saw the lobster salad. "Love Pappadeaux's salads. Thank you."

"I had an idea. Not a great one, but it might help Carbonne and Everhart get honest comments from Pigeon."

Ulysses took a long time to chew a mouthful of the lobster, a lot longer than required. "What makes you think Pigeon wouldn't be honest?"

Sara noticed he couldn't even look at her as he asked the question. She realized any honest response she made would sound negative. So, she ignored the question. "Did you read Kit's report? There was a real bombshell tucked near the end."

Ulysses said softly as if he feared Kit would hear, "Kit's cut-and-paste job was unreadable."

"Too bad. It seems a man named Dan Steele was on a list of employees at Pigeon's plant about seventeen years ago."

Ulysses didn't wait to swallow his food. "What?" He swallowed. "Are you sure? Kit didn't mention it."

"Kit didn't read his own report. He only cut and pasted pieces from various data sets. I slogged through it because I wanted to compare data from the two plants."

"Hmm. That's why I didn't make Kit a data analyst. I'd hoped.... Oh well, it's possible no one thought to ask Pigeon a direct question about Dan Steele. Everhart, the lead agent following Pigeon, is good but he doesn't—I guess you could say—appreciate nuances, like Carbonne does."

It wasn't like Ulysses to be nervous about his decisions. Sara said, "I'm not criticizing anyone, well except Pigeon. Here's what I did, and what I want to do. When I saw Dan Steele on the list, a memory clicked in my mind. I'd seen a strange comment in Dan Steele's VA medical records." Sara shuffled through a file.

"Well?"

"It's here somewhere. Here it is." Sara handed a sheet to Ulysses. "It's a report from a psychologist at the VA. Read the section I marked in yellow.

> *Patient has nightmares because he has overreacted to an accident*
> *at work. He lost his little finger in a meat slicer. Claims now he*
> *can't work in a meat packing plant.*

Sara frowned. "I think the psychologist missed the point. Dan Steele may have had a legitimate fear. I'm not a nervous Nelly, but if I lost a finger in a meat slicer, I don't think I'd ever want to use one again."

"Hmm." He studied Sara. "What's on the next sheet you fluttered by me?"

"I found the old OSHA record for the accident. Routine, except the management response was signed by Pigeon."

"So? He probably didn't even look at the reports before he signed them."

"The plant manager or the supervisor of the unit signed other responses to OSHA reports at Pigeon's plant. There's another hiccup in Kit's report but we can discuss it later."

"You think Pigeon should remember Dan Steele? Did you notify Carbonne?"

"Yes." She checked her computer. "Oh dear. No response to my email. And I missed his message."

"And?"

"You won't be pleased. He doubts Everhart contacted the boy's school as you suggested. So, he's going to question the boy. He thinks it's odd how Pigeon blew up at the marshals within minutes of the boy getting home from school on Monday."

Ulysses drummed his fingers on the table. "I suspect you cleaned up the message."

Sara looked down. She didn't want to be drawn further into agency politics.

"Your silence tells it all." He pounded on his keyboard and scanned his screen. "No time to send someone out to the school now. Better to send two more agents as backup to Belen."

He pounded his keyboard more. Sara noted he drummed the table or his keyboard harder when he was stressed. He seemed to be particularly agitated today. She wanted to suggest he should use a punching bag in the gym.

Ulysses looked at her triumphantly. "I found the name of the boy's teacher. You know this case better than the available agents. Do you think you could talk to her?"

Sara squirmed in her chair. "This call isn't apt to be productive. Teachers don't take calls during class time."

"Hmm. I'll call the principal. Sound official. He'll send the teacher to the phone. I'll let you talk to her because she's more apt to open up to you as another woman."

"Couldn't this call endanger Pigeon and his family if someone is out to get him?" She paused. "I assume that's why he suddenly wanted to go into witness protection."

Sara heard irritation in his voice as he said, "I'm quite aware of the risks, but Carbonne needs pertinent information. While Kit puts through the call, let's create our plan."

***

Ulysses was adamant with the principal when he didn't want to call the teacher from her classroom to speak to the FBI. Thus, Sara wasn't surprised the woman on the other end of the phone sounded scared. She also sounded young and tentative. "I need your help." She named Pigeon's son Noah. "What kind of boy is he?"

"Oh, no. Is he all right?"

"Why do you ask?"

"No reason. The FBI doesn't call…."

Sara wished this call was on Skype or better yet a live visit, because she liked to watch people as she spoke to them. "It's all right to give me gut reactions not facts. Relax. Sometimes we all sense things."

Silence.

"Is Noah boisterous? Or withdrawn?"

"Quiet."

"Did he act odd on Monday?"

"Yes. He screamed hysterically at lunch. I could see an item in his hand and asked to examine it."

Sara thought she'd hit pay dirt. "And?"

"He tries to please me usually, but he ignored me. I asked again. He flexed his hand open for a second and said, 'One of Dad's old stogies.' I saw a thin brown object. A couple of inches long on a yellow piece of paper."

Sara had difficulty concentrating on the conversation because Ulysses was already on another phone whispering. "Did it look like a cigar?"

"We have a no-tolerance policy when it comes to students having tobacco products. If I looked at it, I'd have to discipline him. The other kids were teasing him. I thought it best to not ask more questions."

"What did he do?"

"Threw his lunch away and asked to go to the bathroom."

"What did he do when he came back to the classroom?"

"Didn't talk as the other boys yelled, 'Scream like a girl again!' Most of the time he kept his eyes pinched shut." Silence for ten seconds. "Poor child."

Sara guessed the teacher had withheld pertinent details. "I get the feeling you feel sorry for Noah for other reasons. Can you explain?"

Silence. "Bruises on his upper arms."

"And?"

"If I raise my voice even slightly to him, he cowers like a three- or four-year-old. Although his family has lived in Las Vegas, I guess, for generations, he has no friends."

Sarah thought it was time to push for frank answers. "Do you think he's immature because he's abused at home?"

"There was writing on the paper under the cigar."

Sara noticed the non sequitur. "Could you read the note?"

"No."

Sara tried again. "Do you think Noah is abused at home?"

CHAPTER 17: FBI Agent Carbonne

Ray Everhart took twenty minutes to select the sedan he wanted to drive to the meeting with Pigeon and his family. He insisted the female agent sit in the front seat. Then he whispered his plans for the interview so softly that Carbonne couldn't follow most of the conversation from the back seat. However, Carbonne heard enough to know Everhart had ignored Ulysses's advice on how to prep for this meeting. He emailed Sara.

Carbonne debated in his mind the best descriptors of Everhart. He settled on "arrogant bastard," "control freak," and "general pain in the ass." He finally decided Everhart's flaws made him the perfect person to deal with Pigeon. They were alike in appearance—tall blonds who strutted like peacocks. More importantly, their temperaments were similar. They were both bullies. Carbonne did not regret his decision two months ago to relinquish his role as the lead investigator of Pigeon and his plant to Everhart. He'd rather work with the bums of Albuquerque than Pigeon or, for that matter, Everhart.

After Carbonne had settled his internal arguments, he used his time in the car to scan Kit's report, obviously done without Sara's help. It was dull and disorganized. He couldn't get through it.

Then he saw a useful note from Sara, but he had no time to respond because Everhart had parked the car in the lot of the Harvey House Museum in Belen and was giving an order. "The house where the U.S. Marshals stashed Pigeon and his family Tuesday is about a block away. I'll interview Pigeon, and..."

Carbonne interrupted, "And I'll talk to the boy."

Everhart snickered, "The kid's about your speed."

Carbonne wanted to shout "dickhead" but said, "But I have one or two questions for Pigeon and his wife at the end. Assign a marshal to be present with me all the time."

"We'll see." Everhart pointed over his shoulder. "We'll walk to the house—the white stucco one with the gray roof."

Carbonne cased out the area. Eight empty cars were parked in the lot by the museum. All were painted dull colors and at least five years old. He suspected the volunteers and visitors at the museum were over fifty. The only thing sitting in front of the house was a black garbage can. The marshals either had parked in the garage or in the museum lot.

***

As soon as a woman marshal and the seven-year-old boy had settled at the kitchen table, Carbonne closed the door to the living room where Pigeon, the lead marshal, and Everhart were seated. The woman agent had taken Pigeon's wife to a bedroom. A third marshal roamed the house and checked windows. Carbonne pulled a new red fidget spinner from his pocket and placed it on the table slightly out of the boy's reach. "Bet the last few months have been tough for you. Bought this for you."

The boy didn't look up, but he grabbed the spinner. As the boy stretched his arm, Carbonne could see streaks of black, blue, green and yellow on the child's upper arm. He figured the boy had been abused several times to have bruises at all stages of healing.

"Do you like school?"

The spinner began to whirl around the boy's finger. The boy stared at it for a few seconds, jerked the spinner off his finger, and laid it on the table. "No."

"I didn't either when I was your age. Bet you'll miss your friends at school if you move."

Silence.

Carbonne picked up the spinner. It wobbled around his finger twice. "You do it better than I do. Show me how it's done."

The boy sighed but picked up the spinner and twirled it. He handed it back to Carbonne who spun it poorly again.

"My problem is my fingers are too thick. What do you think?"

The boy glanced at Carbonne as he placed the spinner on the boy's hand. "Hmm. Takes practice."

"Must be someone you'll miss?"

"Not after Monday."

"Guys can be pretty dumb in second grade. Always playing stupid games. Did someone try to be funny with you on Monday?"

The boy stared at Carbonne. "It wasn't funny."

"What wasn't funny?"

Tears welled up in the boy's eyes.

"Want to tell me about it?"

The boy shook his head.

Carbonne pulled out a piece of blue paper from his pocket, unfolded it, and laid it on the table. Then he handed the boy a pen. "How about drawing what you saw? Or how you felt? We'll solve your problem together."

The marshal hadn't appeared to be paying much attention to the conversation at first. Now she stared at the piece of paper as the boy began to draw.

The boy drew a hairpin.

Carbonne was silent because he didn't know what to say.

The boy drew a ragged edge at the bottom of the hairpin and looked at Carbonne.

"I know this is important but I'm not much of an expert on art. I need more." Carbonne tapped the drawing with his finger. "More details."

The boy looked puzzled and drew an oval near the rounded end of the hairpin. Finally, he added a couple more lines.

"Looks like a finger to me. Did someone give you the bird?"

"Not funny." The boy drew little lines all over the finger.

"Hmm. It's a good picture. Why cover it up with lines?"

"No. It was dark."

"An African boy or Native American boy did something?"

"No. It was dark, dry, and wrinkly."

Carbonne put his hand on the boy's shoulders. "Was the finger attached to a hand?"

The boy sobbed.

Carbonne handed him a tissue.

"No. Someone put it in my lunch bag."

The marshal sprang to her feet. Carbonne pulled her sleeve and forced her to sit before he hugged the boy. "If you give me the finger, I'll take it to a lab. We'll learn more about it. Don't you want to know who did this and why?"

"Dad knows. He took the finger."

The woman marshal rushed from the kitchen and pulled the lead marshal and Everhart into the hallway between the living room and the kitchen.

"I guess I brought you the wrong toy."

"No." The boy spun the spinner. "Dad threw my last one into the garbage…" He stared at the red spinner. "…with the finger."

***

Carbonne talked to the boy as Everhart and the lead marshal lectured Pigeon and his wife about how "honesty" and "full disclosure" were necessary in the witness protection program. Carbonne thought they were wasting their time. Pigeon was incapable of either and his wife would never cross him. She wore long sleeves, even though it was over eighty degrees outside, for a reason.

He thought he heard the rumble of a big truck. *The garbage truck!* He tore from the kitchen through the living room and out the front door. The garbage truck lifted the garbage can. Carbonne waved his arms wildly and yelled, "Stop! Don't take the garbage!"

The can was suspended in mid-air. It swung slightly. The driver looked annoyed.

Carbonne thought, *Not as annoyed as he'll be if he doesn't stop.*

The can was lowered to the ground. "Thanks." Carbonne grabbed its handle and pulled the can up the driveway. No one else had exited the house but the lead marshal stood at the open front door.

"You saved it."

"Open the garage door."

The lead marshal yelled the order. The woman marshal who had listened to his interview of the boy stood in the garage. As soon as Carbonne rolled the can inside the garage, she lowered the door.

"Quite a show. Everhart and my boss went berserk before the kid spoke up. First time today."

"What did he say?"

"He saved the finger."

Carbonne sighed. "My fault. As soon as the boy told me that Pigeon threw the finger in the garbage, I should have looked for it. But I wanted to distract the boy from hearing the conversation in the other room. Impossible. Then I heard the garbage truck."

The marshal took off her jacket. "Guess now we find the finger in the garbage. I'm sure no one will come out to help us."

Carbonne nodded. "I've done this before. There is a right way to do it. I'll get newspaper to spread on the floor before we sort the garbage."

The marshal opened the lid and pulled out a black bag. "Bring extra garbage bags too. Unfortunately, this can is stuffed…" She pulled at the bags still inside. "…with three more bags."

He wished he was in his bum attire. He hated to ruin his only good pair of slacks and new shirt. He opened the door from the garage to the kitchen and strode to the living room. Sudden silence. They all stared at him. "Ma'am, either you or your husband must come to the garage and point out the bag most apt to have the spinner and the finger."

The wife began to sob. Pigeon coughed. "Is this necessary?"

"Yes, and it really should be you. You're the one who threw an obviously important piece of evidence away." Carbonne didn't see Noah. "Where's the boy?"

Pigeon glared at him. "I sent him to his room."

Carbonne sidled up to Pigeon and said almost under his breath, "You ass. He didn't do anything wrong." He backed away and said loudly. "I'll enlist the boy to help me search for this buried treasure, like pirates."

Carbonne saw Everhart out of the corner of his eye. The bully bit his lip. He was obviously embarrassed.

The lead marshal followed Carbonne down the hall and pulled him into a bathroom. He whispered, "Many enrolled in witness protection programs are not model citizens, but Pigeon is particularly questionable. You were the first agent to handle him. Do you think he'll testify honestly at the trial?"

"If it were up to me, we'd send the boy and his mother off with you today and put Pigeon back under FBI jurisdiction. Scare him thoroughly. More importantly—get him away from the boy. Pigeon abuses his son and probably his wife."

The marshal nodded. "Pigeon is careful. We've never seen him hit the boy or the woman, but both have bruises on their arms. Monday night after the kid came home from school, the wife went on a crying binge and Pigeon made demands to us. Sorry, I didn't think to really question the kid. He always seemed sullen."

"Typical of abused children."

"My colleague said you were good, really good with the boy. We… we made mistakes. What do you advise?"

"Your marshals and my two co-workers are too demoralized to provide good protection here. Get them all on guard duty until we get backup. Don't call the Valencia County Sheriff's Office for help. It's a leaky sieve to the drug cabal. I'll call Ulysses."

Both men made calls.

***

Afterwards, Carbonne sat on the boy's bed. "Guess we don't get to play pirates. My boss is sending a truck. The lab techs will sort the garbage back at the FBI building. Now let's talk about something important. Have you had lunch yet?"

The boy shook his head as the marshal walking the perimeter of the house stopped at a window at the back of the house and yelled, "Two men, not ours, in the backyard next door!"

Everhart raced to the peep hole in the front door. "A car is parked next door and another one is across the street. Motors on. Two men in each."

CHAPTER 18: Sara

Sara fled Ulysses's office after she made the call to the teacher. She understood why the federal prosecutor had offered witness protection to Pigeon, but he was—she couldn't explain it—so manipulative, so slimy. She studied the data on Pigeon's plant with increased resolve to ferret out his secrets.

Her computer pinged. She worried about Frank as she read his report on his discussions. His gutsy questions could have annoyed or frightened several people at Acoma. However, she didn't worry long because Kit summoned her to Ulysses's office with, "Bring your laptop."

When she and Bug trotted in, Ulysses pointed to a chair and continued his conversations. Two calls at once. She figured she was expected to listen to them to get oriented. One call was in speaker mode. The other came through a headphone that Ulysses now wore.

The agents Ulysses had dispatched to Belen were on the speaker phone. They had passed Los Lunas and thought they'd reach the Harvey House Museum in Belen in less than fifteen minutes. Ulysses snapped, "Not soon enough! Imminent attack at the house—front and back. SWAT is on its way, but you're closer."

Ulysses appeared to be conversing with someone at Pigeon's safe house on his headphone. "Belen Police on the way. They'll make a lot of noise. Might distract your attackers and allow our backup to arrive."

He pointed at Sara. "Use my access code." He handed her a slip of paper. "Could be heading for a hostage situation. Check backgrounds and family connections of Belen police." He cocked his head, typed rapidly, and spoke into his headphone. "Belen Fire Department on the way. How bad is the fire?" He turned to Sara. "Check fire department, too."

Sara thought it was too bad the FBI couldn't hand Pigeon over to the attackers and save the rest. She gave a quick prayer with a more appropriate sentiment. She didn't tune out Ulysses completely, but she focused on his questions.

Kit threw open the door between his and Ulysses's offices. He rushed to lower a large screen. Pictures projected on the screen. "The chief U.S. marshal for New Mexico is also receiving this feed from Everhart."

She no longer heard the feed from the two incoming agents. Instead, she heard Everhart and found it hard to concentrate on her searches. The scene on the screen looked dismal. The kitchen of the safe house in Belen was smoky. She thought she saw rugs rolled up by the door to the rest of the house. Pigeon and his family were huddled in front of the side door to the garage. The woman agent and the lead marshal had their guns focused on the kitchen window facing the street. The other agents and marshals were not visible.

Everhart's voice sounded raspy. "Carbonne shot—probably killed—a guy with a gasoline container on the east side of house but he was too late. The guy already started the fire."

Sara heard distant shots.

"The two marshals started to hose down the house with a garden hose. Shots came from two directions. The marshals are now pinned down on back porch. Injuries unknown."

Sara guessed Everhart must have the camera strapped to his forehead because the view on the screen swung erratically and he wasn't visible on the screen.

More shots—closer. The crash of broken glass. The view on the screen swung rapidly. The large screen showed a shattered front window in the kitchen. Shards of glass everywhere.

The lead marshal said to Everhart, "Think the four men in the cars are ready to move. Maybe we can pick them off."

A sudden view of the side door from the kitchen to the garage. It was ajar and the family were inching out of it. The woman agent nudged them back inside. "The garage is less safe than the house." She closed the door.

The view on the screen swung to the sliding wooden door between the kitchen and the rest of the house. Slowly the smoky living room and hall appeared as the door slid open. The blasting siren of a fire truck got louder and louder. A second deep siren came from the opposite direction. And several shrill sirens came from both directions.

There was a crashing sound. The view swept back to the kitchen, now engulfed in dense smoke. Between coughs, the lead marshal rasped, "Smoke bomb. Bet they're on the move now, but I can't see anything."

Ulysses said, "Everhart—time to move the family to a protected location."

Shots rang from the back of the house. A lot of them.

"They're charging the back of the house," Everhart whispered as the view spun rapidly down the smoky hall. "No place is more protected than the kitchen."

Ulysses appeared to be listening on his headphone. "Okay chief, you focus on the front and the fire on the east side of the house. We'll try to gain control of the rear." Ulysses's voice sounded like a growl as he said, "Everhart—get moving."

The hazy dark hallway opened into a small back porch. Sara immediately wished the scene on the porch was hazier. One marshal was propped against the wall in a pool of blood and water. Bullets must have split the garden hose, lying across his lap, as well as the man's knee or lower leg. A blue rag was tied above his knee. As water spilled out of the hose, the red circle around the marshal's leg seemed to be growing. However, the marshal seemed alert and had a shotgun focused on the backyard. The second marshal was propped up against the opposite wall of the semi-enclosed porch in a pool of darker red liquid. A gun was positioned in her hands, but she didn't appear to be aiming it. Carbonne was not in sight.

Shots came from the east side of the house. Then they heard a response from a different gun. Sara figured one of those shots had to be from Carbonne's gun. By her count, he was the only agent or marshal not accounted for. At least he was still alive.

Ulysses snorted. "Everhart—don't stand there. Help Carbonne before they enter the house. The SWAT should arrive soon to help the Belen fire and police at the front of the house."

The view zoomed to the ground and then moved slowly forward on gravel. The view zoomed up to flames on the front edge of the house and dropped to a man lying on the ground.

Sara held her breath as she studied him. He was bald. A gasoline can lay beside him. It wasn't Carbonne.

The view slid backward along the ground to another man. This one was crumpled in a pile. His hair was dark. It could be Carbonne. Sara wanted to scream, *It's not fair.*

The view moved slowly further back to a third man in a squat position. He stood. "About time you came. Cover me while I check them. No time for fancy shooting. Afraid both are dead."

Sara sighed in relief. Carbonne was shirtless. He'd worn a blue shirt at lunch. She knew the source of the rag used as a tourniquet on the marshal's leg. In the background, she heard a barrage of shots. They seemed to be from several locations.

Carbonne had just begun to move when he said, "Everhart, watch our rear."

The view swung quickly. A shot. The view shifted wildly. A series of shots. The view fell backward and upward to the sky. A hand and a gun were pointed toward the camera. A shot. Then another.

Sara thought the silence was deafening. Then she heard, "FBI— all hands up." The last voice wasn't Carbonne's or Everhart's. The backup agents had arrived, but Sara thought it might be too late. Ulysses must have thought the same because he snorted repeatedly.

"Don't shoot." It was Carbonne's voice. "Get the guns from the attackers, just in case. Attend to the two marshals on the porch while I check Everhart."

Suddenly, Carbonne face appeared on screen. His dark hair was plastered against his head with sweat. He blocked the view of the sky with his body.

"How's Everhart?" Ulysses's voice almost cracked. "An ambulance is on site."

The sky view again. "Looks like gut wounds below the vest." The awful gasps of a critically hurt patient rattled from the speaker.

"Hold on guy. Help is coming." The view was of Carbonne's hairy chest.

"Carbonne, put on his head camera. We need to see the action," yelled Ulysses, obviously hoping if he was loud enough Carbonne would hear him.

Everhart pulled at his earphone. "Yours," he gasped faintly.

Carbonne adjusted the equipment on his head. The view turned to a suited FBI agent being soaked by the spray from a fire hose as he turned over the body of the first attacker by the front eave of the house. A pockmark was on the body armor over the attacker's chest and a hole was in his forehead with blood dribbling down. The agent felt for a pulse, shook his head, and picked up the man's gun. He did the same with the second body with the same result.

The view swung to a man lying across Everhart's feet. The soaked agent turned the body over. Two holes in the forehead trickled blood. The agent felt for a pulse and turned to Carbonne. "Where did you learn to shoot like this?"

"Iraq. After the first shot, realized they had too much body armor for body shots." Carbonne whispered to Everhart, "We did it." The view was of Everhart's ashen face. The sounds of gun shots increased.

Sara noted Ulysses was now listening intently to his headphone, snorting occasionally, and typing madly on his computer keyboard. She saw on the screen views of the backyard and the two new agents as they checked the injured. In the background, she heard an explosion and then another.

Sara did the math. She figured the two attackers, who had been in the neighbor's backyard, were the dead lying at the side of the house.

There had been four men in the cars out front. No one had mentioned seeing intruders in the other backyard but it was possible. So, the third attacker could have come from the car at the front of the house or the backyard of the other neighbor. That meant at least three were at large.

The view jerked to three teams of EMTs running toward the camera with stretchers. As soon as they lifted Everhart onto one, the view zoomed backward on the gravel. The marshals were lifted onto stretchers. The agent, who had been preparing the injured marshals for the arrival of the EMTs, stood.

Carbonne said, "You go with our three to the hospital"

The agent objected.

"See the camera on my head? If Ulysses disagreed, he'd have squawked by now."

Sara looked at Ulysses. She doubted he was paying attention to Carbonne. However, neither Carbonne nor the agent knew it. The agent left with the EMTs.

Carbonne's view focused on the agent soaked by the fire hose. "I can't get a response from the marshal or the agent in the kitchen. Ulysses, what's happening up front?"

Ulysses flipped a switch. The alto voice of the SWAT commander blared in the room. "SWAT got here after four men rushed the front and the west side of the house. The attackers are not responding to us. We have immobilized their cars."

Sara assumed Carbonne could also hear the SWAT commander through his headphone because he was cursing.

Ulysses spoke, "Attackers on east side of house contained. Agents are now ready to enter the house from the rear, but they need back up. Secure the west side."

Sara continued her profiles of the Belen police and fire officers, as Carbonne, Ulysses, and the SWAT commander discussed tactics.

When two SWAT members joined Carbonne, the view on the screen riveted her attention again. First, the view from the camera on Carbonne's head showed the dark sliding door to the kitchen through the smoke in the hallway. Slowly a crack of light appeared at the edge on the screen. Sara shrieked as the view through the slit between the kitchen door and its frame appeared.

Pigeon's wife was tied to a chair near the door to the garage and emitted occasional shrieks. A masked man with a gun yelled, "Shut up!" in response to her shrieks.

The view swept to the other side of the shattered front window. Another dark-haired man appeared with a mask and a gun. His gun arm abruptly moved downward after he said "Will do," into his headphone.

The sliver of a view swept the floor. The woman agent lay curled in a fetal position at the feet of Pigeon's wife. Her back to the camera. Motionless. Next to her was Noah. Motionless.

Carbonne must have moved because the view rapidly swept around the room. Neither Pigeon nor the lead marshal was visible, but it was not possible to see much, except a white refrigerator, along the kitchen wall abutting the rest of the house.

Ulysses gasped. "Where's Pigeon? The marshal? Where's the last attacker?"

The SWAT commander said, "They could be beside the refrigerator on the wall that you can't view, or in the garage. The two gunmen are taking orders from someone on the phone. Might be the fourth assailant."

The horror of the situation became personal in Sara's mind. The marshals hadn't fulfilled the deals made by the federal prosecuting attorney. They had been unable to protect Pigeon and his family and they couldn't keep track of Jack Daniels. Once this immediate crisis was over, she probably would be advised to agree to their protection. She doubted their capabilities.

She picked up Bug and cuddled him. He licked her nose. Agents had already complained she was too identifiable with Bug and suggested he be kenneled. She suspected the marshals would say they couldn't protect her if she kept Bug. Then she'd be truly alone. "Bug, I promise. It's not going to happen."

She stood and handed a note to Ulysses. She'd found nothing odd in her quick search of the Belen police and fire crews. Lots of similar last

names, but none with same last names as those involved in the upcoming
federal trial. She knew the information was almost useless. "I'm going to
make myself useful. Nothing I can do here."

CHAPTER 19: FBI Agent Carbonne

Carbonne felt sweat trickle down his forehead and chest. It was about eighty-five degrees outside and close to it inside. The fire crew had stopped the fire. The smoke had largely dissipated through the bullet-shattered windows, but the wet plasterboard walls of the house steamed dank odors. In the background, he could hear a policeman on a bullhorn telling the attackers to save themselves and surrender.

His view through the slit suggested the gunmen wouldn't surrender. The masked men were well armed. Weapons confiscated from the marshal and the agent lay on the counter near the man with the headphone.

He knew the gunmen would pepper the sliding door with bullets if they thought he was behind it. Carbonne took a final glance at the motionless boy and female agent before he slid back. He motioned to the other agent to move back too.

As he walked to the porch, several shots tore through the sliding door from the kitchen to the hall. He whispered into his headphone. "Must have been noisier than I thought. Means we've lost our view. Has the SWAT established contact with the gunman? He was talking to someone. All I heard was: 'Will do.' Did you hear the whole conversation?"

After what seemed like a minute, Ulysses, said, "The SWAT recorded the short message before the 'Will do.' They traced the contact to a location about two blocks away. They're on the way. Neither party has spoken since."

"What was the message?" Carbonne got no reply.

An FBI technician, who had arrived with the SWAT, handed Carbonne a monitor attached to a wire and an optical fiber cable. Carbonne stepped into the hall from the porch to watch the technician unroll the wire and cable as he crawled to the door and inserted several strands of optical fiber bundles and a microphone in the crack. The agent in the hallway moved forward and prepared to shoot if necessary. The technician cemented one fiber a foot off the floor with a modeling compound.

Carbonne could see Noah's head and upper torso and the woman agent's lower body on the monitor. Both were motionless. He gave the technician a high sign.

The technician placed a second optic fiber higher and adjusted the angle until Carbonne could see the gunman guarding the hostages. He cemented it in place after Carbonne gave him another high sign. The technician quickly placed the microphone and several other optic fibers. Carbonne now had multiple views of the kitchen. All he could hear was Pigeon's wife sobbing.

The SWAT commander spoke, "We have surrounded the house with the burner phone used to call our gunmen. That house is two blocks away. The phone is moving erratically about the house. Infrared detectors indicate one live heat source in the house but have gotten no response to the bullhorn. The heat source seems small for a man. Might be a small woman."

Carbonne waited for more details as he watched the technician seal the last of the cables in place with an ivory modeling compound. The bundles were barely visible when he slid away. Carbonne looked at the multiple views now on the monitor. "Nothing changed. No one talking. The boy and the agent need medical attention."

No response. Time was ticking away. Minutes were important. Carbonne was disgusted. Neither Ulysses nor this SWAT commander seemed to be handling all the action well. "SWAT—the boy and the agent urgently need medical attention.!"

The alto voice of the SWAT commander sounded calm. "We've entered the house with the other burner phone."

Silence.

She spoke again. "The burner phone receiving the gunman's call was tied to a dog's collar. The escape of the dog and two or three men must have been through the exterior door on the west side of the garage. Checked it when agents rushed around the house and garage to help agents at the rear. It was locked."

Carbonne whistled. "So, all the action on the other side of the house—fire and shooting—was a diversion to prevent us for noticing the escape of one attacker, Pigeon, and a dog."

The alto voice said, "Agreed."

Carbonne heard loud noises.

The SWAT commander shrieked, "Found a body in the garage! Knifed!" After a short pause, she said more calmly, "Not Pigeon. Not the marshal. No sign of them, but a knife was left at site." After another pause, "We will now return to the rest of our team at the original house and focus on rescuing the hostages. Ulysses, local police will have to handle the cleanup at the second house."

Carbonne heard sirens wailing a block or two away. A SWAT member on a megaphone probably at the front of the house continued to repeat over and over again, "Let us get the boy and the women agent out. They need medical help. You'd still have three hostages." Carbonne thought it was smart that the SWAT didn't admit they knew the kidnappers now only had four hostages because Pigeon, but probably not the marshal, had escaped. He also noted the man's voice sounded hoarser each time he repeated his plea.

Carbonne could barely hear the SWAT commander's voice because of the background noise. "We're creating more diversions to mask the sound as we enter the garage. Be prepared for action."

Two SWAT team members had joined Carbonne and the other agent on the porch. Carbonne stared at the monitor. The boy moved his hand. "Boy's alive!"

Carbonne thought he heard a groan from the boy. Nothing from the woman agent. But he wasn't sure because the noises from sirens and the man on the megaphone were intense. Pigeon's wife began to hum.

No, she was reciting something. "The Lord is…" She droned on until one of the gunmen slapped her face.

"You've got to act soon. The kitchen's a tinderbox."

"In the garage." The alto voice was steady. "Found the marshal. He's groggy and was trussed up and gagged. No sign of Pigeon."

Ulysses groaned, "Means Pigeon alone escaped unless the attackers had men in a neighboring backyard or a man at the other house."

The SWAT commander said, "Can't worry about him now. My goal is to save the lives of the other three hostages. The message was, 'Clean up in the kitchen and go in five.' If 'clean up' means kill the hostages, we're out of time. We have no clear shot lines to the gunmen through the front window. Hostages are in front of side door from the kitchen to the garage. The door is locked. If we storm in there, they're sure to be killed or injured."

Carbonne gulped. "Clear shot line to the gunman nearest the hostages from the slit by the sliding door. No clear shot to the lead one because of the refrigerator. He's got an arsenal, including an FBI rifle."

The SWAT commander sighed. "No choice. We'll force the lead gunman to the front window with the slow approach of two men in armor. Snipers are positioned in the house across the street and in an armored car. When I say 'star,' shoot the other gunman."

"We need a minute to get positioned by the door."

Carbonne and his two cohorts talked and then scrambled forward down the hall before the SWAT commander said, "Roger."

The voice on the megaphone became conciliatory. "We're sending in a team to carry out the injured. Look out your window. This can end well for everyone."

Carbonne stood by the crack at the door to the kitchen with his gun aimed at the gunman by the hostages. A SWAT team member knelt with his gun also aimed at the same gunman. Another SWAT team member stood ready to push the door open farther for an unimpeded shot. The other FBI agent stood back in the hallway and watched the monitor. They'd agreed the agent would say "ready" when the lead gunman stepped from beside the refrigerator to the window.

The voice on the megaphone repeated. "We're sending in a team to carry out the injured. Look out your window."

The agent whispered, "Ready."

A whining sound. Another. "Star!" bellowed in Carbonne's ear from the headphone.

The crack widened. Carbonne squeezed the trigger. Then again. Blood trickled from the back of the gunman's head as he slumped forward onto the hostages.

Carbonne glanced at the window through the now three-inch gap between the door and the door frame. The gunman wasn't there. Carbonne looked to the floor. The gunman's hand—the one with the gun—moved.

A gun fired from near Carbonne's hips. Blood trickled from a hole in the gunman's head.

Carbonne looked back as the SWAT team member lowered his gun, and said, "I should have warned the sniper out front about the gunmen's Kevlar body armor."

Both SWAT team members raced to pull the gunmen off the hostages. Carbonne took a big gulp of air. No time for nerves. He rushed forward and leaned down to feel the pulse of the boy as a SWAT member cut the bindings off Pigeon's wife. He turned over the woman FBI agent. Her face was bloody. She'd been beaten. He felt her wrist. She had a weak pulse. "Both are alive!"

Pigeon's wife chanted, "The Lord is..." as a SWAT member pulled her to her feet and led her to the hallway. SWAT team members and EMTs stormed into the kitchen from the garage and hallway. The SWAT commander's voice boomed, "Good job!" in his headphone.

CHAPTER 20: Sara

It was easy to say she'd be more useful in her quiet cubicle, but it was hard to make the statement true. First, Sara focused on a detail from Kit's cut-and-paste effort—a detail too trivial to discuss previously with Ulysses. A man named Hank Diaz was the meat inspector at Pigeon's plant at the time Dan Steele lost his finger seventeen years ago. She accessed USDA's employment records. The same Hank Diaz had spent sixteen years as a USDA certified meat inspector at a plant in Belen before he moved to the plant in Grants six months ago.

Maybe this information was relevant to the crisis in Belen, but she had no idea how. She emailed Ulysses and asked Kit to alert Ulysses about her email at an appropriate time.

She reopened the massive FBI file on Pigeon. After a few minutes of going over it again, she still had no idea of what to look for in the file. The phone rang. It was Sanders.

"Sara, I've got flights on a commercial airline booked for tomorrow. I should arrive before noon."

"Considering the usual delays, you'll get here around three. Ulysses will probably have Bug and me sleep here tonight because he has too many more important issues to handle."

Sanders was silent for several seconds. "I know you're stuck in the FBI building until they find a new safe house, but you're not usually so negative."

"Sorry." Sara explained the crisis in Belen. "I think Pigeon outwitted agents and marshals for several months and planned his own kidnapping."

"Perhaps. One thing is sure. He didn't organize the events in Belen without a lot of help. Who does he trust?"

"Good question." She hesitated. "Not his wife. Otherwise, I have no idea. I guess I should look for recurring names in the FBI files on his background. All the stress here has slowed my thought processes."

"You can't always have the answers."

"You sound like the pot when it calls the kettle black. We both are fix-it people and get annoyed with ourselves if we can't meet our own expectations."

Sanders chuckled. "We do share many traits. Maybe I can help you brainstorm, since the New Mexico crew are busy dodging bullets. I bet the agents have focused on Pigeon's activities as related to his packing plant. What do you know about Pigeon's childhood and youth?"

"Nothing, but Carbonne thinks Pigeon abuses his wife and son. That suggests he might have been abused himself as a child. Give me a second." She located the section in the background file on Pigeon labeled *Before 2000*. "Looks like he was born and raised in Las Vegas, New Mexico."

"You know Las Vegas has had an unsavory history for over a hundred years with the likes of Billy the Kid."

"Yeah, Doc Holliday and his common-law wife Big Nose Kate spent time there. However, our Las Vegas is small change in the drug business now." She paused as she stared at her computer screen. "Wait. I doubt anyone seriously read this section of Pigeon's file. Too bad."

"Stop the hype and give me the main points."

"His parents died in a car accident in 1982 when he was twelve. Hit by drunken teenagers. He went to live in with his aunt, a teacher in Las Vegas, New Mexico. An FBI analyst noted he had an extremely strict upbringing. Didn't explain."

Sanders sighed. "So, he might consider his actions with his son necessary, not abusive. What else?"

"Let's see.... Nothing unusual for the only son in a wealthy family in the Southwest, except for his parents' will. It allowed him to inherit a sizable sum when he married or turned twenty-five, whichever came first."

"Let me guess. He got a girl pregnant and married at eighteen."

"Almost right. He married Mary Melendez, a woman of twenty-five with a one-year old son, in 1988. She must have known about the will because he used his inheritance to buy her father's meat packing plant. Odd—he must have been desperate to get away from his aunt."

Sanders snickered. "Or he liked older women."

Sara ignored him. "But not for long. They must have separated. The file has a legal notice filed in the local newspaper in 1989. Basically, says he wasn't responsible for her bills. Can't find another mention of her. Wait. Another analyst's note. Mary Melendez died of a drug overdose in 1995. Can't find any mention of the son."

"But you've got a potentially useful lead."

"Oh, dear. I'm really out of it. How did I miss it?"

"What?"

"The last name of the man killed in the accident at the meat packing plant in Grants was Melendez. His first name might also be relevant. I know of only one other Melvin in this area. It's Pigeon's first name."

"Anything else?"

"The Melvin Melendez killed at the plant was around thirty. He could be Mary's son and Pigeon's stepson. Thanks for helping me focus."

"No thanks necessary. I like brainstorming with you. Looks as if communications among agents in Ulysses's shop aren't optimal."

"You're right. The nastiness level is high here. Several of the agents think Ulysses should retire and are bucking for his position. They want Kit out, ignore Carbonne, and, I imagine, are insulted by my presence."

"Hmm—I'll try to catch an earlier flight. Got to go. Love you. Bye."

Sara wished he'd talked longer but figured he had his own emergencies. At the rate she was progressing it might be three tomorrow before she had useful data for Ulysses. That would be too late to help solve the current crisis in Belen. What would be the quickest way to learn about Melvin Melendez?

She called the Office of the New Mexico Medical Examiner to learn the name of the person who had tried to claim Melvin Melendez's remains. The clerk, a young woman, refused to give her an answer. Sara assumed the clerk was confused and patiently re-explained that she already had a copy of the autopsy by the medical examiner and knew OSHA had requested the remains not be released to the family for cremation or burial. The clerk, in the lilting voice of a girl, not a woman, told Sara to file a special form to learn the name of those requesting the body.

Sara's temper flared. She didn't want to bother Ulysses now. She assumed her most officious tone. "This is Dr. Sara Almquist. I'm calling for Ulysses Howe, special agent in charge of the FBI office in New Mexico. We need to know who requested the body, now."

The clerk choked. "Let me talk to my boss."

The next voice on the phone was that of an older man. "This is the medical examiner. I'm the one who sent the autopsy report on Melvin Melendez to you and the judge. Sorry for the mix-up. My young assistant saw a letter from an attorney requesting the remains and another one agreeing to the request by OSHA." Pause. "That's unusual—both letters noted the client wished to remain anonymous." He gave Sara the name of the attorney.

She decided she couldn't bluff a lawyer into giving her the name of the relative, but realized Ulysses was too busy now to be screening any emails not dealing with the crisis in Belen. She emailed Ulysses anyway.

Melvin Melendez, the man killed in the accident at the meat packing plant in Grants, might be Pigeon's stepson. This lawyer has the answer...

She debated whether to add that the accident might have set off Pigeon because he suspected the accident was really murder, but she decided that the supposition was unnecessary.

It was easy to track police records on Melvin Melendez using Ulysses's access codes. Melendez had multiple arrests for drug possession and petty crimes. Then she noted a pattern. The same lawyer always bailed

Melendez out of jail, got the cases dismissed, or reduced to minor offenses. It was same lawyer who had written the letters to the medical examiner.

Despite his arrests, Melendez always stayed employed, usually in meat packing plants or at grocery stores as a butcher. Finally, she found his birth certificate. As expected, Mary Melendez was listed as his mother. He was born in 1987 in Las Vegas, New Mexico. His father was listed as "unknown."

She emailed the new data to Ulysses.

> *URGENT. Bet Pigeon will lose his focus and make a mistake if he knows we know his secret. He's the father, not the stepfather, of Melvin Melendez.*

Again, she called Kit. He had not interrupted Ulysses during the rescue of the hostages, but now he planned to be heard.

She figured the crisis must be almost over but didn't have the guts to ask Kit for details. She also didn't want to waste his time. Instead, she checked her emails. Nothing from Frank McCoy. She sent the information on Melvin Melendez to him and to his boss at USDA.

Her phone rang. "Ulysses wants you in his office now."

CHAPTER 21: FBI Special Agent Ulysses Howe

"Pigeon engineered his own escape from the marshals! You heard the lead marshal!"

Ulysses thought Carbonne's face on the monitor looked haggard. His dark hair was now a mat of dark curls on his skull. At least he'd found a shirt. He guessed Carbonne had earned the right to vent his frustrations.

Carbonne continued, "Pigeon claimed he heard noises in the garage. The lead marshal opened the kitchen door to the garage and saw something moving behind the large black garbage can. He stepped into the garage and fired his gun when the can moved. Next thing he knew, he was tied, gagged, and blindfolded and his head ached."

"There is another possible interpretation of the data," said Ulysses. "The dog moved behind the garbage can and the attacker, not Pigeon, hit the marshal on the head."

"Doubt it."

"Pigeon's wife, his son, and the woman marshal know the answer, but the agent is comatose. Pigeon's wife is hopelessly incoherent. Maybe you can get the boy to talk?"

Carbonne's voice was weak. "I can't. Besides, Noah didn't talk much to me. He drew a picture of the, I guess, mummified finger. Get a child psychiatrist and Sara to question him. I can't do it."

Ulysses thought Carbonne had let himself become too attached to the boy and needed to focus on the case not the boy. "I suspect the hand at the sewage plant was Dan Steele's. The medical examiner said the hand you retrieved as the sewage plant was missing two fingers. One had been lost years before."

After a long pause, Carbonne continued, "You'd better have the garbage checked pronto. Don't forget Noah's teacher thought there was writing on the yellow paper wrapped around the finger."

"The SWAT has room for the garbage can in one of their vans. We'll find it." Ulysses found it exhausting to psychologically analyze not only criminals but also his staff. However, he had to get Carbonne engaged and out of the funk that followed intense action. "Maybe you'll want to follow up on Sara's new data? Seems Hank Diaz, the USDA meat inspector at the plant in Grants, was the inspector at Pigeon's plant seventeen years ago—at the time Dan Steele lost his finger in a meat slicer. Another interesting note—Hank Diaz worked as an inspector at a meat packing plant and lived in Belen for sixteen years."

"So?"

"I'm sending the agents to pick up Hank Diaz for questioning. Would you like to question him? You can catch a ride from Belen to Albuquerque with the SWAT if you're not up to driving back in the car that Everhart checked out to drive to Belen." He figured Carbonne, after killing three men today, would choose to drive the car back because he needed time to unwind alone.

Carbonne's voice was stronger when he said, "Have them pick up Caleb Steele, too."

Ulysses wanted to say, *I'm the boss.* Instead, he said, "Why?"

"Dan probably told his brother about Hank Diaz."

Ulysses decided Carbonne was engaged, but would still check on him in another half-hour and not mention the mandatory visit with an FBI psychologist yet.

***

Although Carbonne and the lead marshal thought Pigeon had engineered his own kidnapping, Ulysses doubted it for several reasons. The person—*or more likely persons*—who had planned the kidnapping were thorough and prepared for contingencies. Why else would they have hired six men to kidnap a family protected by only three marshals? They had no reason to suspect extra FBI agents would be present to foil their plans. All the kidnappers were from outside New Mexico. That suggested the planners had extensive multistate connections. The planners were also creative, as shown by their use of a dog to distract the police. Those characteristics didn't describe Pigeon. His organizational skills seemed weak. His meat packing plant had not increased its sales during the last ten years and still primarily sold meat in New Mexico. Moreover, the gang leaders on trial would benefit if Pigeon didn't testify at their trial. Killing his family would also warn others not to testify either.

Ulysses recognized several weakness in his argument. One was that all the dead kidnappers were from Texas. In the past, the gang members on trial in New Mexico had used local talent or hired gunmen from Florida and Cuba.

Two, Pigeon had always seemed reluctant to testify against the gang leaders but seemed eager to gain witness protection. The shoot-out may have weakened his confidence in the U.S. Marshal Service or may have given him a chance to disappear until after the trial and avoid having to testify. Carbonne was right that Pigeon was capable of double-crossing the marshals, but Ulysses didn't think he was smart enough to plan his escape.

Another weakness in his argument was the stabbing of the kidnapper. The only clear prints the knife left at the scene were those of Pigeon and the woman marshal. However, there was evidence that someone wearing gloves had handled the knife. It was also strange— sloppy really— that the woman marshal had brought a large knife to the garage to open garbage bags before the attack and forgot it. Pigeon must have found the knife and hidden it until he had a chance to escape his captor at the other house. In doing so, Pigeon had displayed more cunning, physical strength, and ruthlessness than Ulysses thought possible. That worried him. Had he underestimated Pigeon in other ways?

The early search for Pigeon was not promising. Agents and police had canvassed the neighborhood. No one admitted seeing or hearing anything strange, except for the noisy police presence.

An animal control officer had taken the dog to a veterinarian to have its chip traced. The owners were out of town.

Police talked to the owner of the house where the dog was found while the woman was at work at Walmart. She failed to recognize photos of Pigeon or the dog and complained, "My boss will give me a drug test almost every day for the next two weeks because you came here today." The police concluded she used drugs occasionally, but she'd never been arrested even for speeding. Even so, they escorted her to the police station before they told her about the body in her garage and had her look at mug shots of the kidnappers.

The burner phone attached to the dog was probably the best lead for finding Pigeon. Technicians had found three sets of fingerprints on the phone—Pigeon's, those of the dead attacker found in the other house, and a set that didn't match any on file. They also determined someone had used the phone to make one call around ten in the morning, two other calls about fifteen minutes before the shoot-out, and one call immediately before the shoot-out. The first call to another burner phone in Grants lasted several minutes. The other calls were less than twenty seconds. Technicians traced the short calls to burner phones on the Acoma pueblo, in Albuquerque's northeast side, and on one of the dead gunmen in the kitchen. The SWAT had recorded the last call.

***

Sara knocked before Bug paraded into Ulysses's office. It was amazing how elegant the little dog was. An adjective Ulysses wouldn't use to describe Sara. As usual, she carried a pile of papers and a can of diet cola. Her hair almost as messy as Carbonne's but looked clean.

"You've given my staff more to argue about."

Sara's smile disappeared and she sank into a chair in front of his desk. "I thought I was being helpful."

"You were. Great work. One of our lawyers is speaking now to the attorney representing the relatives of Melvin Melendez. Attorney-client privilege is sacrosanct, but billable fees are not. We can trace the source of funds used to protect Melendez through all his criminal escapades."

"I bet the prosecutor is going to learn unpleasant details about Pigeon."

J. L. Greger

"Humph. You better hope not. It will make your testimony more important, and we might have to explore a topic we've both avoided—witness protection for you."

Sara didn't look teary-eyed as Ulysses had expected. Instead she said defiantly, "That's why I'm working hard to get the evidence you need to find Pigeon and force him to talk."

"Don't give me the lecture on how he engineered the whole kidnapping hoax."

"Don't plan to. You need facts and evidence, not theories. I thought of a few new angles to get data on Pigeon and this mess of confusing clues." She frowned. "Please note: I assumed the accident at the meat plant in Grants, Dan Steele's murder, the shoot-out today, and my strange package were linked. That may have been a mistake, but I had to start somewhere." She glanced at a hand-written list on a pad of paper.

Ulysses smiled in amusement. Although Sara was a whiz at searching data bases, she always kept her to-do lists and lists of ideas on paper. "I'm listening."

"Frank McCoy's report from earlier today is important. I bet you haven't had time to read it." She stared at Ulysses.

"What's your point?

"He asked provocative questions at the Acoma Pueblo. Agents should interview the Lewises in Potters Place and the two Acoma officials he spoke to."

"His boss at USDA gave me the same advice. Evidently, they require investigators to call in at certain times. Frank missed two call-ins. Do you know where he is?"

"Last I knew he was on his way to talk to Elijah Wood at the El Malpais ranger station off State Road 117."

"Well, we should have answers soon. The Cibola County sheriff and Acoma Pueblo police are looking for him."

When he drummed his fingers on his desk, Sara said, "Cool it—I've got more points on my list. I've tried repeatedly to contact Elijah Wood. Phone, Twitter, email—nothing. So, I profiled him too. A typical young Gen Y—still lives with his parents on the Zuni Pueblo, drinks too much occasionally as evidenced by citations, and has only a part-time job as a USDA meat inspector. He turned down a full-time position as a meat inspector in Nebraska. He either likes lots of spare time or has another job which—by the way—he hasn't reported to his USDA employer."

"Typical of today—lots of dead ends."

"Are you speaking literally or hypothetically?" Sara looked at her list. "Talked to Lydia Griegos. The Veterinary Diagnostic Lab confirmed *Yersinia pestis* infection in the prairie dog, and surprisingly, in the sheep samples sent to me."

"Why are you surprised?"

"The sheep had no characteristic buboes in their lymph nodes. Lydia says occasionally livestock are found to have *Yersinia* infections without that characteristic symptom."

"Why do I care?"

She handed Ulysses a list of names and phone numbers. "Once they were sure of the data, state health and agricultural officials acted. They talked to physicians at Indian Health Service, the environmental officer at Acoma Pueblo, and health and agriculture officials in Cibola County. No one admitted to actually seeing plague symptoms in humans, sheep, or cattle. But the pueblo environmental officer admitted talking to one of the Lewises." She stared at him. "Someone lied."

"What do you mean?"

"It is doubtful only one sheep acquired a *Yersinia* infection from the prairie dogs. State ag and health officials figure at least one rancher has sold off a lot of sick animals fast—probably two or three days ago—before the New Mexico Department of Agriculture could demand they be destroyed, and the carcasses burned."

"Did they do more than talk?"

"State ag officials have already demanded data on the sale of sheep to meat packing plants throughout New Mexico during the last week. Ag officials will inspect all ranches and farms that sold sheep in the last week. Health officials have already published a health alert on plague in prairie dogs on the Acoma Pueblo and in surrounding areas. All TV stations in New Mexico have agreed to announce it on their evening news tonight."

"Should yield a few crank calls."

Sara looked surprised. "This is a big deal! Ranchers and farmers lose a lot of money when a whole herd is destroyed. That's what the state ag officials will demand to prevent the spread of the plague if they find even one infected animal in a herd. It can break a rancher or farmer financially and emotionally. That's a motive for murder."

Ulysses sighed. "All that's interesting. Useful even, but not for finding Pigeon or even Dan Steele. And although I sent agents to pick up Hank Diaz, we have nothing to tie him to the current situation."

Sara blinked. "In all the excitement, you must have missed several emails. The burner phone call to Grants bounced off a tower near the meat plant. That might tie Diaz in. The lab got useful prints from the hand, which Carbonne retrieved from the sewage plant, after a lot of processing. The prints matched ones on file for Dan Steele. I think you've found Dan Steele or at least part of him."

Ulysses coughed. He depended too much on Sara for updates because he didn't have the right people in place. Too much squabbling among his staff. "I missed both of them. He stared at his computer screen and scanned his unread messages.

"That's why I left your office in the middle of the hostage crisis. I figured someone should attend to boring, but potentially important, details."

Ulysses had his best brainstorm of the day, but Sanders would kill him if he lured Sara into a permanent position with the FBI. His short conversation with Sanders today suggested Sanders was willing to make a commitment to Sara.

"One more thing. Have you found a place for Bug and me to stay tonight?"

CHAPTER 22: FBI Agents and FBI Agent Carbonne

The agents in Grants found no one at Hank Diaz's home. A neighbor, an elderly woman, claimed he seldom got home before six in the evening and often didn't come home at all because he spent his nights with "loose women."

They went to the meat packing plant and found the front door locked even though the plant didn't officially close until three. They circled the building. Lights were on in one office. The doors at the delivery platform were locked. However, a side door was unlocked. They called the Grants police and waited for them to arrive as backup because they feared what they'd encounter.

Guns drawn, they entered the plant, and knocked on the door to the main office. No one replied. They walked through the dark business office to a brightly lit side office.

Caleb Steele had his back to them. He was yelling into the phone. When he finally noticed the agents, he waved them to be seated as he continued his tirade. The agents demanded he hang up the phone after they determined the regional director of the USDA meat inspection service was on the line.

The agents spent several more minutes unraveling Caleb's problem. Hank Diaz had gotten a call around ten and disappeared immediately. Caleb had repeatedly called Elijah Wood but gotten no response. He'd even tried the number of a new backup meat inspector Frank McCoy, who was supposed to stop by at three, but got no answer. Thus, he'd been forced to shut the line down at eleven, three hours early, and send all his employees home because he had no USDA meat inspector.

The agents couldn't get him to focus on their questions. He kept raving. "I've got to call the plant owner now. He'll be furious!"

Finally, the agents threatened to take him to Albuquerque where "someone more knowledgeable" wanted to question him. They expected him to resist.

Instead, he said, "Let's go."

***

Carbonne plodded to the car that Everhart had parked in front of the Harvey House Museum less than two hours before. He didn't like Everhart and hardly knew the woman agent. Still, he dreaded the drive home alone. He wondered whether he should apply for a desk job in the agency. Maybe back East. He had better conversations with the bums at the VA than with the macho agents and police in Albuquerque.

He started the car. The heat was stifling. He stepped out and called the ICU at University Hospital in Albuquerque. Noah's condition had been upgraded to fair. The woman marshal had died. Everhart, the woman agent, and the other marshal were in critical condition. Physicians planned to release the lead marshal from the hospital after one more test.

The car was no longer a blast furnace, only a hot sauna. He didn't want to drive back to Albuquerque alone, especially in this car. However, the ride in the van with the SWAT would be worse. They would be celebrating the rescue of the hostages and the fact none of the SWAT had been injured. He didn't feel like celebrating. Left to his own devices, he would have eaten and drunk too much in Fat Sat's Bar and Grill on the I-25 bypass at the edge of Belen, spent the night in a nearby motel, and rolled into Albuquerque tomorrow around noon. Ulysses had eliminated that option. He guessed the agents driving from Grants with Hank Diaz and Caleb Steele would arrive in Albuquerque in two hours.

The car reeked of a putrid odor. The fleet crew must not have cleaned the car adequately. He opened the trunk to look for decaying evidence or food. It was empty. He sniffed again. It wasn't the car. He looked at his blood-stained, sweaty clothes and realized that he was the source of the stench. Then he remembered there was a Walmart at the edge of Belen.

***

He wore a new shirt, slacks, and underwear when he strolled out the front door of the superstore and spotted a van selling slices of pizza and cold drinks. The pizza wasn't as good as the thin crust slices sold in Philadelphia, but it was tasty.

He scanned his emails in the hot car as the air conditioner slowly lowered the temperature. Sadness washed over him when he read the report from the medical examiner that Sara had sent. He'd never met Dan, but he'd delved into his life so much that Dan felt like a friend—another lost soul who fit nowhere. Sara's emails on Frank McCoy also worried him. Last night with Sara and Frank had been one of his best since he came to Albuquerque. Brainstorming and laughing with smart, kind people.

His phone rang. "Where are you now?"

"Parking lot in front of Walmart in Belen."

"I'm short on agents." Ulysses paused.

"Let me guess. You want me to drive to Grants." Carbonne fiddled with the GPS system built into the car." You know it'll take an hour and a half to get there from here."

"No. How would you like to interview Frank McCoy? He'll arrive soon at the helicopter port on the roof of University Hospital's new wing. The Acoma police found him injured and muttering. The only words clear to the EMTs were 'three,' 'trucks,' 'Indians,' and 'Sara.' In no particular order."

"What happened? Will Frank be all right?"

"Frank rolled his car into a deep ditch around noon. No one reported the accident and the Acoma police didn't find him until a few minutes ago. His car wasn't visible from the road. He's lost a lot of blood and has internal injuries."

Carbonne groaned. "You know I hate bedside interviews in hospitals."

J. L. Greger

"Didn't figure you would want to do it. Sara's already at the hospital. However, I'd like fresh eyes to look at the photos of the accident scene and wanted to update you on new data from Sara before we interview Caleb Steele in about an hour, maybe two."

Carbonne recognized the real purpose of Ulysses's call—it was a check to see whether he was all right. He appreciated Ulysses hadn't told him to report to the psychiatrist the FBI had on call. He suspected the psychiatrist was unavailable this afternoon and Ulysses would give him the message after they interviewed Caleb Steele.

"I'm sending photos of the accident scene now. They were taken by the Acoma police."

Carbonne stared at the photos. "Most likely scenario is Frank fell asleep at the wheel. Except, there's a lot of loose gravel on the road. Not only at the site where the ruts show he left the road but also apparently for miles in either direction. Do gravel trucks use the road?"

"I asked the Acoma police chief the same question. He replied, 'Don't underestimate my officers. The officers thought big trucks might have blocked the road and forced Frank into the ditch. They knew a few good pictures beat fancy theories.' The Acoma police chief also said big trucks usually avoided this road. Now take a look at the next photos."

A beat-up pick up was parked in the lot by a lodge, apparently the ranger station of El Malpais. At least that's what a sign in the first photo indicated. The pickup truck had a long, deep dent on its rear right bumper in the second photo. The paint in the dent was red, the color of Frank's car, in the third picture.

"Do the guys at the scene think Frank's car swerved to avoid hitting the pickup truck and spun out of control?"

"Yes. We're towing the truck and Frank's car back here because Acoma Police don't trust their local body shop technicians to do the analyses."

"Anything else?"

"Technicians determined Pigeon used the burner phone attached to the dog collar to make two thirty-second calls to other burner phones on the Acoma Pueblo and in Albuquerque shortly before the shoot-out in Belen. The technicians couldn't identify the exact locations of the phones. However, agents circulating in the northeast neighborhoods of Albuquerque, the vicinity of the second call, spotted a black Camaro resembling Jack Daniels's car. They chased but lost it."

"You're guessing the call to the Acoma Pueblo area was to Elijah Wood because El Malpais ranger station is near Acoma land?"

"Problem is Hank Diaz and Elijah Wood have disappeared. The agents in Grants spent an hour searching for Hank Diaz before they picked up Caleb Steele. The Cibola County Sheriff's deputies can't find Elijah on the Zuni Pueblo. The ranger said Elijah left the ranger substation before ten today."

Carbonne was silent for ten seconds. "Your hypothesis could be wrong. Sara pointed out that Frank McCoy might have riled several people on the Acoma Pueblo. Pigeon could have called one of them."

"So, you've read all your emails."

"I've learned to open Sara's first."

"Even before mine?"

"Especially before yours."

CHAPTER 23: Sara

Bug strutted down the glassed-in hallway between the old and new parts of University Hospital and slowed whenever a child approached. He expected them to pet him. The two agents with Sara were used to setting the pace and often had to stop and wait for Sara and Bug to catch up with them. Finally, the older male agent stopped and stared down his thin nose at Sara. "We really should try to be less obvious."

Sara was annoyed and wondered why Ulysses had assigned this old-fashioned agent to be her guard. She knew the other agents called him "Old Tom" behind his back. His gray hair, the white lines on his tanned face, and his gaunt, slightly stooped frame made him look old. It was more. His thin lips never turned upward and his gray eyes flashed anger when he looked at Sara and even Bug. She bet he saw himself as Wyatt Earp reincarnated.

However, Sara realized Old Tom was right. She scooped up Bug and hurried to the elevator in the new wing of the building. She also realized escorting her and Bug was stressful. Before they left for the hospital, she'd overheard Ulysses fume about her safety to Old Tom and the young red-headed agent, Ian Homes, through the open door to Kit's office.

Old Tom put his foot in front of the door of the first available elevator to keep her from entering. With his arm clapped on Sara's shoulder, he guided her into an empty one while Ian blocked the entrance to other passengers. Once the door closed, he said, "The child psychiatrist will meet us at the entrance to the Pediatric Intensive Care Unit. So, we won't have to show our badges to gain entrance."

Sara shrugged. "If not, I'll say 'pet therapy' at the hall monitor. The nurses and docs in the PICU know Bug and me. They always buzz us in immediately for our weekly visits."

Old Tom sighed. "So, you'll be recognized."

Ian snickered. "We're guarding a local celebrity."

Sara blushed "Most don't know my name, but they'll recognize Bug."

The elevator stopped on the fifth floor. Old Tom briskly led the entourage toward the Pediatric Intensive Care Unit but slowed his pace when he saw a casually attired, bald man slouched at the entrance.

The man looked up from his phone and smiled. "What brings Bug here? You usually visit in the morning."

Before Sara could answer, Old Tom showed his badge. "She's with us. We have an appointment with the child psychiatrist."

The bald man laughed.

Sara said, "This is the child psychiatrist. He dresses casually because kids are more apt to talk to someone who doesn't look like he's about to poke them with a needle."

The psychiatrist flashed the card on his lanyard in front of the monitor. The double doors to the unit opened. He led the way down the hall to the last room. A man in a suit and a university security agent nodded to Old Tom and slid the room's glass door open.

The sight was familiar to Sara. A young boy curled in a fetal position in a hospital bed with monitors and bags of solutions attached by long tubes to one arm. "Would you like a visitor? A special visitor— Bug." Sara held Bug up so the boy could see him.

The boy's eyes widened, but he said nothing.

Old Tom said, "We…."

The psychiatrist pulled him back and whispered, "Let her do her thing."

Sara approached the bed and brushed Bug's tail on the boy's free hand. "Tickles, doesn't it?"

The boy's lips quivered.

"Would you like Bug to sit next to you? He'd like to get to know you."

The boy struggled to pull himself up a bit. Sara lowered Bug into an empty space next to the boy on the bed. Bug promptly repositioned himself.

"He wants you to pet him." Sara showed the boy how to scratch behind Bug's ear.

Old Tom stepped forward and leaned over the boy. "We have questions." The psychiatrist pulled the agent back before he could say more.

Sara watched the boy. "You're really good at petting. Do you have a dog at home?"

The boy looked up. "Used to. Dad said the dog barked too much. Made Mom take it to the pound."

"Bug's special. He doesn't bark."

The boy nodded.

"Your dad had a lot on his mind lately. Has he been grouchy?"

The boy looked down but continued to pet Bug.

"You know adults sometimes misbehave, like kids, especially when they're afraid."

The boy's head jerked up. "My dad isn't afraid of anyone. He gets mad." He stopped petting Bug. "Then he hits Mom and me."

The child psychiatrist circled to the other side of the bed. He touched the bruises on the boy's upper arm. "Is that how you got these?"

The boy looked down. "Dad says only babies are tattletales. I'm not a baby."

Sara put the boy's hand back on Bug's shoulders. "You're certainly not a baby. You're in second grade."

The boy kept his head down.

"Do you remember the man with dark curly hair? You drew a picture for him." Sara swept Bug's tail along the boy's hand. "We want to understand what happened today after you talked to him."

The boy looked up at Sara. He didn't smile but he didn't seem afraid either. "I didn't get to play pirate with him in the garage."

Sara didn't understand the comment but figured it didn't matter. She knew Ian was recording the conversation. "That's too bad. What did your dad do?"

The boy began to pet Bug again.

"Did he yell at you and your Mom?"

The boy shook his head. "Talked to Mom. She cried. The lady in a suit came over."

"What happened next?"

The boy was silent. Sara sat on the bed and put Bug on her lap. The boy remained silent. She mouthed to the psychiatrist, "Help."

The psychiatrist frowned. "What did your dad do?"

The boy's head jerked up. "Whispered to Mom."

"What else?"

"Hit the lady. Over and over. She fell. Kicked her." He burst into tears.

Sara normally avoided hugging children when alone with them. There were plenty of witnesses now, and she couldn't be charged with sexual abuse. She hugged the boy. "What did your mom do?"

"Cried."

"Anything else?"

"Yes." He gulped. "Dad slapped her. Told her to shut up"

Sara kept her arm around him. "What did you do?"

"Hit him. He shouldn't hit Mom and the lady."

Sara felt drained just listening to the boy's story and couldn't even guess how remembering these details made him feel. She looked at the psychiatrist and mouthed again, "Help."

The psychiatrist bent toward Sara and the boy. "You're a good man. You tried to help your mom and the lady. What did your dad do?"

"Hit me hard over and over. Shook me."

"Anything else?"

The boy shook his head and sobbed violently. Bug licked the boy's hand. Sara usually didn't allow Bug to lick patients, but it seemed right.

The boy whispered, "Bug knows."

Sara decided Noah was at his emotional limits but decided to ask one more question. "Did the masked men hit you, too?"

Noah looked up at her. "What masked men?" He burst into hysterical tears again.

Old Tom stepped forward. "One more question. Where was the marshal?"

The boy moaned and rocked back and forth without speaking.

The psychiatrist stood and grabbed Tom's arm. "The boy can't answer more questions today." He walked around the bed, opened the door, and summoned a nurse and an aide. He pointed to the agents. "Please leave now."

After the aide had replaced Sara and Bug at the bedside, the psychiatrist shooed Sara and Bug out of the room. Before he closed the sliding door, he said to Sara, "Don't know—don't want to know—how you got roped into this, but you and Bug were good today." He pulled the curtain shut.

Bug flattened on the floor. Sara picked him up and cuddled him. He placed his front paw on her arm.

Old Tom tried to peer into the room. "We need to know if the marshal was present. Had the attackers entered the kitchen? Did they hit the boy too?"

"Seems to me that Noah was unconscious by the time the attackers entered the kitchen." Sara thought a minute. "Or he's suppressing memories."

Ian shook his head. "Doubtful the marshal was present. He's already said when he stepped into the garage, the woman agent was talking to Pigeon's wife."

"Not good enough." Old Tom shook his head.

"It'll have to be enough for now." Sara knew her next comment was inappropriate, but she spoke anyway. "You might as well hear my comments before I email Ulysses. He will listen to, but maybe not agree with, them. Looks to me like Pigeon's actions were premeditated, except his inability to control his temper. Not the actions of a victim."

Old Tom coughed.

As they entered the elevator, Ian said, "Ulysses should add a dog or two to our crew in Albuquerque. We, even the psychiatrist, couldn't have gotten the boy to talk as much if Bug hadn't come along with us."

"Humph. Bet the dog doesn't work on Pigeon's wife. We need her to fill in the boy's story. She's in the old wing of the hospital."

Sara hated to admit it, but she was sure Old Tom was right.

They had left the elevator when Old Tom's phone rang. He turned his back on Sara and the other agent. Sara noticed he said "yes" twice during the short call. When he turned back to them, he looked more tired than moments before.

"Frank McCoy was injured in a strange car accident. It might be an attempted murder. The helicopter should land on the hospital's roof momentarily. Ulysses wants us, particularly Sara, to question him. The EMTs say he keeps groaning 'three,' 'trucks,' 'Indians,' and 'Sara.' Our questions have to be focused. He's not expected to survive."

Sara wished Sanders was here with her. Today felt like one long battle, and her side was losing. She wanted to curl up with Sanders and Bug and wake up when it was over. She thought for a moment. She guessed Ulysses, Carbonne, and these agents felt the same way and chided herself.

When she refocused, Old Tom had his hand on her shoulder. "Are you all right? I thought you were about to faint." He'd lost the angry tone in his voice.

"I'm not delicate, but I am tired. Can we skip the rooftop scene and go where they're taking Frank?"

Both agents peered at her. Old Tom said, "Time is critical."

"I know, but the frantic scene at the heliport is always noisy. I don't think questions will be possible. And I need to think about my questions based on the emails Frank sent me. He talked to residents of the Acoma Pueblo this morning and was on his way to talk to Elijah Wood, a member of the Zuni Pueblo."

Old Tom turned away to speak into his headset. Sara only heard him say, "McCoy spoke to several Native Americans," before Ian pushed her forward toward a chair close to the elevators. Less than a minute later, Old Tom joined them and gripped Sara's arm. "Don't like this open area. We're going to wait in a prep room by surgery."

"Wait. You said Frank had an accident—I assumed a car wreck—but gave no details. Two-car? What about the other driver?"

Old Tom pulled Sara to her feet. "Let's go." They moved so rapidly that Bug loped to keep up. Old Tom whispered into his headphone the whole way. Once they were shoved into an empty curtained area, Old Tom rolled his eyes. "These three-way calls are impossible to decipher." He paused. "I'll tell Sara." He focused on her. "Looks like a single car accident, except there was a lot of gravel on the paved road. They're guessing based on Frank's words, that three trucks forced him off the road. Ulysses said you might as well guess the scenario, too, while we wait for Frank to be rolled in."

Sara shrugged. "The drivers of the three trucks were Native Americans whom Frank didn't know. They could be the husbands or relatives of the two women he spoke to from Potters Place. Someone should go house-to-house in Potters Place, the little village near the Acoma Pueblo. What are there, five or six houses there? Of course, one driver could be Elijah Wood."

Old Tom repeated her comments into the headphone.

Sara bit her lip. "No idea why he mentioned me, except he was thinking about our emails. Tell Carbonne he did good work this afternoon."

Old Tom snorted at her last comment but repeated it before he turned back to Sara. "You and the wild man Carbonne work together a lot?" He didn't wait for an answer. "Patient should be here soon."

The noise outside the curtained area increased. The curtain was pulled back. A long white form with tubes and monitors was rolled into the alcove.

Ian whispered to a man in a navy jacket with blood smeared across his khaki slacks and then pulled Sara outside the curtained area. "Don't think Frank can respond to questions. This would be a good time for us to take a break. Maybe get a cup of coffee."

Sara nodded. "I'd like to squeeze his hand and say a few words to him. He doesn't know anyone here. It sounds silly but semi-conscious patients sometimes respond to touch."

He grabbed Bug's leash from her hand and shoved her back into the curtained area. The nurses parted slightly. Sara squeezed Frank's hand and leaned toward his face. Gauze bandages covered Frank's right eye and forehead. A ventilator mask covered his lower face. He was unrecognizable. Physicians were examining his abdomen. Red was everywhere.

"You're safe now. Hang in there." It was probably her imagination, but she thought his fingers moved slightly. She grabbed the opportunity. "Did big trucks force you off the road?"

His fingers tightened again on her hand.

"Was Elijah Wood the driver of one truck?"

His fingers didn't move.

She thought he'd probably lost consciousness but remembered the gravel on the road. She might as well try. "Were they gravel or dump trucks?"

His fingers tightened again on her hand.

A nurse pushed her aside. "No more questions. Time for surgery." The gurney jerked away.

Ian handed her Bug's leash. She immediately picked up the dog to prevent the gurney from hitting him. Old Tom leaned toward her. "What did you get?"

Sara watched the gurney surrounded by medical staff in dull green scrubs rush down the hall. She hated that shade of green. Tears washed down her face. Bug snorted and licked her arms.

"What did you get? Couldn't hear your questions."

Ian held his hand up. "Give her a few seconds." He pushed her into a chair.

"Might be my imagination, but I think he squeezed my fingers in response to two of my questions."

"Exactly what did you say?" Old Tom spoke into his headphone. "We got more."

                                                    J. L. Greger

Sara repeated her questions and Frank's responses and added, "Might only be a response to the first voice he recognized. He once said I reminded him of his first wife."

Old Tom whispered into his headphone. He announced to the blood-stained agent who had accompanied Frank on the helicopter from the accident scene, "Someone who isn't worn out has to guard Frank McCoy. I'll wait here outside surgery. Why don't you and Ian take Dr. Almquist back to the building?"

Sara was shocked he'd used her title. No one else did. She was also hungry. Nervous hungry. She's eaten too big a lunch to be really hungry. "Could we get a snack at the food court across the hall from the ER? Bug can't enter the food court, but we could eat in the reception area, by the mosaic horse statue near the food court."

The blood-stained agent nodded. "I'm hungry too."

Old Tom frowned. "Get the food while Ian brings the car to the emergency room entrance." He looked at his watch. "I'll take Dr. Almquist and her dog to the exit in exactly ten minutes."

***

The FBI sedan sped away from the hospital. The bloodied agent slurped his beverage and looked back and forth between Ian, who was driving the car, and Sara. "What did you do to get Old Tom assigned to you today?"

Sara fed a bit of her peanut butter cookie to Bug. She didn't want to be drawn into office politics. "What do you mean?"

"He's here on loan. I've heard a rumor that he wants a part-time staff position when he turns fifty-seven, the mandatory retirement age for federal law enforcement officers. However, the staff openings here are only for outreach in schools."

Ian coughed.

The other agent snickered. "Don't be coy."

Sara figured Ian couldn't risk his answer being quoted or misquoted. She had less to lose. "I suspect Ulysses wanted Tom to be exposed to a bossy woman, like me, and a child. Sort of a test of his patience. He was fine."

Sara's phone rang. She recognized Carbonne's voice.

"The agents bringing Caleb Steele to Albuquerque got squat from him. You and I are going to play good cop/bad cop with him."

"Wouldn't it be better if Ulysses and you did the interrogation and I handed you details as needed?"

"Ulysses would rather be silent. That's scarier to the person being interrogated."

CHAPTER 24: FBI Agent Carbonne

Carbonne knew he looked like a wild man. He'd been too tired to detangle his black curly hair or shave the stubble on his face before he entered Ulysses's large office. Sara didn't look much better as she sat across the conference table from him and thumbed through files. Her lips were pressed thin in a determined look. Ulysses frowned as he sat hunched at his desk and drummed his fingers slowly. No wonder Caleb Steele looked terrified.

Ulysses had decided they wouldn't tell Caleb about his brother or the shoot-out in Belen until they had questioned him thoroughly about the accident in the Grants meat packing plant. Carbonne knew if Caleb slipped and indicated he knew or suspected Dan was dead, Ulysses would treat Caleb as a murder suspect for the death of Melvin Melendez. Revenge was a common reason for murder.

However, Caleb never mentioned his brother. He denied knowing more about the death of Melvin Melendez than what was already in OSHA and police reports. But the interview was rocky because Caleb couldn't seem to focus on their questions. He kept complaining he'd never had to close the plant before today because no USDA meat inspectors were available. Finally, he said, "The owner can't afford more losses."

Sara followed with a little fib, which Carbonne and Ulysses had hatched. "We think the owner of the plant where you work plans to sell it."

Caleb gulped. "To whom?"

"Do you know…" She stopped because she couldn't say Pigeon, his FBI code name. "Do you know Melvin Mueller?" When he didn't answer, she added, "Be careful."

Caleb sighed. "He's related to Melvin Melendez, the man killed in the accident in my plant."

"What else?"

A long silence. "I think Melvin Melendez said Melvin Mueller was his stepfather."

Sara's voice was sharp with annoyance. "You must know Melvin Mueller owned the meat packing plant in Las Vegas where your brother Dan worked."

Caleb shrugged. "I guess so."

"Did your brother tell you about the plant?"

Caleb was slow to answer. "Dan's not… much of a… talker."

Carbonne decided it was time to play the bad cop. He slammed the table with his first. "Come on, man. He certainly told the psychologists at the VA about the loss of his finger in a meat slicer."

Caleb didn't have a good poker face. Carbonne tapped Sara's foot lightly with his toe. The cue for Sara's next question.

"Did you know your brother kept his finger?"

Carbonne thought Sara had delivered the bluff well. Her pitch usually went higher if she was uncertain. This time her pitch hadn't changed as she spoke.

The tic over Caleb's right eye speeded up. "He got emotional whenever the plant or his accident was mentioned. He's a bit odd at times, but he'd never keep that kind of memento."

Sara kept her voice even. "I thought you said he never talked about the plant."

"He raved and ranted, not talked."

"About what?" Sara's voice was smooth.

Caleb was silent for ten seconds. "Lack of safety in meat packing plants."

Carbonne decided it was time to give Caleb a jolt and yelled, "Get real, man. What did he call the plant where he lost his finger?"

　　　　　　　　　　　　　　　　　　　　　　　J. L. Greger

Sara said quietly, "Remember we've talked to the psychologists at the VA."

Caleb turned pale. "A hole that made a battlefield look tame."

Sara gave Caleb a motherly smile—the way she looked at Bug. "What about the management of the plant?"

Caleb leaned forward on the table with his head cradled in his hands. He muttered, "Dan didn't take orders well and imagined insults, even as a kid. Came back from the Middle East angry. And he wasn't lucky." He looked past Sara to Ulysses at the desk.

Ulysses continued to remain remote as he scanned his computer screen and typed.

Caleb gulped. Gulped again.

Carbonne held his breath He thought Caleb was almost ready to spill secrets or at least things he didn't want to admit.

"The owner of the plant motivated workers by threats." Gulp. "And meted out punishments after the slightest disagreement."

Carbonne again tapped Sara's foot with his toe.

Sara reached her hand toward Caleb's hand. "Were accidents really punishments in the plant?"

Silence. "Dan thinks so." Silence. "Maybe Dan did keep the finger. Is that what he told you? I don't know."

Carbonne noted Caleb spoke of his brother in the present tense. Either he was really clever, or he didn't know his brother was dead.

Ulysses must have noticed, too. The folds around his mouth sagged as he stared at Caleb. "Mr. Steele, we believe your brother is dead. I'm sorry."

Caleb inhaled deeply. "I was worried. He seldom disappears for this long." He hung his head. After a few seconds, he began to sob.

Sara rose and patted his shoulders. Ulysses brought the box of tissues on his desk to the table. Carbonne thought it was strange that Caleb didn't ask how his brother died.

Sara sat down. "Think. If not your brother, who might have kept the finger?"

Caleb raised his head. "What? Why are you asking?"

Carbonne was surprised Sara had asked the question so quickly. He guessed she was right. Caleb was more apt to give gut reactions now. "Man, it's important. Would Hank Diaz keep it? He worked in the plant then."

Caleb wiped his eyes. "He's a snitch, but not crazy."

Sara attacked immediately. "We've heard that you and Diaz often argue. Not uncommon for a plant manager to disagree with a meat inspector. But what do you mean he's a snitch?"

Caleb eyed her and then Ulysses. "Guess being a snitch is the job of a meat inspector."

Sara frowned. "We both know that wasn't what you meant. Does Diaz report to someone besides USDA? That's officially his employer, isn't it?"

Silence from Caleb.

Carbonne decided it was his turn to play good cop and use a line they'd planned for Sara. "Hey man, if you have the right info, we can protect you. We know the meat packing industry is a jungle."

Sara winked at Carbonne. "Your problems are not so different from those Upton Sinclair mentioned in *The Jungle*, his famous book on the meat packing industry in the early 1900s. They depended on cheap immigrant labor then. You do, too. Maybe also undocumented workers."

Caleb straightened in his chair. "I run a clean plant. The owner and I agree. We don't hire undocumented workers. We collect urine samples on Mondays to check for drugs."

Sara nodded. "So, who does Hank Diaz tattle to? And about what?"

Carbonne was surprised Sara had not followed up on Caleb's comment on drugs. Most managers believed random drug tests were more effective than routine tests to detect employees with a drug problem. He studied Caleb and decided this was not the time to ask another question. Sara's questions appeared to have threatened Caleb. He sat hunched over the table and chewed an imaginary cud.

Ulysses cleared his throat. "We know you're under tremendous pressure. You might qualify for witness protection. If you read the

Albuquerque Journal, you realize we know meat packing plants have been involved in the shipment of drugs in New Mexico."

Caleb lowered his head farther.

Ulysses left his desk, pulled out a chair and sat at the table. His voice was low. "We've made mistakes in whom we trusted. We need to learn what you know and suspect. Let's start with Sara's questions. Tell us about Hank Diaz."

"Life was good at our plant until USDA assigned Diaz to be the meat inspector there six months ago." Caleb sighed, "We had one of the best safety records in the state before Diaz came. I didn't want my plant to be like the one where my brother was injured."

Ulysses frowned. "How did a USDA meat inspector affect the safety in a plant?"

"He went to the owner and said our line was slower than necessary. The owner insisted I speed up the line. When I gave warnings to employees for sloppiness or rule violations, he buddied up to them. Last week when I announced the initiation of random drug tests, he went to the owner again. I can't help but think Melvin Melendez would still be alive if I'd instituted random drug tests despite the owner's comments."

"What makes you say that?"

"Hmm. Melvin Melendez was not a happy man. Like Dan. Suspicious. Maybe *paranoid* is a better word. I think they were friends because they both thought Melvin Mueller was the devil incarnate. On the day of the accident, Melvin was in a good mood. I even asked him whether he was high. He laughed."

Before Carbonne could ask a question, Sara leaned forward. "Was Melvin Melendez one of Diaz's friends?"

Caleb answered quickly, "No."

"How did you know? There's so much to watch in a meat packing plant. I went with my father when he sold steers to a local plant when I was a child. It was a busy place. It would be hard to identify friends, except by who ate together at lunch."

Caleb gulped. "I have my sources."

"Like the Native Americans from Potters Place?" Sara pulled a list of names from a file.

Caleb shook his head. "You got it wrong. All wrong. Mel Melendez was my chief source of gossip in the plant. He had a love-hate relationship with Hank Diaz. They were cousins. Not really but related somehow. Seems like everyone in Las Vegas, New Mexico, is related. Said Diaz was kind to him when he was a kid, but Diaz would never cross his stepdad, or as he called him—'the old devil.'"

Carbonne thought this was a time for the key question. "Do you know why Diaz was so loyal to Melvin Mueller?"

Caleb shrugged. "No, but my brother might have known."

Sara began to explore what Caleb knew about the Native Americans who lived in Potters Place and worked in the plant. It quickly became obvious they gave Caleb no problems and seldom spoke to him.

Carbonne's mind drifted. He doubted Sara's questions would yield much. Besides, her tone of voice would change if she uncovered anything useful. Then he could tune her back in. He stretched back in his chair. Maybe Dan Steele's death wasn't related to the package Sara received. Maybe he was killed because he knew Melvin Melendez's secrets. Obviously, Melendez had lived in Pigeon's house at one time. He probably knew Pigeon's secrets. Carbonne decided he was overthinking the situation. Pigeon didn't like screwups in his family. Look how he treated his wife and Noah. And Melvin Melendez was a screwup.

Carbonne noticed Ulysses wasn't listening to the interview either. He was at his desk with his chair turned so his back was to the group. He cocked his head and made occasional comments, but mainly listened to his headphone. That was odd. Ulysses was as big on details as Sara.

Ulysses rotated his chair to look at those at the table. "I've been attending to business. Caleb, U.S. marshals are prepared to bring your wife to Albuquerque and to protect both of you, if you agree to work with us."

Caleb gave a sigh of relief. "I have something that might interest you." He reached into his briefcase and pulled out a sealed manila, letter-sized packet. The packet was labeled.

To be opened upon the death of Melvin Melendez

In the bottom corner of the packet, someone had written:

Delivered to Caleb Steele by Melvin Melendez

Underneath were both men's signatures.

"Mel gave this to me about two weeks before his accident. It's been in my safe at work since then."

Carbonne wanted to yell, "Why did you wait so long?"

CHAPTER 25: Sara

Sara admired Ulysses's patience and thoroughness. Instead of ripping the packet open, he called analysts. They took the packet to the laboratory and processed it and its contents for DNA and fingerprints while he waited for two marshals to arrive at his office. In the meantime, Sara took Bug for a walk, and Carbonne took a shower.

***

At the beginning of the session, Ulysses noted the four envelopes were already opened when a technician unsealed the outer packet. The outer packet had clear fingerprints from Melvin Melendez and Caleb Steele. The inner materials had many smudged prints but clear prints only from Melvin Melendez and Melvin Mueller. He also assured the marshals present that Caleb Steele would be available for questioning after the group had assessed the packet's contents.

Sara never saw a group go from bored to excited so fast. None of the four letters were signed. All were short. All were posted in Albuquerque. The handwriting, actually printing, on the letters and envelopes was similar, at least to Sara's untrained eyes.

The first letter was yellowed with age and in an envelope postmarked in 1989. The note said:

That wasn't an accident. Shame on you.

The investigators stared in amazement at the slip of the paper. Sara volunteered to search the Las Vegas police logs and the local newspapers for accidents around the date of the postmark.

The second was postmarked in 1995. It said:

Smart way to kill Mary. She showed me the money you gave her. You knew how a drug addict would use it. Shame on you.

The Mary mentioned was probably Mary Melendez, Pigeon's first wife and Melvin Melendez's mother. Melvin would have been a child of eight in 1995. He could have printed it, but it was doubtful. Sara determined the postmark was three days after Mary Melendez's death.

The third was postmarked 1998. It said:

Don't get ideas. I have the finger as insurance. Can't you behave?

Sara recognized the postmark as being two days after Dan Steele's accident in Pigeon's plant.

The fourth note was postmarked in 2010. It said:

You're a rapist of young girls as well as a murderer. You're hopeless.

All those around the table doubted rape charges were filed, but Sara agreed to scan stories in the Las Vegas newspaper during 2010 for mention of Hank Diaz and Melvin Mueller. All thought either Diaz or Pigeon had written the notes and the other had received them. The question was: which one was the serial murderer?

***

The group's interview of Caleb was short and boring. Sara thought the most revealing part was Caleb's reply to the question: Why didn't Melvin Melendez take these letters to the police or FBI? "No police officer would have believed Mel. He had a police record. They would have charged him with theft and notified his father Melvin Mueller."

His mistrust of the police was also evident in his response to the follow-up question: After Melvin was killed, why didn't you take the letters to the police? "You don't get it. No one would have listened to me. Dan and I even discussed my choices after Mel's death. I figured I was safer if no one knew I had the letters."

At the mention of Dan, Ulysses's head had jerked up. "How many others knew about these letters? I assume your secretary and others have access to your safe at work."

"Just Dan and me. The packet was as I left it."

"Dan was an open book with his psychologist at the VA and I bet to others. If he knew where you stored the packet, you may have gotten him killed." Sara regretted her comment to Caleb even before he moaned.

***

Sara sat in her cubicle with Bug and sorted out her thoughts and emotions. Her comment to Caleb Steele had been needlessly cruel. The interview, really this whole day, had made her feel guilty. Every time she guessed wrong or wasted time during the investigation, she endangered the lives of others.

Most of all, she was afraid. She was glad to flee Ulysses's office when the marshals began to explain the witness protection program to Caleb and his wife. She knew the limitations of this program in term of the safety and comfort of the witnesses. She shuddered as she thought about Pigeon's wife and son and even her ride to work this morning. She also understood how the protection she'd received made her feel like a caged animal. She didn't want to think what the next few months would be like.

Although Ulysses hadn't told her about new threats against her, he'd been more protective than usual. When she returned to the FBI building from the hospital, Ulysses had told her "Old Tom" had been in the Secret Service at the White House for years. It only made her more nervous to realize that Ulysses thought she needed so much protection.

The truth about Old Tom bothered her in another way too. It was another example of how she misjudged those around her. Old Tom wasn't angry, just cautious. She wondered how many of her assumptions had biased her interpretation of other data today. She needed to calmly reevaluate her assumptions on this case. Even that was an assumption. She had to accept that she might be investigating several cases with only incidental links.

She looked at her new computer messages. The FBI lawyers had been efficient. They'd determined Pigeon had paid Melvin Melendez's legal fees over the years. Before the shoot-out, she'd hoped Ulysses could use this information to get Pigeon to cooperate. Now it was useless. The problem was to find Pigeon, not to get him to talk.

She needed to focus on Hank Diaz now. Caleb Steele hadn't been much help. He knew Diaz's ex-wife had gone back to her maiden name and still lived in Belen, but he couldn't remember her name. Ulysses had asked the Belen police to find her. Everyone in Ulysses's office was

J. L. Greger

surprised when the Belen police chief called back fifteen minutes later. She was the clerk at Walmart whom his officers had already questioned.

Ten minutes later, the Belen police chief called again. After the County Animal Control Unit did not return the dog to its home because the owners were on vacation, the Belen police had questioned the owners' neighbors. One claimed that a woman in Belen always kept the dog when the owners were away. The Belen police chief had sighed when he called Ulysses, "Same woman." Ulysses had sent agents to question her.

Sara opened the email from these agents. The best way to summarize the ten-page transcript of their interview was to say that Diaz's ex-wife was a mess. She kenneled dogs because she was desperate for money. On Tuesday and Wednesday, she had taught the already well-trained golden retriever to enter her dog door to retrieve bologna left on the floor because Diaz had threatened to tell police about her side business. She sold drugs. The agents had found a small cache in her house. She had no idea about Diaz's location but thought his current girlfriend—Gina—lived on Gibson Boulevard in Albuquerque. Then she asked to be taken into custody because she was afraid to remain in her house while Diaz was free.

The agents took her to the Belen police department. When the police booked and fingerprinted her, they found her prints matched the second set on the phone attached to the dog collar. After ten minutes of interrogation, she admitted she'd bought the phone for Diaz on Tuesday. The Belen police promised they would question her again in two hours to see whether her story had changed. They expected it would.

Sara came to several conclusions. First, the Belen police were much better than Ulysses had thought. Second, Hank Diaz had begun to plan Pigeon's escape or kidnapping as soon as Pigeon was transferred to the safe house in Belen. Third, the Albuquerque police and FBI analysts didn't need her help to find Gina.

She was too tired to think, but she might be able to solve one mystery. She typed a couple of questions to her old pal, Gil Andrews of the Mercado police.

Bug suddenly stood, did his down-dog stretch, and wagged his tail. There was a knock on the door.

"Sara? It's me."

She flung open the door. Sanders pushed a bouquet of yellow roses toward her, but she mainly noticed his eyes twinkling as he leaned forward and hugged her. "I missed you." He parted her lips with his tongue and kissed her slowly.

***

Sanders concluded the description of his visit with Maria by saying, "Sara, it doesn't make sense. Your testimony against the Butcher Don and Maria will be dramatic—even a highlight of their trials, certainly to the press and the jury—but there are other witnesses. Neither Ulysses nor I can figure out why the gangs are focused on you."

"Is Maria jealous of me?"

He groaned. "I left out her comments on me. Believe me, she's not jealous. Remember, she said you saw too much again."

"Someone else made a similar comment recently. Funny, I can't remember who. Wasn't out of place at the time. If I had to guess, I'd say I someone at the VA, but so what. Pretty much all the men involved in this case, except Pigeon, served in the military. Most go occasionally to the VA for medical services."

He brushed her hair back from her face and kissed her forehead. "Let's be logical. Except for Hank Diaz and Caleb Steele, it's difficult to imagine the employees at the meat packing plant in Grants as being organized enough to plan a hit on anyone. Jack Daniels may hate you, but I doubt he has the authority to order someone killed. While you've profiled him, you've never met Pigeon. However, I suspect he knows of you."

Sara pulled herself away. "I'd never count Jack Daniels out of any illegal activity." She shivered. "He scares me. Lot of heads rolled at APD because I fingered Jack and he sang to stay out of prison. I bet several police officers hate me because I unleashed Jack. More important, I bet Jack kept a few cases back so he could collect favors in the future."

He pulled her back and put his arm on her shoulder. "I don't know the details as well as you, but I think Pigeon and Hank Diaz might be able to order a hit. We should work a few new angles on them."

Sara again pulled away and began to pace. "I can't take being cooped up much longer in this building. I can't concentrate. I've run out of ideas. And I can't relax either. Let's be honest—Ulysses doesn't even want to see me because he doesn't know where to keep me tonight."

Sanders grabbed her hands. "I solved the last problem. I rented three adjoining rooms at Sandia Resort and Casino tonight. We'll be in the middle room. Agents will be in the rooms on either side of us. Ulysses won't have to worry about the federal per diem rate and you won't have to cook."

Sara kissed him. "Nice try, but he doesn't have enough agents here. Most of the agents are worn out from this afternoon's romps in Belen, Grants, and at the ranger station in El Malpais. You may think I look tired, but Carbonne looks worse. Ulysses even had to recruit a secret service guy, checking out his retirement, to guard Bug and me at the hospital today."

"Ulysses emailed me about your rendezvous. You and Bug gained an admirer today. Tom has agreed to stay on here for a few days. Four agents grabbed a ride on the same military jet as I did from Washington." He looked at his watch. "So, you see we don't have to wait here much longer. Ulysses or Carbonne will bring the new crew by after they're briefed."

***

Sara had no desire to gamble at casinos. As the daughter of a sharecropper farmer in the Midwest, she'd learned early not to waste money. However, she always told others that she exhausted her urge to gamble while writing grant applications and doing research. She thought they were exercises in gambling—betting you could learn what others had missed. Honestly, she didn't know why she'd never placed a bet on a roulette wheel and had only pulled the levers on slot machines a few times.

Yet, she loved occasionally walking through casinos. She liked the noisy gongs and bells, the garish lights on the slot machines, and the intensity of the people as they made wagers at the tables. She wished she could have made students look as intently at the board when she lectured as the casino regulars did at their cards or the roulette wheel.

Thus, she was disappointed when the agents and Sanders rushed her from the hotel entrance to the elevators. All she got was a whiff of food from the buffet and a glance at the smoky but glittering casino. There was no need to argue. The agents were right. The fewer people who saw her, the better for her own safety and the safety of those around her.

Their room was a typical nice hotel room. This one had a Southwestern motif in a turquoise and brown color scheme. The view didn't matter. Agents closed the shades before she entered the room. Besides, it was almost dark outside, and the room faced the golf course not the city.

At least, Bug was pleased. He paced around the room, jumped onto a comfortable armchair, and waited for her to place his food and water cups on the matching ottoman.

She wished she and Sanders could go to Bien Shur, the restaurant at the top of the hotel. It had a well-known chef, but Sara had never fancied the food. Too many big slabs of expensive meat. She wanted to revel in the panoramic view of the surrounding mountains from Bien Shur. At night the twinkling lights of Albuquerque were beautiful.

It was time to be realistic. She looked at the menus provided through room service. She usually enjoyed the food in the Council Room Restaurant and the buffet, but nothing looked interesting tonight.

Sanders alternated between studying the menu and looking sadly at her. He was obviously hungry. He was also cautious about "heat" in Southwestern food.

"The green chili stew and the posole are good here and not too hot. I think I'll have a bowl of stew and a salad." She looked at the movie guide on the desk.

He studied the menu more before he placed their orders. "We could watch a movie until dinner arrives." He petted Bug as he watched her. "I suspect you're too tense to enjoy a movie. I have an alternate idea. Work-related, but fun."

She knew he was trying to please her. "I'm game."

"I watched my staff in Havana change photo images—the hairstyle, hair color, clothes—of people in a crowd. They got some amazing results and identified men and women whom I would have sworn weren't in the crowd."

"Let me guess. You want me to think more about Pigeon and Diaz." She knew she sounded too negative. "Okay." She put on her happy face and placed her laptop on the desk. "I'll pull up photos of Pigeon, Hank Diaz, Dan Steele, and even Caleb Steele." She thought about the tangles of long, gray wig-hair Carbonne had pulled from Dan's hand. "Let's start by giving them long, gray hair."

Sanders pulled up another chair to the desk. He muttered to the computer as he struggled at first to manipulate the program. Soon he showed her four photos and pointed to the altered photos of Caleb and Dan Steele. "They must be the brothers."

Sara blinked. "I hadn't realized how much they looked alike when their hair styles were different. Their beefy red faces look silly with the long gray hair. I'm sure I didn't see them."

Sanders nodded. He pointed to the original and altered photos of Diaz. "I hadn't noticed all the gray in the eyebrows of the original."

Sara stared at the original and the altered photos of Pigeon. "I might have seen him before… Not with gray hair or short hair." She looked at all the photos again. "One point worries me. All of the original photos are several years old."

"Shouldn't matter much in adults."

"Maybe, but Dan Steele's medical records indicated he saw a cardiologist as well as a psychologist regularly."

"So?"

"They often advise patients to lose weight. I should have thought about that sooner."

There was a knock on the door to the next room. Two minutes later, an agent knocked on the door between the two rooms. "Mr. Sanders?"

Sanders opened the door.

"We've got your dinners." The agent rolled the cart in and left.

Sanders rolled the cart toward the desk. "It's easier to eat from the desk than the cart."

Sara didn't move her computer. Instead she typed rapidly. When she finished, she announced, "Sent the altered photos to Carbonne." Suddenly she felt better, much better. Sanders had done it again. He knew how to manage her moods. "After dinner, I have an idea on how to have fun." She blew into his ear and ran her fingers down his neck.

"I'll eat quickly."

CHAPTER 26: Mercado Police Chief Gil Andrews on Saturday

On Saturday morning, Chief Gil Andrews called Barb Lewis into his office. "My friend Sara, you know the woman who got the package of tripe?"

Barb nodded. "We thought it was a bomb because of the ticking clock."

"Yes. Sara sent me a strange email. She asked whether you were from the Acoma Pueblo and whether your parents lived in Potters Place."

Barb bit her lower lip so hard it bled. "Did she say why she was curious?"

"She said a woman at Potters Place had bragged that her daughter was a police officer and she was too honest to work in Albuquerque. Sara, being Sara, had remembered the young woman officer on our bomb squad had 'great' black hair."

Barb, a normally calm, smart police officer, twisted her cap in her hands. "I don't usually talk about my work to my family. When we spend a weekend in our historical home on top of the mesa, we stay up late and tell tales. You see, my family spends only four or five weekends a year on the mesa. There's no running water or conveniences. Ma cooks constantly the week before one of our stays on the mesa top. It's like a camping trip with lots of time spent repairing our ancestral house and the old church. The church was built about four hundred years ago and requires constant work."

He knew Sara was right. No one who was innocent gave such a long intro to a simple yes or no question. "I don't need a cultural tour of

Acoma. I know your heritage is with the Acoma Pueblo. Where do your parents live? What do you suspect?"

Barb twisted her cap more.

"Sit down. What happened?"

"Ma asked me several odd questions lately. It seems my family has followed the newspaper accounts of the arrest of the Butcher Don and the preparations for his trial."

"Not surprising. The Mercado police force was key to his arrest. They were proud of you and figured you had an inside scoop."

She looked down. "You don't understand. Most of the men in my family work at the meat packing plant in Grants. They also raise sheep. Anything affecting the meat industry can threaten their livelihood."

He remembered his previous conversations with Sara and the session he was forced to attend at the state lab. State health officials had ordered him, and for that matter Barb, too, to take antibiotics daily for a week because they might have been exposed to the bacteria causing the plague. He'd almost forgotten to take his pill this morning. He'd also seen alerts from state health and ag officials. He reached in his desk drawer and pulled two pages from a file. "Will your story eventually get around to the plague alert on the Acoma Pueblo?"

Barb gulped. "Look, I don't know what my family did. I can only repeat Ma's questions. I really don't think they broke any laws. My parents are good people."

"I'm sure. Tell me what she asked."

Barb closed her eyes as if she was remembering the scene. "It was a week ago. My extended family gathered at my uncle's house for dinner. After we'd eaten my aunt's lamb stew and my ma's peach pie, my father and uncle began to talk business. My uncle had spotted evidence of plague in a prairie dog colony near where he and my father sometimes grazed sheep. He'd talked to the tribal environmental officer. The environmental officer pointed out the colony wasn't on pueblo land, and he had no authority there. The Cibola County extension agent didn't answer either of my uncle's two calls." She twisted her cap again.

Andrews leaned back. "So far, I don't understand why you're nervous."

"Ma listened for a while and said, 'We, the people of Acoma, need someone to speak for us. Someone people listen to. I've read in the papers about a woman scientist who consults with the FBI and police. She got them to listen to veterans.' Then she turned to me. 'Doesn't she live in Mercado? Have you met her? Can't you talk to her?' I said, 'No.' and found an excuse to leave."

"What else?"

"Nothing."

"Your cap wouldn't be a twisted lump if that was the end of the story."

"Last night I called Ma to tell her I'd visit on Sunday. She asked me about my week. I…"

"You told her about the false bomb alarm. No problem. I told my family about it too. It was weird. What did she say?"

"Odd things. She asked whether the samples in the package that the bomb squad opened were sent to state officials. She seemed to know the answer because she said several state officials had talked about plague to the leaders at the pueblo and to the men at the plant yesterday. She seemed pleased and said, 'Someone listened to us.' Funny, she said it twice."

He noted Barb's voice had lost the singsong sound of many pueblo women by the end of her answer. She had her usual confident voice. "Anything else?"

"No. Wait. She complained about a man. He came to visit her at the school where she works. She called him a bad man but wouldn't explain why." Barb shook her head. "That's so like my mother. She tells me something is bad and then says, 'Don't worry.'"

"Most mothers do. I'll report this info back to Sara and the FBI."

Barb flinched.

"You haven't done anything wrong. Doesn't sound like your mother acted illegally when she helped to mail the package to Sara." He put the pages back into the file. "Well, the package could be considered a threat and potentially a dangerous bioterror agent, but Sara won't file charges. But Sara or the FBI might still want to talk to your mother about the man who frightened her."

"She didn't say she was frightened. You don't understand the old women of Acoma. 'Bad' doesn't necessarily mean evil. It could mean she felt the spirit of death was over him or he looked angry."

"Okay. Don't tell your mother about this conversation."

CHAPTER 27: Sara

She and Sanders lingered in bed snuggling and talking about a small problem until light streamed around the edges of the drapes. When Sanders had booked the room at the hotel, he assumed Bug as a pet therapy dog would qualify as a service dog. Sara had doubted his assumption and found a baby carriage in a storage area of the FBI building. Thus, Sara had wrapped Bug in a blanket, put him in the baby carriage, and rolled him by the front desk of the hotel to the room last night.

Bug had played his role perfectly but this morning he stormed across their bed four times, snuffling. He needed a walk and he was tired of waiting. Finally, Sara tossed on clothes, wrapped Bug in a blanket, and put him in the carriage, while Sanders convinced an agent to bring a car up to a rear entrance. Sara, accompanied by another agent, pushed her baby out to the car. The agents drove several miles on Tramway Road to an area where people walked their dogs. When Bug was satisfied, she and her agent escort returned to the car.

The driver looked at her in his rearview mirror. "We're going directly to our building. The ruse wasn't a success. Sanders will join you after he's settled accounts at the hotel. It may be an hour."

***

Sara and Bug slunk into their cubicle because she looked like an unmade bed. However, she didn't feel like sitting. Besides, she couldn't work because she'd left her computer, phone, and purse in the hotel room. It was too late for pride. She left a note for Sanders on the door to her cubicle and walked Bug inside the building.

When they passed Carbonne's office, she saw light streaming under the door. She knocked. No one answered. She and Bug passed the vending machines. She wanted a diet cola. No, she *needed* the caffeine in a diet cola, but she had no money. They continued walking. She thought she heard voices in Ulysses's office. She knocked.

Carbonne opened the door. "Looks like you just rolled out of bed. Never seen you look so... casual."

The words came tumbling out as she vented her unhappiness. "Bug and I were thrown out of Sandia. I think everyone is annoyed with us. The agents wouldn't even talk to me in the car. All my stuff is in the hotel room."

Ulysses couldn't suppress his laughter as he looked at her. "We were about to look for you. The agents should have told you they were needed here. If they were annoyed, it was because they liked the cushy assignment with you at Sandia."

"Okay, do you have a diet cola in your undercabinet refrigerator, or can you give me money to hit the vending machines?"

Carbonne knit his eyebrows. "Don't you want to hear our news?"

"I need my caffeine and fluid first."

Ulysses pulled a can from his refrigerator and reached for a glass.

"I don't need a glass or ice." Sara grabbed the can. "Thanks." She took a swig, then another. She sank into a chair by Carbonne in front of Ulysses's desk. "Carbonne, did you like the photos I sent you?"

He shrugged.

Sara felt like someone had depleted the bubbles in her soda. "Oh. I thought they would be part of your news."

"They are. You got me thinking last night. Called the marshals first thing this morning."

Ulysses sighed. "I was trying to let him catch up on his sleep. He didn't know two agents and two marshals were going to debrief Caleb Steele and his wife here at seven-thirty. If you don't mind, I'll let Carbonne tell you the details while I finish these memos. I have to do my own typing because Kit doesn't work on weekends." Ulysses turned to his keyboard.

"Got to get the kinks out." Carbonne stood and stretched. "To make a long story short, I showed Caleb Steele the picture from his brother's driver's license. He snorted when he saw it. Seems Dan Steele lost eighty pounds in the last two years. I was lucky. Caleb had a photo of his wife at her birthday party last month. Dan was in the background."

"Do you want Sanders to apply long gray hair to the photo?"

He continued to stretch. "Pulled in a favor from a woman in the photo lab. After she played with the photo Caleb supplied, we compared it to the image of the gray-haired man at the UPS Store on Central."

"And?"

"Two bad quality photos. Might not hold up in court as a match but sure looks like Dan Steele delivered the package you received to the UPS Store."

"So, did Dan Steele fake the loss of his driver's license to further hide his actions?"

Carbonne finally sat down. "Doubt it. His pals at the VA described him as slow and honest."

"What are you hinting? Do you think the use of the gray wig was a bit creative for Dan?"

"Yeah."

She noted Ulysses had stopped typing and appeared to be listening. "Wonder who suggested it? Any chance it was Caleb?"

"Doubt it." Carbonne pulled his hands through his hair, which was messy as usual but neater than Sara's hair. "I sat in for only part of the interview with Caleb and his wife this morning. Good people scared by the recent events in their lives. Couldn't help but feel sorry for them. Normal. Not the type I see most of the time."

"Humph." Ulysses looked away from his computer. "Give her the facts she needs."

"Gotcha. Caleb Steele loved his brother but didn't really understand him or know much about his activities. Caleb's wife pitied Dan. Recognized he was 'hopelessly damaged'—her words not mine. Appears Dan didn't tell them he was sending a package, but he had raved last weekend about the reappearance of plague near Acoma. The wife thought Dan was too 'disorganized' to assemble the box without help. Caleb said Dan was a 'lousy' butcher."

"Okay. Let's assume Dan Steele sent the package to me but needed help to assemble it. Any chance his cohorts waited for him outside the UPS Store? Would they show up in the store's hidden camera pictures through the windows?"

"Already looked."

"Maybe we could check whether any employees at the plant were sick or on vacation on Tuesday. They might have come with Dan to Albuquerque. Of course, it would be even better if we knew who Dan saw the night before, when the package was prepped."

Carbonne leaned forward. "Caleb could get us into the plant today or tomorrow. He and his wife want to collect a few items from their home and the plant before the marshals take them out of state on Monday."

"Hmm. No wonder you're at work on a Saturday. You don't have much time to question Caleb in person. Did you ask him about Dan's friends?"

Ulysses's computer pinged. A minute later Ulysses announced, "This is a better day than yesterday. Gil Andrews answered your questions. Luckily he cc'd me." He handed a page from his printer to Sara.

Carbonne stared back and forth between Ulysses and Sara. "Care to fill me in?"

"Native Americans living in Potters Place and working at Caleb Steele's plant probably helped Dan Steele assemble the box I received." She handed the page to Carbonne.

"How do you figure?"

Ulysses didn't give her a chance to answer. "In typical Sara fashion, she put disparate data together. Gil Andrews confirmed her suspicions. I think Gil's deputy, Barb Lewis, will help you interview her parents and other relatives tomorrow over Sunday dinner."

Sara finished her cola. She was still thirsty but felt embarrassed to ask for a second can. "Maybe they'll talk more if you assure them I won't press charges for sending the package of tripe and other goodies to me."

Ulysses muttered. "It was infectious and thus dangerous. Better not make promises until necessary. This case has already provided us with too many bad promises. Carbonne, you'd better get the details worked out with this Barb Lewis, ASAP. Her shift ends today at noon."

Sara turned the can in her hands. "Any news on Pigeon?"

Ulysses reached into his refrigerator and handed her another diet cola. "You eyed the old can like an old wino looks at an empty bottle. I said this was a better day than yesterday. Not a *perfect* day. No sign of Pigeon. His escape was well planned, exceptionally well planned. However, Tom and the child psychiatrist brought Pigeon's wife and son together. Both seem better. Pigeon's wife responded lucidly to simple questions. She's glad Pigeon is gone. So much so, we're concerned she could have helped plan his kidnapping."

Carbonne frowned. "The woman I saw couldn't utter a simple sentence. Doubt she was involved in any plot."

Ulysses groaned. "Abused women are hard to assess. A couple of officers from the APD's Special Sex Crimes Unit have agreed to help our agents interview her this afternoon."

Carbonne's phone rang. He said, "Yes," listened, and said, "Thanks." His voice was at a higher tone and sounded more upbeat afterwards. "Got to go." He rushed to the door. "Wish Sanders better luck tonight."

Sara smirked. "What makes you think he didn't have good luck last night?"

Ulysses shook his head after the door closed. "What do you think of Carbonne?"

She swallowed hard because she hadn't expected the question. "He's dedicated, bright and organized or he wouldn't get so much done. Easy for me to work with."

"Ulysses nodded. "And?"

"Unhappy. Lonely. Several of your agents haven't accepted the concept that we don't all have to be alike. They may parrot diversity platitudes to you but they don't believe them."

Ulysses looked at his hands. "One of the reasons I was sent here. That's why I scoured the nation to get a woman to lead the SWAT and asked Carbonne to stay here. He's not a minority, but he relates better to minorities, women, and outsiders in general than most of the agents here."

Sara sympathized with Ulysses but wanted to hammer in her point. "Everhart treated both Kit and Carbonne badly, but Carbonne risked his life to save Everhart." Sara paused and glanced at the ceiling. "That's why both Carbonne and I feel badly about Frank McCoy. We didn't have to work to get his acceptance."

"Speaking of Frank McCoy, the news is good. The docs in the ICU say he's moved from an unconscious state to a stuporous one. Something about his pupils responding to a light. I'll send Carbonne and you to question him if he regains full consciousness." Ulysses pulled a sheet of paper from his desk. "Since you're stuck here today, you might as well continue to track Pigeon's history. I relooked at our and the marshals' files on him. Seemed complete for the last ten years, but sketchy before…"

"Hmm. Especially the way he got his father-in-law's business…"

"I agree." He handed her a page. "These codes will give you access to a couple of files I pulled from archived court and police records but didn't have time to study."

There was a knock on the door. Sanders, looking perfectly groomed, stepped in. He stared at Sara. His lips quivered. "Know I shouldn't say this, but you look like you had one hell of a night. Hope it was." He leaned over and kissed her. "All your stuff is in your office." He looked at Ulysses. "I assuaged the hotel. Don't know how they figured out Sara had a dog, not a baby, in the carriage. The FBI should have no problems if they need to use the hotel again. I, on the other hand, shall not return there. They didn't like my comment that Bug was better behaved than any child."

Ulysses laughed. "I know. The agents sent me a message."

Sara picked up Bug, stood, and hugged Sanders with Bug squirming between them. "Thanks for defending Bug's honor. We're sorry we messed up your plans for a grand weekend." She turned back to Ulysses. "Bet Jack Daniels trailed us and turned us in."

Both men said simultaneously, "Don't be paranoid."

CHAPTER 28: FBI Agent Carbonne

FBI analysts used the tip from Hank Diaz's ex-wife and identified eighteen Ginas, Virginias, Reginas, and Eugenias who lived on or near Gibson Boulevard in Albuquerque. Agents with the help of Albuquerque police visited the homes of all the women early, between six and eight, on Saturday morning. All the women, most of them fresh out of bed, were annoyed and denied knowing Hank Diaz.

Agents had narrowed the list to the five most likely candidates to be "the Gina" on the basis that no husband or boyfriend was present in the house and the woman was between sixteen and fifty in age. Albuquerque police agreed to monitor those five houses and wait for Hank Diaz to appear.

***

Two police officers in an unmarked car spotted a blue Fiesta pulling into the garage of one of the Ginas around nine. The officers thought the driver was a male and there were no visible passengers.

The young officers showed Carbonne their photos as soon he arrived at the small stucco bungalow with elaborate black ironwork over each window. Their bleary photos had no clear views of the face of the driver. Carbonne wasn't eager to enter the house because he wasn't up to another hassle. Police files indicated Hank Diaz had a bad temper, and the two APD officers were rookies. He called for FBI backup and returned to his car.

Before other agents arrived, the garage door opened and the blue Fiesta began to back out. The female officer jumped from the police car and rushed forward, yelling, "Stop! Police!"

The Fiesta rolled backward. At the last second, the woman officer jumped aside, and the male officer pulled the police car in front of the driveway. The Fiesta hit it.

A woman jumped from the car. "He's loco!"

Carbonne glanced inside the Fiesta and its trunk. No bodies—dead or alive. He ordered the woman officer to run to the back of the house to prevent anyone exiting through the back door or windows. The male officer locked the woman in the back seat of the APD car. Carbonne ran through the garage and into the house, yelling, "FBI!"

No one was in sight in the kitchen or living room. A door slammed at the back of the house. It was not an outside door. More likely it was the door to a bedroom.

He inched down a hallway with his gun drawn. One door was open; one was closed. This could be a trap. He heard the roar of sirens becoming louder and louder. He wanted to avoid a confrontation until better backup was present. He thought he saw drops of blood on the floor near the open door. So, he started with the hopefully easier room first and nudged the closed door open.

The green bedroom had two closed doors, probably to a closet and a bathroom. Carbonne stepped back from the entrance and focused on the open doorway to a beige room. The room appeared to be used as an office but had another closed door. It could be a bathroom, but more likely was a closet. The door was slightly ajar.

He thought he saw the door move slightly, but he knew his imagination could be in hyperdrive like the rest of his body. He heard the tramp of feet in the living room behind him. "Come out with your hands up! I don't want to shoot!"

He heard a slight rustle from behind the door and hard breathing behind him in the hallway.

"I know you're in there."

A low voice from the behind the door in the beige room said, "Are you the crazy bastard from Belen? How do I know you won't shoot?"

"Throw your gun on the floor. Keep both hands up and walk slowly." He needed to give directions to what he presumed were agents or police in the hallway behind him without diverting his attention from the doorway to the small beige room. "A man is about to come out. If his hands are up, don't shoot. If he has a gun in his hand, shoot."

He heard an object hit the floor in the beige room and could hear the snorts of more than one police officer or agent behind him.

A man emerged from the beige room. His hands were up, but one was wrapped in a towel. He was a middle-aged, dark-haired with some gray, and thin. He looked like photos of Hank Diaz.

Carbonne kept his eyes focused on the man. "Drop the towel."

The towel fell to the floor revealing a cut on the man's hand seeping blood.

Carbonne called to those behind him. "I haven't checked out either room. There is a woman APD officer in the backyard. She might be edgy."

Two agents streamed around him and Diaz into the beige room. A door opened and then closed. "Clear. I've got the gun."

A scratching noise came from the green room. Diaz looked like he was about to speak. Carbonne kept his gun steady and whispered, "Don't."

Diaz ignored him. "Little bastard's in there." One agent slapped cuffs on Hank, gagged him with a white handkerchief, and called for more help.

Carbonne recognized the agent who rushed past him and stood at the doorway to the green room as Ian Homes. Carbonne stepped backward and covered him. Ian moved slowly forward and opened the door on the far wall. "The window's open. Why didn't the officer in back yell?" He moved from the bath to the other door. Clothes bulged out as he opened the second door in the green room.

Carbonne motioned toward the bed. "Come out from under the bed!" He waited ten seconds. "I'm too old to crawl under it. Easier to shoot. Pillows muffle sound but don't stop bullets."

Ian had finished checking the closet and winked at Carbonne as he aimed his gun at the bed also. "The metal coils of a mattress might deflect bullets, but I doubt it."

"I'm coming out." First, a leg emerged from under the bed.

Carbonne said, "Don't make me nervous. Throw out your gun. Then let's see your hands and arms."

Grunts as the man twisted under the bed. A gun slid across the floor. Carbonne kicked it further from the bed. The woman APD officer, who must have been summoned from the backyard, picked up the gun.

The man's leg disappeared. A right arm emerged from under the bed, followed by his head, looking downward., and then his left arm. He slid forward.

As his feet were ready to clear the bed, Carbonne said, "On you back."

The man complied.

Carbonne gaped at the young man with an unexpectedly wholesome look—big black eyes and a lower face that looked as if he seldom needed to shave. "Who are you?"

"Elijah… Elijah Wood."

Carbonne kept his gun aimed. The woman officer checked under the bed, while Ian patted Elijah down, turned him over, and cuffed him.

CHAPTER 29: FBI Special Agent Ulysses Howe

Carbonne plunked into a chair in Ulysses's office. "I need a break before I do the paperwork. Don't want to do it too fast, or you'll send me out again."

Ulysses chuckled and reached into his refrigerator. He handed a bottle of water to Carbonne. "Believe it or not, agents and analysts had been less suspicious of the Gina you investigated than the other four Ginas being watched. They thought they gave you a break and you'd only have to babysit two rookies."

"Some break. Wouldn't have gone in if Gina hadn't bolted. What have you got?"

Ulysses returned to staring at his computer screen. "Bits and pieces. Diaz won't talk. Gina can't stop, but it's gibberish. She screamed at agents and insisted they, not the APD, take her away before either man emerged from the house."

Carbonne stopped guzzling the water. "Who's she afraid of besides Diaz? Jack Daniels?"

"You and Sara have a fixation on Jack." He scanned his computer screen. "So far, her story isn't logical. We only believe a couple of points. Elijah Wood arrived at her house after midnight last night. No vehicle. The local police saw Hank's arrival this morning in the blue Fiesta."

"What does Elijah say?"

"Nothing." He continued to scroll through messages. "This is interesting. The blue Fiesta that Diaz arrived in this morning is registered to Elijah Wood." Pause. "Oh my. They found blood in the trunk."

"A little slow about checking out the car."

Ulysses groaned. "Saturday isn't usually a big day for the lab crew. I had to call reinforcements in."

"Tell you what, I'll question Elijah Wood with Sara's help. He should be easier to crack than Diaz. Can't take a screaming woman, like Gina, today."

"I'll have Ian tell Diaz that Gina and Elijah have a lot to say. Perhaps he'll become more talkative after he stews about it for a couple of hours."

***

Ulysses couldn't believe it was a Saturday. The building was humming. Carbonne and Sara were interviewing Elijah Wood. Ian Homes was in a room with Gina. He thought calling Ian's session with Gina an "interview" was being generous.

The phone rang. The agents and marshals working with Caleb Steele and his wife had made progress after Caleb gave the access to the plant's employment records. Only one employee, George Lewis, had missed work at the plant on Tuesday. Friday was another story. Three employees claimed a vacation day on Friday—three of the Lewises from Potters Place.

Ulysses flinched at the news. Had George Lewis tracked Dan Steele to Albuquerque? If Frank McCoy had been forced off the road by three trucks, as was believed, those three employees could have been the drivers of the trucks. No wonder the two Lewis women whom Frank had talked to on Friday before his accident were so nervous. He reminded himself to not make unnecessary suppositions.

The agents in Grants also reported that they tore apart Dan Steele's apartment while the marshals checked his bank accounts. They noted Caleb Steele, as Dan's nearest relative, gave them permission but they didn't allow him to watch. Ulysses realized the agents had heeded his advice to not trust anyone involved in this case.

They noted that Caleb was shocked when they showed him Dan Steele's will. He had left his meager savings to Melvin Melendez because he "needed money to get away from his father Melvin Mueller." Both the marshals and the agents thought Caleb cared less about the allocation of

Dan's money than about learning Melvin Mueller was Melvin Melendez's *father*, and not his stepfather.

Ulysses forced himself to remain alert as the agents reported more boring but necessary activities. He wasn't sleepy when they talked about the man who Caleb believed had bought the plant ten years ago. The man, a semi-retired veterinarian, didn't own the plant. He was the manager of a trust, which actually owned the plant.

The agents replayed a section of their interview for Ulysses. The raspy voice of an old man said, "Now don't think this bit of a charade on my part reflects a lack of trust on the part of the owners in Caleb Steele. The meat packing industry is competitive, actually cut-throat is a better description. The available labor force is problematic in regard to citizenship, criminal records, and substance abuse. The owners and I believe Caleb has done a good job of giving second chances to those who were willing to work hard, especially veterans. Also, that way we don't have to worry about illegal immigrants on our payroll. We all, especially Caleb because of his brother, will not allow drugs or alcohol in the plant."

The agents finally stopped the tape and skipped to the veterinarian's comments about Hank Diaz. "Neither Caleb nor I were pleased when Hank Diaz was assigned to be the USDA-certified meat inspector at our plant six months ago. The owner of the meat packing plant in Belen, where Diaz was an inspector, used to run a clean plant, but over the last ten years rumors have circulated that his meat shipments sometimes hid other items. Caleb and I decided we had to be fair to Hank. Besides, the USDA meat inspector doesn't control the plant, the owner and manager do. However, Diaz was a troublemaker from the start. I'm sorry to say I listened to him and forced Caleb to speed up the line and didn't let Caleb institute more drug tests. Probably cost one young man his life."

Ulysses thought the old veterinarian must have broken down and cried. The tape was a blur of sounds. The old man continued slowly, "I've read the OSHA report. I plan to tell Dan on Monday to set the speed on the line as he thinks best. I also intend to call an old friend at USDA and see whether he can get us another USDA-certified meat inspector. Diaz is a troublemaker, and his young backup Elijah Wood is unreliable."

Ulysses complimented the agents on a great job. The agents didn't reply for ten seconds. Then one said, "There're two problems. The veterinarian was cooperative in every way but one. He won't give us the names of the owners. We'll have to get a court order. And the marshals have reneged on their promises. They decided Caleb and his wife don't need to be permanently relocated under the witness protection program. They think he only needs short-term protection until his brother's murder investigation is concluded. Besides, Caleb Steele has little to share, except the packet of notes, which we already have."

Ulysses sighed. Court orders were harder to get on weekends. He didn't think he should request another favor from a judge until he'd assessed all the current problems. With his luck, he might have to make several requests to judges today. He also couldn't be angry with the marshals. It was logical that they didn't want to promise long-term protection to Caleb Steele as they had to Pigeon and Jack Daniels.

He told the agents to continue to troll for clues. The rumors that the old veterinarian and Caleb Steele had heard about the meat industry of New Mexico might be a way to validate Pigeon's stories. Ulysses was sure no jury would believe Pigeon's statements now without additional backup. Of course, the main challenge was to find Pigeon.

***

After a knock on his door, Ian Homes appeared before Ulysses could say "enter." "Wasn't easy, but I did it. First, you should know Gina isn't Hank's girlfriend. She's his younger sister and a nursing assistant in Ward Seven, the psych ward, at the VA. I gave up interviewing her fairly quickly because I don't know the details like you, Sara, and Carbonne do. I let her spin her story. It's biased but might give you a couple new leads."

Ulysses waved the red-haired agent to a chair at the table. "Analysts can listen to the recording later. Give me the major points."

Ian thought for a second. "Gina believes Pigeon killed his aunt, his first wife, Gina's and Hank's sister Lily, and their niece."

"Does Gina have evidence?"

"No. I think the woman has worked in a psych ward too long. She flits from one topic to another and never completes a thought. She talked about a finger, Lily being smart, and someone being distraught when Lily was killed, but she never named the person. She kept saying, 'I had to warn him. He's not perfect, but I love him.' Almost sings it like a song lyric."

"Do you know whom she warned? And about what?"

The redhead scowled. "If I did, I would have told you. I assume Diaz, her brother, because she said several times, 'Pigeon ruined Hank's life.' Seems Pigeon framed Hank Diaz for a series of robberies in 1987 but recanted his story after Diaz was indicted. She hinted Pigeon and his then girlfriend may have committed the robberies, but I'm not sure. The net result was Diaz wasn't convicted but had a blemished police record and couldn't get a decent job immediately after he earned his B.S. in agriculture. He had to accept a job with a butcher in Mercado."

"Did she mention the butcher is the Butcher Don?"

"Of course not, this is a biased account." Ian looked at his tablet. "Oh, this might be important. She thought Diaz shouldn't have accepted the job as a USDA meat inspector in the plant in Las Vegas. Then her story got confused again. Something about the boss's anger and a finger. I assume the boss was Pigeon. But then she rambled on about Lily again. Said she was too nosy."

Ulysses shook his head. "Do you think analysts listening to the tape will glean more than you did from Gina's comments?"

"I doubt it. But I'm sure Diaz took the position as meat inspector in Belen to get away from Pigeon." He paused. "At least, Gina thinks so, but then she started her refrain, 'He's not perfect but I love him,' again."

Ulysses hadn't thought Gina would have anything more valuable to share than had Diaz's wife in Belen. He guessed Diaz talked more to his sister than his wife. "I'm sorry to do this to you. You've got to talk to Gina again. Learn more about this Lily and Diaz."

"Is that all?"

"No. See if you can get the answers to these question: Did Diaz rescue Pigeon from Belen? Why? Really push her." He thought for a few seconds. "Take an hour break. I'll see if I can get someone familiar with this case to help you."

***

Ulysses feared he'd made a mistake when he allowed Carbonne and Sara to interview Elijah Wood, and ordered Ian and another inexperienced agent to interview Gina. He had no choice. Those familiar with Pigeon and this case, except Carbonne, were dead or incapacitated. Everhart had died last night. Physicians feared the female agent kicked by Pigeon would have permanent brain damage and might never return to work at the FBI, at least as a field agent. The injured marshal on the porch was expected to survive but wouldn't work again for at least a month. Physicians said the lead marshal was fit for work.

He called the lead marshal on the case to ask whether he could help interview Gina and Hank Diaz. The man leapt at the chance.

He pulled a can of diet cola from his refrigerator. Sara was right—the caffeine in cola seemed to sharpen his thinking. And he needed to think. Pigeon could be charged with the attempted murder of the female agent and his son Noah. Enough to release the prosecutor and the U.S. Marshal Services from their promises to provide him with long-term witness protection. It was a minor point now. Pigeon might be dead. The lab had identified the blood in the blue Fiesta as Pigeon's. However, the amount was not enough to prove he was dead.

Ulysses sipped his cola. He was ashamed of himself, but he hoped Pigeon was dead. Yes, it would complicate the prosecutor's case against the Butcher Don, but it would improve the lives of Pigeon's wife and son. Besides, Pigeon was replaceable now. Diaz and others knew as much about the Butcher Don as Pigeon did.

If Ulysses understood the notes in Melvin Melendez's packet correctly, Pigeon had killed several times, and Hank Diaz knew it. It didn't make sense for Diaz to rescue Pigeon from Belen, especially if he later killed him. But a lot about this case wasn't logical.

CHAPTER 30: FBI Agent Carbonne

Carbonne hated interviewing teenage boys. They usually answered questions literally and supplied little additional information on which to base the next question. Thus, the interviewer had to struggle to extract data and deal with their smug sneers. He looked at Elijah Wood's profile. He was twenty-five and had earned a B.S. degree in agriculture, but he looked and acted like as teenager. Still this was better than interviewing a hysterical woman.

"I did what Mr. M told me."

Sara flashed her most motherly expression, the look she usually reserved for Bug. Carbonne figured she hadn't guessed how hard this interview would be. "Is Mr. M... Melvin Mueller?"

Elijah Wood's eyelids no longer drooped. For the first time, he looked alert. "Yeah."

"Why did you do what Mr. M told you? Did you owe him a favor?"

The young Native American shook his head. "I do odd jobs for him. He pays well."

"What type of odd jobs?"

"Mainly follow people. Deliver items." The young man stared back at Sara as if he thought he'd given a complete answer.

"Tell us about what you did on Thursday—two days ago? What did you see? We want to understand your job."

"I followed Hank Diaz."

"Why?"

"Mr. M told me to."

Sara's voice was louder. Carbonne guessed she had finally realized the kid would be difficult. "Do you know why Mr. M asked you to follow Hank Diaz? I thought they were friends."

Elijah stared at Sara with a blank face. "How would I know?"

Carbonne leaned forward to within six inches of Elijah's face. "Look son, this interview will be a lot easier and faster if you tell us all you know or suspect."

The boy grinned as if he'd gotten great advice. "As usual, Diaz arrived at Gina's house about seven. I expected he'd stay the night as he usually did. I was bored. So around eleven I was ready to go home. Then the garage opened, and Diaz's car went to the Embassy Suites. You know, the one near campus."

Sara's voice was softer. She was obviously pleased because he answered with more than a phrase. "What did you see?"

"She met…"

"What do you mean 'she'? I thought you were tailing Hank Diaz."

Elijah looked confused. "I did. When Diaz's car left, I assumed he was the driver. But I was wrong, Gina was the driver. I didn't know until she entered the bar." Elijah grinned as he had done before when he completed an answer.

"Okay," Sara shook her head in disbelief. "Sorry I distracted you. Whom did she meet?"

"A tall man."

Carbonne spoke because Sara didn't. "More?"

"Typical Anglo. Sunburned. Not young, not old. Blue long sleeve shirt."

Carbonne was surprised but figured he was jumping to conclusions. He knew he wasn't the only one when Sara gasped. "How long did they talk?"

Elijah tilted his head. "Neither of them even finished their beers. Gina went home. I called Mr. M. He was pissed because I didn't hear their conversation, except a couple of words."

Carbonne wasn't sure whether the boy was intentionally annoying or was extremely dense. "This isn't a game. Tell us everything."

Sara bit her lip. "Give us more than one- or two-word answers to our questions. Like, except what words?"

Elijah looked surprised. "I'm trying. I heard them say 'Pigeon' several times. Seemed to make Mr. M mad. Real mad."

Sara nodded. "Did he tell you to go home or give you an order?"

"He gave me orders."

"And?"

"I was to get an old truck. He didn't care how. And take it to the ranger station at El Malpais and park it in the back lot. Leave the keys under the front mat."

Carbonne figured the young man stole a truck and would be reluctant to admit it. He made a note on the sheet of paper in front of him to return to the topic later. "Any other orders?"

Elijah knit his brow as if to think. "To go to Belen and wait for him."

Sara sighed. "Where in Belen? When?"

"Parking lot by the old museum."

"Were you to go there immediately?"

Elijah frowned. "No, it was the middle of the night. I was to be there by ten the next morning and stay until he called."

"What car were you driving?" Carbonne tried to remember the cars he's seen as he walked from the Harvey House Museum to the safe house in Belen yesterday.

"My lightning blue Fiesta. Mr. M bought it for me."

Carbonne knew all the cars in the lot were empty when he and the other agents arrived. None were lightning blue. "Did you get there by ten? Did you leave the car to get food or go to the bathroom?"

Elijah's voice sounded annoyed for the first time. "I was in the car from ten on."

Carbonne was pleased. He'd caught Elijah in a lie. "What did you do when you heard all the sirens and saw all the police cars as you waited? Weren't you curious? Scared?"

Elijah flushed. "No. Didn't matter. Mr. M told me to wait. I closed my eyes and listened to my music. Suddenly he banged on my window. I hadn't seen him coming. He jumped in and directed me to the back lot of a thrift store on Main Street. Only a few blocks away. Hank Diaz was there. In his car." He stared off in the distance.

Carbonne saw Sara jot a note on the page in front of her. Probably to have someone check for Hank's car. He was glad Sara spoke before he made a sarcastic comment. "Did they argue? Were they yelling?"

"No. After a while, they got in my back seat. Mr. M told me to take back roads to Albuquerque."

"What did they talk about?"

Elijah shrugged, "Don't know. Mr. M told me to listen to my music on my headphones. I guess he didn't want me to hear him talk." Elijah grimaced. "I forgot—Diaz brought a big bag with him."

Carbonne wondered, *when do we get to the blood?*

Sara spoke before Carbonne could ask his question. "Do you know what was in the bag?"

"Not at first."

Carbonne thought Sara showed remarkable restraint. She asked quietly, "What was in the bag?"

Elijah frowned. "Booze, limes, and glasses. First, they had beers. When we got to Albuquerque, Mr. M told me to turn onto Gibson Boulevard. I thought we were going to Gina's house, but he told me to stop at Dion's Pizza. Then, Diaz made a big show of putting salt on the edge of Mr. M's glass before he poured in tequila and added a lime slice. Mr. M handed me twenty dollars. Told me to get a pizza and walk to Gina's. I said it was a long walk." The young man gulped and gulped again.

Sara touched Elijah's arm. "We know Mr. M gets angry easily. What did he say and do?"

"Yelled, 'Don't ever cross me!' but calmed down. Diaz took my keys and drove way."

Carbonne looked at his watch and wanted to scream. Not much from Elijah for all the effort. "Wasn't Gina surprised when you showed up? What time was it?"

Elijah shrugged. "No, she's used to Diaz showing up at all hours. I've been with him at times."

Sara waited for Elijah to finish, when he didn't, she asked, "What time was it?"

Elijah shrugged again. "Maybe midnight. She told me to bed down on the sofa in the living room."

Sara slid a note to Carbonne. He read it silently:

Now we check his memory.

After he nodded, she leaned toward Elijah. "Did anyone stop by or call before Diaz arrived?"

"Nada. Boring." Elijah shrugged.

"Are you sure?"

After a long pause, "I forgot. Someone rang the doorbell. Gina ordered me to her den in back before she answered the door."

"What did she say afterwards?"

"Nothing."

"What did you do?"

"I lazed around and watched cartoons until Diaz arrived."

Sara forced a grin. "You're doing great. Are you thirsty?"

"No, want to get this over."

"What did Gina do when Diaz came in? Did he knock?"

Elijah looked at her blankly. "Don't knock when you come in from the garage. As soon as he came in, Gina asked 'Where's Melvin?' Diaz ignored her."

Sara touched Elijah's arm. "What happened?"

"Diaz told me to go to Gina's bedroom and stay there until he called for me."

"Weren't you scared?"

Elijah hung his head. Sara leaned over and touched his shoulder. "You made a mistake to work for Mr. M, but you may be able to save yourself from prison time if you answer our questions honestly. Could you hear what they said?"

Elijah closed his eyes and spoke in a monotone slowly, like he was in a trance. "Diaz yelled, 'You crazy bitch! Heard a crash. Not sure what. Gina started to really scream and cry. Suddenly, he ran in. His hand was bleeding. Pushed me into the bathroom. Grabbed a towel. Closed the door." Elijah gasped for air.

Sara said, "You were scared. What did you do?"

"Figured I'd better get out of the house fast. Opened the window in the bathroom. Couldn't get the grill in front of the window open. Odd rattling noise—maybe the garage door opening. Couldn't open the grills on the bedroom windows either. Couldn't squeeze into the closet. Crawled under the bed. Heard someone run by in the hall. More footsteps—different than before. Quieter. Door to the bedroom opened. Footsteps. Yelling." He pointed to Carbonne. "Mainly you."

"What did you do?"

"Hoped no one would see me. Didn't want to be arrested. All I did…" Elijah hung his head again. "…was get the truck."

Carbonne slid a blank pad of paper and a pen to Elijah. "I think you told the truth some but not all of the time. You can do better when you write it all down." He stood and opened the door. "Start from the beginning when Mr. M told you to follow Diaz on Thursday. Include all the details, even those you forgot to tell us."

Sara patted Elijah's shoulder again as she left. "Quite a story. I was scared for you as I listened. I'll find food and a beverage for you now."

Elijah was already hunched over the page. He looked up hopefully. "Maybe a Dr. Pepper and a corn dog?"

She rushed out.

Carbonne stood and watched the boy as he wrote. He cursed Pigeon and Diaz silently. Elijah could be charged with abetting the presumed murder of Pigeon and abetting the attempted murders of Gina and Frank McCoy, but in reality, he was a bystander. Well, except for the theft of a truck.

Elijah looked up, "Do you want me to write about how I followed your car on Thursday night before Mr. M told me to follow Hank Diaz?"

Carbonne thought, *Forget the innocent bystander bit.*

CHAPTER 31: Sara

Sara returned to her cubicle hoping to have a long talk with Sanders—actually to listen to his account of the checkout at the hotel. She expected it would be much funnier than his short comments when Ulysses was present. Sanders was a good mimic of voices and mannerisms.

All she found was Bug curled in his bed and a note.

> *Time to end the cat and mouse game with Jack Daniels. I will*
> *talk to Ulysses before I act. May take several hours.*
> *Love,*
> *Sanders.*

Sara's first reaction was to worry Sanders might be reckless. If she hurried, she might be able to stop him. Bug was ready for action and loped beside her as she sped to Ulysses's office.

Light filtered under Ulysses's office door. He was either talking to himself or someone was with hm. She was ready to knock. Then she realized this was a mistake. Sanders would ask if he wanted her advice. He didn't need to be nagged, especially when others were present. Ulysses, Carbonne, and Gil seemed to enjoy taking jabs at him. There was no need to fuel their barbs.

Bug wagged his tail and pulled her away from the door. Although Ulysses didn't like her to leave the building unless necessary, she and Bug needed fresh air. They wandered from one grassy spot to another among the parking lots around the building. The coolness of the morning had disappeared, and the sun beat down on them. Finally, they sat in a shady spot within the gated area, not far from the sentry.

This was the last weekend of the state fair. If she hadn't been imprisoned at the FBI building, she would have wandered around the fair yesterday and watched the livestock judging. Usually the longhorns were shown on the second Friday of the fair. Then she would have wandered over to the Home Art Building and spent several hours comparing the quality of red- versus blue-ribbon baked products, quilts, and other handicrafts. Throughout her teen years, she'd shown her 4-H baking, sewing, and handicraft projects at county and state fairs. Funny—she rarely thought about her lonely teen years on the farm, but she still loved fairs. They brought back the happiest moments of her youth.

Sanders sat down beside her. She hadn't noticed his approach. "We've been searching for you. Ulysses feared you'd been kidnapped. Then the sentry reported you and Bug had been sitting by his post for the last half-hour."

"Didn't seem that long. This weekend is the end of the New Mexico State Fair. I've gone every year, except this one, since I moved here."

Sanders looked surprised. "I didn't know you liked carnival rides and shows."

"I don't. I like watching the judges. Makes me remember how much I liked learning by observation, not from books, when I was young. Guess that's why I became a scientist."

He squeezed her shoulders. "And today those memories helped you escape the pressure of this case and the confines of the building. You know, this may be about over. All the known main characters, except Jack Daniels, are in custody, presumed dead, or in the hospital."

Sara sighed. "Note you said all the 'known' characters and 'presumed' dead. The more we dig, the more we find old connections, wrong assumptions, and new possible bad guys. A bottomless pit. Carbonne and I thought Elijah Wood was an innocent dupe after we interviewed him for an hour. Then Carbonne discovered Elijah had tailed Carbonne and Frank on Thursday night when they came to my safe house."

He squeezed her shoulder again. "Carbonne told me. He also said the APD and FBI questioned Elijah Wood yesterday morning after they caught him following you. They did a quick license plate check and released him because he seemed like a dumb kid, who agreed to one foolish assignment from Jack Daniels."

"I think he's the ultimate con man. He convinced the agents and police that he thought Jack's name was Mr. Smith and I was his wife. He claimed Mr. Smith gave him one hundred dollars to follow me and see whether I was cheating on him." She shook her head. "The worst part is a jury would believe his stories. Carbonne and I did for an hour. He's really perfected his dumb kid act. He only slipped after I left. So, Carbonne and I interviewed him again. Now we're not sure what to believe. Other agents will have to grill him again and try to determine what parts of his story are true."

"What do you expect? He was coached by two experienced liars, Pigeon and Jack Daniels." He kissed her lightly. "Now I want to snare Jack Daniels. He knows details on all the characters and will squeal on them if given the right incentives. And I've got the perfect bait to get him out of hiding."

Sara wanted to scream *no* but said, "I guess I could be the bait again, since you're here."

"Not you—me. He'll follow me because he knows I'll lead him to you." He twirled a few strands of her hair around his fingers. "You've set up the scene perfectly. I bet he or an associate has spotted you outside the building. If I leave with a blonde wearing your pink knit top, I think he'll follow me. Though you have pointed out a problem. The state fair will snarl traffic in a large section of Albuquerque. Hmm… We may have to alter the course a bit."

"I know you're experienced at spotting a tail and losing it, but it's not the same as catching the tail. The agents spotted Jack Daniels's old black Camaro several times during the last couple of days, but he always lost them."

"I've got to try. This stalemate can't go on. You and Bug won't be happy in sequestration for several more months before the trial."

***

Sara forced herself to tackle Pigeon's and Diaz's pasts again. It was more useful than worrying about Sanders or fretting about her future.

J. L. Greger

This time she examined the archives of *The Las Vegas Orbit*, the newspaper in Las Vegas, New Mexico. She began her search in 1985 when Pigeon was fifteen and Diaz was seventeen. She looked for names related to the case and articles on the packing plant in Las Vegas, which then was owned by Mary Melendez's father.

She found articles in 1987 confirming Gina's ramblings. Hank Diaz had been charged with a string of thefts at the meat packing plant and other businesses in Las Vegas when he was nineteen. The case was dismissed because a juvenile, the prosecution's main witness, had recanted his pre-trial testimony. She emailed Ulysses to see whether he could get the court records unsealed because she suspected the minor was Pigeon.

She found the obituary for Pigeon's aunt in 1989, a week before the postmark on the first note in the packet Caleb had delivered. No cause of death was listed in the obituary.

She had finished her second diet cola before she spotted a short item in the business section of the paper about a lawsuit against Melvin Mueller for negligence in his meat packing plant in 1992. This time, a twenty-year-old college student had been injured. It appeared the case had been settled out of court, like all the other five complaints against Melvin Mueller that she'd found. Nothing unusual, but the student's name was Franklin McCoy. She felt like she was searching through a friend's underwear drawer as she looked for Frank McCoy's name in the newspaper archives.

She didn't have to look long before she found Frank's name again. He married a local girl Lily Diaz in August 1993. She had been walked down the aisle by her older brother, Hank Diaz. The blurb on the wedding noted the groom was a student majoring in agriculture at Kansas State University in Manhattan, Kansas. Sara checked Frank's online resume at the USDA website. He'd received a B.S. in agriculture from Kansas State in 1994. This must be the Lily that Gina raved about to Ian Homes

Sara thought of the fourth note in Melvin Melendez's packet and searched through the archived newspaper files for 2010. The search was easy. Frank's wife Lily and teenage daughter were killed in a one-car accident near Taos about two weeks after the fourth note was posted. The accident report indicated the driver had fallen asleep at the wheel, and the car had rolled into a ravine and exploded. Sara felt a chill. The accident sounded a bit like the scene at Frank McCoy's accident, only the ditch had been shallow compared to the ravines around Taos.

CHAPTER 32: Sanders

Sanders was glad Sara had asked few questions about his plan to trap Jack Daniels. He doubted she'd like the plan which he and Ulysses had concocted. The agent posing as Sara was young, dark-haired, and trimmer than Sara. She looked a lot like Maria. On second thought, he decided Sara wouldn't be jealous. The blonde wig didn't highlight the agent's features well.

He drove the green Subaru Forrester, which he rented yesterday from Hertz, because both he and Ulysses figured Jack Daniels had already pegged it. Two other agents had left the parking garage five minutes before in a gray 2010 Honda Civic. Two more agents were ready to follow him in a newer black Honda Civic.

Sanders drove a little more slowly than usual from the FBI building before he turned east on Montgomery Boulevard. He didn't want Jack Daniels or his helpers to have trouble spotting and following him. He turned onto Jefferson Street and took the Hospital Loop to the Donut Mart. The woman agent stayed in the car while he went inside. So far, he'd not noticed a car following him. He returned with two donuts. Then he took back streets toward San Pedro Drive.

An agent's voice blasted from the phone. "Think an old red Chevy is following you. Haven't seen Jack's old Camaro yet. When are you planning on turning south toward the VA?"

Sanders replied, "Change of plans. The state fair is in session. I'm heading northward. Then east on Osuna Road along the golf course. We give up when I reach County Line Barbecue on Tramway Road. That way if we fail to catch Jack Daniels, at least I'll get carryout barbecue to take back to Sara and the crew."

The trip was a bust. As Sanders drove back to the FBI building on Tramway Road, he apologized to the woman agent for wasting her time. An agent had traced the license plate number on the red Chevy to a middle-aged woman who lived alone. No one spotted another car tailing him. At least the barbecued ribs, brisket, and sausage perfumed the air with a better aroma than the sickening musk odor the rental agency had sprayed in the car.

As they passed Tramway Terrace, the woman agent thought she saw an old black Camaro. Sanders assumed she was mistaken, but he spotted the Camaro three cars behind him two stop lights later.

Sanders drove slowly to allow the tracking cars to converge at the stop for Comanche Road and Tramway Road. The FBI cars with the aid of two marked Albuquerque police cars boxed the Camaro in.

Sanders was surprised that Jack Daniels didn't try to escape. In fact, he didn't recognize Jack Daniels when he first stepped out of the Camaro. The usually pompous man slumped over his car and apathetically answered police questions.

The APD officers reluctantly allowed the FBI agents to take control of Jack when they saw their warrant for him. Sanders suspected they would have liked to exact revenge on the man who had ratted out so many officers.

Carbonne, Sara, Sanders, Ulysses, Ian, the lead marshal in Belen, and another young agent ate barbecued meat, slaw, corn, and baked potatoes in the observation room and made bets on how long it would take to get a useful piece of information out of Jack Daniels. It was obvious he wasn't nervous. His snoring almost shook the interview room. Ulysses and Carbonne left the observation room after thirty minutes.

Ulysses entered the interview room quietly and then slammed a heavy book on the table. Jack Daniels raised his head, rubbed his eyes, and looked at Ulysses. "Finally, the A-Team. I want you guys to know I did nothing illegal—well, nothing major. All I did was prove the marshals were lousy monitors. You can't remove my witness protection for their inadequacies."

As agreed beforehand, Carbonne didn't speak as he noisily turned on a recorder and waved to those behind the mirror. They had all agreed Jack would know they were in the observation room and Carbonne's openness might annoy him. Jack, in the past, talked more when he was annoyed.

Sanders leaned back to enjoy the show when Ulysses pointed at Jack. "I suggest you listen closely because I'm too busy to play your games today."

Jack closed his eyes.

Sanders figured Jack thought he knew all the details of the case. This interview would only work if Ulysses surprised and scared Jack.

Ulysses's initial comments were dry. "We know Melvin Mueller, better known by law enforcement officers as 'Pigeon,' called three people during the shoot-out in Belen. We captured Hank Diaz and Elijah Wood at the home of Gina Diaz this morning."

Jack snorted but didn't open his eyes. Sanders guessed Jack already knew.

"They all have a lot to say about you."

Jack opened his eyes.

Sanders knew Ulysses was bluffing. Gina had made only one comment about Jack Daniels—Diaz didn't trust him. Elijah Wood had claimed he'd never heard of Jack Daniels.

Ulysses continued in a monotone. "I don't think you can survive, even in witness protection, if you don't cooperate and help us put Pigeon and Hank Diaz away permanently."

Jack must have recognized the bluff, he turned toward Carbonne. "First you have to find Melvin Mueller."

"Ahem." Ulysses looked at his phone.

Sanders was sure Ulysses had not received a new text or call. He waited to see how well Ulysses could act.

"An update on Frank McCoy. He's regained consciousness. Carbonne has to leave."

Carbonne looked shocked as he ran from the room. Sanders and Ulysses had planned this move. It was a sham and would only work if Carbonne didn't know it was a sham.

Ulysses continued, "We know Frank McCoy and Hank Diaz worked together against Pigeon and everyone helping him—like you. Don't you want to talk before Frank McCoy does?"

Jack stared straight ahead.

"As Frank McCoy regained consciousness, the nurses mentioned he said 'Jack' a lot."

Jack gulped. "Frank McCoy's no choir boy."

Sanders heard Sara sigh. He leaned over and hugged her.

Sara whispered, "I liked Frank. I'd hoped my discoveries were red herrings. I know Ulysses is bluffing on several points, but FBI analysts must have confirmed my discoveries."

"I could have told you that you have bad taste in men." Sanders hugged her again.

***

Once Jack Daniels began his fifteen-minute monologue, he seemed to revel in being the center of attention. Daniels explained that after the Butcher Don had been arrested, Frank McCoy decided to take tighter control of the transport system for drugs through Texas and New Mexico. Before, the Butcher Don had controlled the movement of drugs in New Mexico. Pigeon and Hank Diaz had been minor links in the transport chain through Las Vegas and Belen, respectively.

The key points weren't surprising, but Sanders was sure Ulysses was happy to have his guesses confirmed.

"Frank McCoy knew Pigeon was a loose cannon and planned to install Diaz, his one-time brother-in-law, into the drug lord position in New Mexico." After his comment, Jack had eyed Ulysses. "You don't seem surprised. Sara must have done a good job of researching the background of all the characters. Though Frank McCoy bragged he'd snowed her."

Sara pulled away from Sanders and sat down at the table in the observation room. He decided he shouldn't leave Sara for long stretches of time in the future. She was lonelier than she admitted and had obviously found Frank McCoy interesting—too interesting. He sat down next to her and put his arm on her shoulders.

Ulysses, however, showed no emotion in response to Jack's comment. "How did you get involved in this transition of power?"

Jack said, "I saw a window of opportunity as soon as the Butcher Don was arrested. I warned Melvin Mueller. Oh hell, I'll call him Pigeon. He deserves the tag. Pigeon did what I expected. He paid me well to keep him informed and cozied up to you Feds." He laughed, "You fools thought you manipulated him into providing you with evidence. He was afraid you'd never make the offer of witness protection. Although he was crazy, he hedged his bets when it came to his own safety."

Throughout his monologue, Jack insisted that he'd not broken major laws and only gave hypothetical advice to Pigeon and Elijah Wood on how to ensnare Hank Diaz. "It was easy. Diaz was eager to add the packing plant in Grants to his drug shipment network and agreed to arrange an accident for Melvin Melendez. Pigeon got three birds with one stone. He got rid of the son who had been a weight around his neck his whole life." Jack grimaced. "Though the kid must have done something lately to tick Pigeon off." Jack stared into space.

Sara whispered into Sanders's ear. "Pigeon must have noticed the blackmail notes were missing and figured his son, Melvin Melendez, had taken them. I bet Ulysses keeps Jack guessing."

They both stared as Ulysses drummed his fingers on the table. "What were the other two birds?"

Jack returned from his reverie with a jolt. "Pigeon had a recording of Diaz announcing Melvin Melendez's accident at the meat packing plant in Grants. Up to then Pigeon had nothing concrete on Diaz, but I think Diaz had stuff on Pigeon. And third, he'd tested Elijah Wood's mettle. I admit I didn't see the potential that Pigeon did in the kid."

Sanders was surprised. Ulysses didn't ask the location of the recording. He figured Ulysses must now more than he'd admitted.

After Jack bragged a bit, Ulysses asked, "What did Pigeon think when he received the mummified finger in his son's lunch sack?"

Jack stopped chuckling. "He knew his rival Frank McCoy had arranged a hit on him. Pigeon immediately had Elijah Wood set up a hit on Frank. A much better scheme than Frank's plan to kidnap and eliminate Pigeon. Still can't figure out why Frank bothered with the kidnaping. Maybe because he or Diaz wanted to retrieve something from Pigeon." Jack sat quietly for almost a minute. "More likely Frank wanted to make Pigeon beg for his life. I knew a cop who worked the scene at the accident that killed Frank's wife and daughter. He said there was a suspicious amount of gravel on the road, but the cop in charge didn't note the gravel in the accident record and closed the case quickly. My friend also said he never saw a man cry as much as Frank McCoy did at the scene of the accident."

Sanders felt Sara shiver.

Ulysses stood and walked to the door.

Jack seemed to shrink in his chair. Sanders thought he understood Jack Daniels for the first time. Jack knew he was an also-ran but liked attention. Confident women like Sara and young, active men like Carbonne reminded him that the best was past for him. Jack shrank in his chair because he knew he'd lost Ulysses's attention. After the trial of the Butcher Don, he would disappear completely into the oblivion of a safe, boring town with no friends. Sanders guessed Jack would drink himself to death in a year if an off-duty APD officer didn't get him first.

Sanders watched as Ulysses stopped. He guessed Ulysses had come to a similar conclusion and now would give Jack one last chance to bask in the limelight.

Ulysses turned to look at Jack. "Whose side was Diaz on?"

"He was definitely in Frank McCoy's pocket. Frank had been Diaz's brother-in-law. But it was more than that. Diaz's mother had worked as a housekeeper for Pigeon's parents and then Pigeon's aunt in Las Vegas. Rumor has it that Diaz transferred from being a meat inspector in Pigeon's plant in Las Vegas to the plant in Belen after they had a fight. One of many. Neither talked about it, but I sensed Pigeon was afraid of Diaz. Everything changed about two weeks ago, just before Melvin Melendez's accident. Pigeon told me he had control of Hank."

"I want all you know." Ulysses sat down.

Jack shrugged. "Let's face it. Elijah Wood couldn't have turned Frank McCoy's kidnapping plan into an escape for Pigeon without help from Diaz. He knows Belen like the back of his hand and had access to, shall we say, hourly laborers. He also had Frank McCoy's trust. Of course, Pigeon knew how to stage fatal accidents. He'd done it before." Jack paused and waited for a question. When Ulysses remained silent, he said, "Sara's snooping isn't much different than mine."

Ulysses waved his hand as if to say he'd heard enough. "What was your role in Frank McCoy's accident? If you're honest now, we might not file charges."

"Pigeon didn't need my advice. Didn't ask for it." Jack swallowed. "His call to me was an order to watch Gina. He knew she'd met with Frank. I was surprised Elijah didn't kill her as soon as he arrived at her house last night."

Ulysses sat down and stared at Pigeon. "Do you think Pigeon is dead?"

"For the first time in four months, I can't reach him on any of his phones."

"Where's his body?"

He paused. "I'd guess some place around Las Vegas where Pigeon and Diaz camped when they were boys. They have a long history."

Sanders heard a sniff. Tears streamed down Sara's face. She shook her head. "I wouldn't want to do police work full time. You see too many lives wasted over greed, revenge, and stupidity. At least when I work on public health issues in Bolivia or Cuba for USAID, I'm being constructive. And I'm tired—very tired."

CHAPTER 33: FBI Special Agent Ulysses Howe

Ulysses entered the observation room. He thanked Sanders for locating Jack and then turned to Sara. "Are you up to one more task today? You may like this one. Tom, or Old Tom as you call him, would like you and Bug to visit Noah. He's convinced Pigeon's wife—her name is Rose—has one more secret. And he says if he's wrong, Bug will make his day."

"Who will go with me to the hospital?"

Ulysses scratched his head. "Good question." He looked around the room. "Carbonne plans to help Ian question Gina one more time. I thought Sanders might take a crack at Jack along with the marshal and you." He pointed at the other young agent.

Sara noticed Sanders was not surprised.

The young agent stared at Sanders. "But he's new to the case."

Sanders chuckled, "Jack Daniels and I became well acquainted during the capture of the Butcher Don. Let's talk strategy." He motioned the marshal and young agent to a corner table.

Sara shook her head. "You planned this as carefully as your interview with Jack. Who's left to go to the hospital with Bug and me?"

Ulysses smiled. "Me."

***

Noah and Rose sat on the day bed by the window in Noah's hospital room and played the game, Candy Land. Bags of solutions, all connected to the boy, were suspended on a pole by the bed. As soon as the boy saw Bug, he screamed, "Bug, you came!"

"I think the men…" Sara waved her hand between Ulysses and Tom. "They want to talk to your mother. Are you willing to teach Bug and me to play Candy Land?"

The boy looked closely at Bug who sniffed the board. "He might need your help."

***

Tom gave Rose a fatherly smile as she settled onto a chair in the next room. As he pulled up a chair, he said, "Your husband, Melvin Mueller, was abusive to you and the boy." He motioned at Ulysses who had also pulled up a chair. "We know he was narcissistic and brutal."

Ulysses leaned forward. "We found your husband's treasures in the attic of the safe house in Belen. Thank you for the hint. Witnesses have now provided enough evidence for us to indict your husband on several charges. He's going away for a long time." Ulysses was careful not to admit that Pigeon was probably dead, because he thought she might be less cooperative if she knew. "The stronger our indictment, the longer the time. Now's the time to tell us all you know."

The dull look in Rose's eyes didn't change.

"For example, why did he abuse your son? It's not normal." Tom patted her hand. "I think I can guess but I need you to admit the truth."

Tears welled up in her eyes.

Tom lowered his voice. "Was your husband Noah's father?"

Rose looked at her lap and whispered, "No."

"How did he find out?"

"He saw a picture of my son in Hank's wallet a couple of weeks ago." Tears ran down her cheeks. "After that, he hit Noah and me more and more."

Ulysses handed her a tissue. "Why didn't you leave?"

She stared at him. "Couldn't. The marshals and agents wanted him to be happy. No one cared about me and my son… until the man with curly dark hair arrived yesterday."

Ulysses couldn't fit the pieces together in his mind. Why did Hank Diaz cross Frank McCoy and help Pigeon to escape? He could have had a normal family life with Rose and Noah after Pigeon was dead. Or maybe Jack Daniels had been right. He thought Frank McCoy wanted to see Pigeon beg for his life. Perhaps Diaz did, too. He also wondered why all three gunmen didn't try to escape with Pigeon? Obviously, Diaz didn't want to see Noah and Rose harmed.

He doubted she could answer these questions, but he asked anyway. Her answer to all his questions was "I don't know," except to one. She said Pigeon whispered just before he left, "Now you can see if these gunmen take my advice or your lover's advice on how to clean up here."

CHAPTER 34: FBI Agent Carbonne on Sunday

Carbonne knew it would happen, and sure enough it did. Less than ten minutes after the Sunday dinner began, Barb's mother, Eunice, asked, "How long have you dated Barb?"

Ulysses and the Acoma police chief after a long discussion had decided the best way to interrogate the Lewis family was to have Carbonne wear a wire. Thus, Ulysses had ordered two cars with two agents each to follow Carbonne and Barb to the Lewis home in Potters Place after they picked up the Acoma police chief. The agents were told not to enter the house unless they felt Carbonne needed help or he summoned them. Ulysses had advised Carbonne to admit he was an FBI agent working on cases related to the Butcher Don when Barb introduced him to her family, but to not give details of his work. Carbonne was pleased no one in the family asked any questions.

Carbonne suspected the four agents parked close to the home had roared when Eunice asked her question. He was sure this would not be the last time he was embarrassed today. He was mentally prepared for the question and looked at Eunice as she passed a big bowl of potato salad to him and said, "How did you convince Dan Steele to deliver the package with prairie dog and sheep guts to UPS?"

All conversation at the table stopped. Barb gasped. He was sorry that he'd embarrassed her, but he'd been told that her boss, Mercado Police Chief Gil Andrews, had prepared her for his questions. On the drive to Acoma, he'd decided she was nice and toyed with the ideas of asking her for a date if the interview went well. He decided he could forget that idea.

Eunice didn't miss a beat. "We at Acoma are ignored by government officials. No one in the state health and ag departments listened to us when we told them the plague had reappeared and was a threat to the sheep and the people of Acoma. I decided they might listen to the woman scientist who I read about in the paper. She got help for homeless veterans several months ago."

Carbonne noted her voice had lost its singsong lilt. Eunice sounded determined. Now was the time to de-stress her a bit. "You were lucky. Sara Almquist, the woman scientist, has already agreed not to press charges, even though the package was dangerous. But Sara wants details." He pulled a sheet with scribbled notes from his shirt pocket. "I don't have a farm background. I need her notes. Where did the sheep come from? The whole flock is apt to be infected."

Barb's father now spoke. "You know you could destroy the farmer?"

Sara had prepped Carbonne for this question. "Yes, but time delays mean state agriculture officials will have to destroy more animals. They'll arrive at Acoma tomorrow ready to act."

Barb's father and uncle whispered a bit. Barb's father spoke again. "It's from George's flock." He motioned toward his brother, who also had short gray hair. "He noticed ten dead prairie dogs on the second day after he allowed twenty sheep to graze in a new pasture last week. We'd seen plague on our lands twenty years ago. He knew what to look for. It's something you don't forget."

George interrupted. "This has been a drier summer than usual. My sheep were stressed. So, I rented access to additional land for my sheep and released twenty animals there. After I saw the prairie dogs, we talked." He pointed to his brother. "I left the twenty animals on the rented land but bought additional alfalfa hay for the rest of my flock and kept them away from those twenty sheep. It was expensive, but I had no choice. Two of my sheep on the rented land had bloody diarrhea two days later. I butchered one and noticed odd bleeding spots on the animal's gut. I was worried."

Carbonne read from his notes. "Sara says state agriculture officials will ask more questions and run tests, but what did you do to prevent contamination of the rest of your flock?" He now looked at George. "How many of your animals are sick now? Sara says there's a chance all your animals have been exposed because you worked with both flocks."

George straightened. "I knew the risks immediately. I ordered my son to care for all my sheep except for the twenty on the rented land." He pointed to a young man further down the table. "I took care of the twenty sheep and didn't go back into my sheds or near the rest of my flocks. I left my boots and clothes in a box on the contaminated pasture. I hosed myself down with a soap solution when I left the rented field every day."

Eunice interrupted. "We looked up old bulletins from the Cooperative Extension Service He followed their advice on how to prevent contamination of our livestock, but we were scared."

George nodded. "After two days, four sheep had died. It was obvious I'd lose all twenty. I couldn't get help from the county extension agent, state officials, or the pueblo environmental officer. So, Eunice called Dan Steele."

Barb's father added, "Dan's a good man. He believes in environmental concerns and like his brother Caleb understands the problems of ranchers."

Eunice added, "I called Dan on Monday because he always goes to the VA on the second Wednesday of the month. George killed another sheep and packaged key tissues. I gave Dan the hair from one of my grandchildren's Halloween costumes because we didn't want him to be identifiable in photos taken at the UPS Store. You know they all have cameras."

Carbonne reviewed his notes. "You haven't answered Sara's question. How many animals are sick now?"

George gulped. Tears streaked down his wife's face, "None. I took the day off from work on Tuesday, killed the rest of the sheep on the rented pasture and burned their carcasses and even my boots. My son is still tending the rest of my sheep. None are sick."

Carbonne eyed his notes. "Remember, I'm reading the questions given me. Are you sure you didn't take several to the meat packing plant?"

George sighed. "You can check at the plant. I called in sick on Tuesday to do the work. If I sent any of the twenty animals to the plant, I'd contaminate the whole plant. We would have to close for several days to decontaminate it. Bad for business. It would lose money."

Carbonne thought George's last comments were strange. Why would he care if the plant lost money? But that reinforced what he already knew. As a city boy, he didn't understand farmers and ranchers. He looked around the table. No one was eating. He'd destroyed this dinner. He might as well continue. "It sounds to me like you behaved responsibly. However, you were lucky. I don't think anyone but Sara would have thought to send the package to a vet diagnostic lab."

Barb nodded. "No one on the bomb squad did."

Carbonne stared alternately at Eunice and George. "You could have spread the plague with your box. State health officials told me those handling contaminated meat sometimes develop the plague."

All those around the table now were studying their laps.

"Unfortunately, I have more bad news." Carbonne cleared his throat. "The FBI believes Dan Steele was killed in Albuquerque on Wednesday morning."

There were gasps from the Lewises.

Carbonne studied the faces around the table, particularly George's and his brother's faces. They all looked shocked. "I found Dan Steele's hand—I should say his butchered hand—at the sewer plant on Thursday. We have a photo of him wearing a gray wig at the UPS Store on Tuesday. He reported his driver's license lost to Albuquerque Police early on Wednesday morning but didn't show up for his medical appointments at the VA on Wednesday afternoon."

Eunice had tears in her eyes. "You can't think we're involved? Dan is—or was—our friend."

Barb stared at Carbonne is disbelief. "They all have alibis. They were all at work on Wednesday."

Carbonne said softly. "I know. We checked."

Eunice sighed, "The bad man on Friday knew."

"Ma, don't go into your superstitions. Now's not the time." Barb sounded annoyed. "I already had to explain to my boss that you didn't mean evil when you said bad."

Carbonne was pleased Eunice had given him the perfect transition into another difficult question. "Eunice, why did you call Frank McCoy 'bad?'"

She looked puzzled.

"The man who talked to you and your sister-in-law is named Frank McCoy. Was he nasty? Did he threaten you?"

Eunice looked at her sister-in-law. "No threats. Too nosy. But good because he got a state ag official here later in the day."

Her sister-in-law nodded in agreement.

Carbonne tried again. "Why did you call him bad?"

She looked down. Her voice reverted from that of a confident woman to a singsong high pitch. "I felt doom around him. Sadness."

Carbonne took a deep breath and texted the agents and the Acoma police chief in the cars to come to the house. "You were right. He had an accident about an hour later."

Everyone gasped.

"But it wasn't an accident. He was run off the road by three trucks." He looked around the table. They stared at him expectantly. "The FBI knows three of you took off work on Friday."

Silence. A knock on the door. Barb rose from the table and let the agents in. They said nothing.

Carbonne stood. "Where were you on Friday around noon?" He pointed at George, Barb's father, her brother, and her male cousins.

Eunice sucked in her breath. "Tell them. No more secrets."

Barb's father spoke slowly, weighing his words. "We have an airtight alibi. We had a business meeting with the manager of our family trust. You see, we're the owners of the meat packing plant in Grants. The manager of the trust is our old veterinarian. Ma…" He pointed at Eunice. "Call him now."

Eunice pulled out her phone, dialed, and handed it to Carbonne. When an old man answered, Carbonne identified himself and asked questions. He quickly realized this was the man that agents had talked to yesterday. After the short phone conversation ended, Carbonne said, "Why the secret?"

Barb's father spoke slowly as before. "We can't work in the plant if everyone knows we own it."

George quickly added. "We could, but it would be awkward. We wanted an honest, clean place to process our meat."

Barb's father said, "When the past owner wanted to close the business ten years ago, we knew we had a problem. We needed a place to sell our animals. None of us could do it alone, but we could if we pooled our resources. We also knew we didn't want to run the plant. We're ranchers."

George nodded in agreement with his brother's statement. "And Caleb Steele is a good manager."

Carbonne shook his head. "I'll be blunt. How did Melvin Melendez's accident happen in your well-run plant?"

Eunice said, "Tell him."

Barb's father hesitated. "My son told me Melvin Melendez was high on the day of the accident. I ignored him."

For the first time, a younger man spoke. "No, you said Melvin was often strange."

"Then I noticed Diaz was acting odd. He's not helpful around the plant, but that day he checked several pieces of equipment along the line, including the hide remover."

Barb's father spoke even more slowly, pausing frequently. "We were concerned when Elijah Wood walked in an hour later… and Hank Diaz ran out. I called Elijah out to the pen to see if he knew what was wrong with Hank. He acted dumb as usual. Then I heard the screams."

Carbonne and the other four agents questioned family members for another two hours. They made no arrests but warned all the men to not leave the state until the FBI contacted them again. Before they left,

Carbonne asked one last question. "We are all puzzled. Why did you put an old alarm clock in the package you sent Sara?"

Eunice waved her hand. "That was my idea. I thought the bomb squad in Mercado would be called if a ticking package was delivered to Dr. Almquist in Mercado. That meant my daughter would be called to examine the package. Eventually, she'd tell me about it. I figured it was as if I sent a letter by certified mail through the post office."

Barb didn't speak during the ride back to Albuquerque.

CHAPTER 35: FBI Special Agent Ulysses Howe

"I remembered something important."

"Sara," said Ulysses as he put his phone on speaker mode so that Ian Homes could hear. "I thought you were going to relax today and enjoy time with Sanders."

"I did. That's why I finally remembered a minor incident. You know I think better when I relax. Anyway, as we cooked Sunday dinner, Sanders pestered me to think about Bug and my weekly pet therapy visit to VA patients last Tuesday. He was convinced that Maria's threat was based on a recent event. I had a nagging feeling that the event had occurred at the VA. After a while, I remembered that I saw a young biker, too young and healthy to be among the guys assembled at the picnic bench by Building Two at the VA." Sara sighed. "After dinner, Sanders and I played with photos of our suspects. I was sure the young man was Elijah Wood when Sanders put a long black braid, a black shirt, and headband on Elijah's image."

"Is that it? You can identify Elijah Wood as being at the VA at about the same time as Dan Steele."

"No, there's more. Remember, I told you that I'd never met Pigeon, but his face looked strangely familiar."

"And I told you that your imagination was working overtime because you'd seen so many photos of him."

"Well, as I thought about Elijah, I remembered thinking how pathetic the man sitting next to Elijah looked—a tall, pale man dressed in black. Sanders played with photos. It all clicked when he put black hair, biker's regalia, a black sleeveless T-shirt, and a headband on Pigeon's image. Then I remembered there were three of them—a biker son and I assumed his dad and mom. The latter two were attempting to look young with long black hair, but they really looked ridiculous."

"Not sure how your memory works, but this might be the wedge we need to get Elijah Wood and Gina Diaz to talk." Ulysses smiled at Ian. "Ian had a successful afternoon with Jack Daniels. Of course, it was the result of the tip that Rose gave me. This morning agents located Pigeon's blackmail tapes in the attic of the garage of the safe house in Belen. I'll let Ian tell you."

"I worked with Jack Daniels all afternoon. I began by playing the tapes we found in the attic of the safe house for him." Ian glanced at Ulysses. "I'd like to thank Pigeon's wife, Rose, personally for telling us where to find Pigeon's tapes." His gaze returned to the phone on Ulysses's desk. "In the first tape, Diaz discreetly said, 'Thanks for getting Melvin Melendez in the mood. He didn't survive his accident.' Now listen to what Elijah Wood told Pigeon."

Ian played the second tape. Sara thought she'd gag as Elijah gave a lurid description of how he killed Dan Steele and dismembered the body. Elijah ended his message to Pigeon with, 'It was as easy as butchering a sheep. I could do the same to Jack.'"

Sara exhaled loudly. "Boy, I didn't see that coming. How did Elijah contain himself so well when Carbonne and I interviewed him on Saturday? In this tape, Elijah's voice sounds different—higher, more excited, and alert."

Ulysses shook his head and sighed. "I've arranged for an experienced psychiatrist from Quantico to talk to Elijah before his arraignment. I'm concerned any lawyers defending Elijah will make an insanity claim. However, he's not requested a lawyer yet. At least, the tape unnerved Jack. Again, I'll let Ian explain."

Ian spoke more rapidly this time. "As Jack listened to the last tape, he began to shake. Afterwards, he said, 'Don't know which crazy bastard is worse.' Then he supplied one detail after another on Pigeon and Elijah." Ian looked at his notes. "I won't go through them now."

Ulysses clapped Ian on the shoulder. "He did such a good job, I had only one question for Jack Daniels. Why did you stick around and work for Pigeon? Jack said, 'Pigeon liked to brag about his exploits. Made it clear he'd have me killed the same way if he ever suspected I crossed him.'" Ulysses cleared his throat. "I think that comment also explains Diaz's behavior for the last thirty years. He was trapped as long as Pigeon was alive."

Sara sighed. "Never would have thought Jack Daniels would be the first one to crack, but that tape was chilling. Who's the lucky one who gets to interview Elijah?"

"Carbonne." Ulysses didn't add that he was still debating whether he would participate in the interview or watch it. He doubted his rank would impress Elijah, but thought Ian's time would be better spent with Gina Diaz. "Carbonne is due back from Potters Place any minute. He had a good day. The Lewises are innocent except for the bad judgment of sending you the contaminated package."

"Good. I was rooting for them. And how's Frank McCoy?"

"Weak. Tom thinks he's holding on… waiting for something."

"Oh. Wish I could help."

Ulysses had sensed the attraction Sara felt for Frank McCoy and didn't want to extend this discussion, especially with Sanders probably listening to Sara's comments. "Thanks for calling. We've got a lot of interviews to do yet today."

***

Carbonne slid across the table a doctored photo of Elijah as a biker with a long black braid, black headband, and black T-shirt with the sleeves cut off. For the first time during the interview, Elijah didn't yawn and close his eyes in boredom. He tensed.

"Is this how you looked last Tuesday when you met Pigeon—I mean Mr. M—at the VA?"

Elijah began to shake violently. Ulysses wondered if he should summon a medic when the young man continued to shake for more than a minute.

Carbonne was less sympathetic. He slid another photo across the table. "We know you had a long braid. Look at this photo. We found it at your home. Why did you cut the braid off?"

Elijah stopped shaking but didn't speak. He just stared at Carbonne.

"Your mother said the photo was taken several months ago at Easter. She was helpful when agents talked to her and searched her trailer on the Zuni Pueblo."

Ulysses thought Carbonne's characterization of Elijah's mother was so false that Elijah would know Carbonne was lying. Elijah's mother had admitted the agents to her home only after the Zuni police chief had shown her a warrant, and all she said during the hour-long search of her residence was, "Elijah is a good boy," over and over again. Ulysses figured he was right when Elijah yawned and began to close his eyes.

Carbonne responded in anger. "Do you know what we found in her freezer?"

Elijah opened his eyes and gasped.

"We've got it here? Do you want to see it?"

Elijah shook a bit and then began to hum.

"The lab crew say it's a finger."

Elijah's humming became louder.

"We think it's Dan Steele's finger—his ring finger. Did you cut it off after you killed him? Or did you cut it off while he was still alive? The lab thinks the latter."

Elijah kept humming.

Carbonne repeated the questions several times and got the same response. Ulysses slid a note across the table to Carbonne before he stood and left the interview room.

Elijah blinked. "Glad he's leaving. I like your woman partner better. She's nice. Too bad…" He began to hum again.

Carbonne thought Elijah was referring to Sara. "Why is it too bad?"

Ulysses watched Carbonne and Elijah from the observation room.

Carbonne repeated, "Why is it too bad? If you answer questions about my partner, I might arrange for you to get a corn dog—as I remember that's what you wanted the last time we talked."

Elijah licked his lips. "Mr. M didn't like her."

"Why?"

"She saw us at the VA."

"What do you mean? Who are 'us?'"

"Mr. M., Gina, and me."

"Why were you there?"

"Mr. M wanted to talk to Gina." Elijah shrugged.

"Why?"

"Don't know." Elijah looked down.

Carbonne reached across the table and lifted Elijah's head. "I don't believe you. I think you know why Mr. M wanted to talk to Gina."

Elijah shrugged. "The dried-up little finger made him nervous. I thought it was cool."

Carbonne blanched, thought for a couple of seconds, and smiled. "Help me understand. Did you put the dried-up finger in Mr. M's son's lunch bag?"

Elijah began to hum.

"Don't know about you, but a corn dog sound pretty good to me. Cut the crap. Did you put the dried finger in a red lunch bag in a school locker?"

"No. The kid left his lunch bag on his bench while he was on the playground before classes began."

Carbonne sighed. "Did you put the dried finger in the lunch bag then?"

Elijah nodded.

"Who gave you the dried-up finger?"

Elijah smiled. "The crazy broad—Gina."

Elijah closed his eyes. "I like mustard on my corn dog."

"You haven't finished your end of our bargain. Why was it too bad Mr. M didn't like my partner?"

Elijah sighed.

"Maybe two corn dogs?"

"Mr. M told me to go to her house and take care of her after I was through with Dan, but she wasn't there."

                                                    J. L. Greger

Carbonne stood and raised his hand. Before Carbonne could do something foolish, Ulysses put on the intercom and said, "Mr. Carbonne report to me *now.*"

"Add a Dr. Pepper to the order, and I'll tell you who drove the gravel trucks." Elijah groaned. "Guess you'd better send in a lawyer for me, too."

***

The lawyer for Gina Davis stopped Ulysses before he entered a second interview room. "I'm letting this interview go on because it's obvious Gina Diaz has done nothing criminally wrong. Furthermore, her comments and actions are proving that she is a confused woman, incapable of knowing the consequences of her actions."

Ulysses knew the lawyer's second comment was true when he opened the door to the interview room. Gina Diaz was stroking Ian Homes's hand as she said, "Oh dear, you're interrupting my talk with my favorite redhead." She pointed to the marshal sitting at the table. "Of course, he's been here the whole time, too."

Although Ulysses empathized with Carbonne as he sorted through the diabolical thoughts and actions of Elijah Wood, he pitied Ian for enduring the ramblings of Gina Diaz. Both interviews had lasted for over two hours.

Gina began to sing. "He's not perfect, but I love him." She closed her eyes as she sang her ditty several times.

The marshal cursed under his breath, "Not again. Took us an hour to learn she's talking about Pigeon, not her brother Hank Diaz.

"What?" Ulysses sat down. "Do you have everything on tape?"

Ian nodded.

Ian smiled as he gently pushed Gina's hands onto the table. "Tell my boss, why you were angry with your brother Hank and your sister Lily."

"Must I?" A tear dripped down her cheek when Ian nodded yes. "They ruined my romance with Melvin Mueller, the richest boy in town."

"How?"

"Lily wrote those awful letters to Melvin. They scared him. I don't want to talk more."

"Oh please, Gina."

Gina began to stroke Ian's hands again. "But he wasn't scared after I found a dried-up finger in a dresser drawer in the guest room at Lily's house." She blushed. "He was grateful. I wanted to keep him grateful. So, I didn't let him have the finger until… he was in danger. Then I gave it to Elijah Wood—such a nice boy—to deliver to Melvin's son, Noah."

The marshal impatiently said, "We don't need all the details now. What did Melvin do?"

Gina smiled. He told me to meet him at the VA by Building Two—near where I worked. He said he'd be dressed as biker. I wanted to look my best." She pulled her hands through her hair. "So, I wore my wig with long black hair." She batted her eyelids. "You know my hair used to be black… and long."

CHAPTER 36: Sara on Monday

"Sara, a day away from the building was good for you. You look better, and your clues helped us interview Elijah Wood and Gina Diaz." Ulysses hesitated. "First, I'd better tell you—Frank McCoy died a couple of hours ago without ever talking."

Sara had prepared herself for the inevitable, but tears still welled up in her eyes. "I remembered last night who had told me 'I'd seen too much.' It was Frank McCoy. That suggests he had widespread contacts with the drug cartels and explains Maria's comment to Sanders." She wiped a tear from the corner of her eye.

Ulysses cleared his throat. "Unfortunately, everything we've learned in the last twenty-four hours has confirmed our suspicions. Frank was a drug czar in Texas and was in the process of replacing the Butcher Don in New Mexico."

"Let's change the topic. How did the interview with Elijah go? Did my clues help?"

Carbonne must have been eager to change the topic too because he stopped pulling a bottle of water from Ulysses's refrigerator. "The interviews yesterday made our conversation with him on Saturday look easy. We…"

Ulysses interrupted, "The bottom line is that Elijah killed Dan Steele on orders from Pigeon. It seems Pigeon was upset that Dan had recognized him at the VA and spoke to him. Evidently Pigeon and Elijah were at that time discussing how to arrange Frank McCoy's accident."

Carbonne added, "Elijah also killed the kidnapper who escaped from the safe house with Pigeon. We assumed Pigeon had done that murder, but Elijah tripped himself up by lying that he waited for Pigeon in his car at the museum. He actually waited for Pigeon in the garage of the house where we found the dog. Now some weird stuff. Elijah complained Pigeon wouldn't give him 'time' to collect a 'souvenir' after Elijah stabbed the kidnapper."

Sara blinked. "I don't understand how Pigeon turned Elijah from an errand boy into a killer."

Ulysses nodded. "We don't know, but Elijah said Pigeon cut off Elijah's braid before they left the VA on Tuesday and told him he could 'earn it back' by killing Dan…" Ulysses placed his hand on Sara's shoulder. "…and you."

Sara shuddered. After thirty seconds, she said, "I guess… I really did see too much." She blinked repeatedly. "I owe you two and the marshals my life for putting me in protective custody."

Ulysses pulled a diet cola from his refrigerator and handed it to Sara. "Are you ready for more?"

Sara nodded. "Have you found Pigeon? I'll feel safer when I know he locked up."

Ulysses settled back in his chair. "First, we have to tell you about Gina Diaz. Let's say that Gina triggered many of the actions of the last week after she overheard one of Hank's phone conversations and realized Pigeon might be in danger. She panicked and gave Dan Steele's mummified finger—that she'd had for years—to Elijah Wood and asked him to put it in Noah's lunch sack on Monday. As expected, Pigeon rushed to meet her at the VA on Tuesday."

"Wait." Sara held up her hand. "This doesn't make sense. How did Gina get Dan Steele's finger?"

Carbonne winked at Sara. "Love is blind. Seems she's had a crush on Pigeon since they were kids together in Las Vegas."

Ulysses drummed his fingers on the table. "Let's get to the bottom line. In 2010, Gina spent the weekend at Frank's and Lily's home and took a dried-up finger from a box in a dresser in their spare bedroom. Gina had heard rumors and showed the finger to Pigeon, but insisted on keeping it. Lily and her daughter were killed in an accident several days later."

"What will happen to Gina?"

Ulysses shook his head. "I've had long conversations with federal and state prosecutors and everyone's lawyers this morning. Gina won't be charged with anything if she testifies at the upcoming trials. We all believe she didn't understand the consequences of her actions, and still doesn't." He paused. "I might as well summarize the prosecutor's decisions in regard to the others. A federal prosecutor will arraign Elijah Wood tomorrow for murdering Dan Steele and one kidnapper, abetting the murder of Frank McCoy, and racketeering. None of us ever want him released because we think he'll kill again. The prosecutors and the U.S. Marshal Service will honor their commitments to Jack Daniels. We all think Pigeon and Elijah took the fun out of criminal activities for him."

Sara thought for a second. "Where's Pigeon? And what about Frank Diaz?"

Ulysses glanced around his office, picked up a gift bag from his desk, and placed it in front of Sara. "Before I forget, let's take time for a bit of fun. This is from Tom. He wanted to be here today but after spending forty-eight hours at University Hospital supervising all our injured agents, suspects, and victims, he had to take a break."

Sara pulled a bag of dog treats from the gift bag and read the note.

Sara and Bug,

After I leave the Secret Service in a month, I want to develop a canine unit, which uses dogs to relax witnesses and to generate interest among school children in the science and non-violent aspects of criminal investigation. Thank you.

Tom, not "Old Tom"

Sara swiped at her eyes. "Bug and I are touched. Please thank him."

"Back to business." Ulysses opened a file on his computer. "This morning, we tackled Hank, Diaz, who for more than twenty hours had refused to talk to agents."

Sara interrupted, "Before I forget, I have something to add. I talked to Lydia Griegos this morning before she left to inspect farms in the Acoma area and collect samples. She thought it unlikely that she'd have to order the rest of the Lewises' sheep destroyed." She turned to Carbonne. "Gil Andrews called me and gave me the details of *your* trip to Potter's Place. He thinks you really impressed Barb."

Carbonne reddened. "Doubt it."

"Gil says Barb hopes you'll call her." She handed Carbonne a slip of paper with Barb's phone number. She laughed at Carbonne's shocked expression. "Don't underrate yourself."

Ulysses roared with laughter. "Our budding Casanova shocked me when he started his questions with Diaz by saying, 'I know you love Rose and your son Noah. If you could start over, what would you do?' That was a great psychological approach."

Carbonne didn't blush this time. "Just because I go undercover as a bum, doesn't mean I'm insensitive." He turned from Ulysses to Sara. "Diaz said he'd marry Rose, officially adopt Noah, change his name, and forget his past. Then he was ready to answer questions."

Ulysses scanned his computer screen. "Although Frank McCoy's plan to kidnap and kill Pigeon was ostensibly to take control of the drug trade in New Mexico, it was really about revenge... and love. Frank wanted to know why his wife and daughter were killed—and hear it from the suspected killer. Thus, Frank hired gang members to kidnap Pigeon from his home in Las Vegas last Thursday, but Gina warned Pigeon by arranging for Elijah to put Dan's finger in Noah's sack on Monday. Like I said earlier, Gina set in motion many of the events of the last week."

Carbonne interrupted, "I want to remind Sara of a major point. Only Gina and Pigeon knew Lily was the writer of the four notes that Caleb Steele gave us. Diaz heard Gina's story for the first time on Friday night from Pigeon."

Sara gasped. "No wonder Diaz was angry with Gina on Saturday morning. Are you sure Frank McCoy didn't know about the letters?"

Carbonne shook his head. "Asked Diaz. He said if Frank had known about Lily's letters to Pigeon, he would have known the motive for his wife's murder. There would have been no need to kidnap Pigeon. But he suspected that Gina finally told Frank something about Lily's notes at the bar on Thursday night. The main detail that Gina and Hank agreed on was Lily was too gutsy for her own good, even at seventeen when she wrote the first note."

Ulysses cleared his throat. "Back to Pigeon's kidnapping. Diaz reported Pigeon had called him on Monday night, and made it clear he would kill Rose and Noah slowly and painfully if Diaz didn't help him escape from Frank McCoy. Diaz was frantic. He told Pigeon to request a safe house in Belen. Then he went to work adapting Frank McCoy's plans into a fake escape. He admitted he knew Frank was right—it was time to stop Pigeon, but first he had to separate Pigeon from Rose and Noah."

Sara frowned. "I don't understand. Why did Diaz get into a car with Elijah and Pigeon at the thrift shop in Belen? He'd already separated Pigeon from his family. It was suicidal."

Ulysses nodded. "Bothers me, too. There are a couple points to consider. Diaz thought his presence at the meat packing plant in Grants during the kidnapping in Belen gave him an alibi. Pigeon ruined the alibi when he called Diaz at ten and threatened to kill Noah if Diaz wasn't at the thrift shop in Belen by one. Diaz was also unsure whether the kidnappers with Rose and Noah would take Pigeon's advice or follow his earlier orders."

"Okay," Sara frowned. "That explains why Diaz rushed to Belen, not why he got in the car with Elijah and Pigeon."

Ulysses looked at the table and spoke slowly. "The SWAT, really all of us, may have misinterpreted the kidnappers' last message… and acted too quickly. Diaz claims 'clean up' meant—leave no fingerprints or evidence behind. The last two gunmen planned to sneak away." He gulped. "I think Diaz told the truth because the Belen police found two unclaimed cars parked four blocks from the safe house."

Carbonne interrupted, "We all feel bad about their deaths, but we'd given them plenty of chances to surrender."

"Diaz was shocked when Pigeon showed up without any of the kidnappers. Then Pigeon rattled him more by bragging that he thought Noah was dead." Ulysses frowned. "I think he overplayed his hand and Diaz decided he had nothing to lose."

Carbonne snorted. "Don't forget Diaz had a backup plan. He brought not only booze, like Elijah said, but also Rohypnol, the date rape drug."

Ulysses scanned through a computer file. "A federal prosecutor will arraign Hank Diaz tomorrow for the second-degree murder of Pigeon, aka Melvin Mueller, and manslaughter in the death of Melvin Melendez."

Sara stared at him disbelief. "Why not first-degree murder for both?"

Ulysses drummed the table with his fingers. "The prosecutor was convinced it was impossible to convict Diaz for the first-degree murder of Melvin Melendez because the defense could claim it was an accident that got out of control. He originally had planned to charge Diaz with first-degree murder for the death of Pigeon."

Carbonne interrupted again, "Until he heard the tape of my interview. Diaz asked about Frank McCoy as soon as I started to talk to him. I told him his brother-in-law was dying. Diaz agreed to a 'full confession,' if we would take him to Frank's bedside."

Ulysses shook his head. "I was opposed, but Tom agreed with Carbonne. He thought Frank was waiting for someone as he kept moaning 'Lily.' I gave in."

Carbonne wiped tears from his eyes. "Diaz grabbed Frank's hand as soon as he entered Frank's room at the hospital and whispered, 'Old friend, I avenged Lily. She knows. I dumped his body in the ravine where he killed her. Thanks for letting me save Rose and Noah. Be happy with Lily. Tell her I miss her.' Frank died less than five minutes later with Diaz holding his hand."

Ulysses glared at Carbonne. "After the prosecutor listened to the tape of Diaz's comments to Frank, he said, 'If the jury hears this tape, I'll be lucky to convict him of second-degree murder."

Carbonne laughed. "The prosecutor isn't sentimental. He knows Diaz will provide better testimony against the Butcher Don and many gang leaders in the drug cartel than Pigeon. Diaz is believable and has kept good records. The prosecutor only had to promise to create new identities for Rose and her son and get them out of the Southwest immediately."

Ulysses smiled. "This morning, we had another major success. The Inspector General at USDA asked the FBI to review the records of all meat inspectors in FSIS, beginning with those in Texas and New Mexico." Ulysses closed his computer lid. "It will take time, but it is apt to strengthen our case against the Butcher Don and his cohorts."

Sara wiped her eyes. "On a more positive note, I have a question. Do all these new developments mean that I don't need protection before the trial, because much of my testimony is now supported by statements from Jack Daniels and Hank Diaz?"

Both Ulysses and Carbonne nodded yes.

"Can I travel internationally?"

Again, both men nodded yes.

"Good. Sanders figured as much and stayed at my house today to apply for our visas to India and to book our flights. Sanders, Bug, and I will fly to Washington next week. Bug will spend two to three weeks in his favorite dog spa, while Sanders and I spend a couple weeks in northern India during Diwali, the Hindu festival of lights. I think he has a surprise for me at the Taj Mahal."

Carbonne snorted, "About time he got up his guts."

Sara sniffed. "He's got plenty of guts. But it's not easy to be romantic when I'm worrying about a pound of flesh. You know this case was about revenge, like *The Merchant of Venice*, but sheep tripe and prairie dog guts are viscera not really flesh."

Ulysses shook his head as he pulled a bottle of champagne from his refrigerator. "I have one more announcement. After the trials for the Butcher Don and his cohorts are over, I'm retiring. In the meantime, Carbonne has agreed to leave the streets, clean up his act, and be the assistant director here." He popped the cork.

Carbonne chuckled, "Sorta."

THE END

THE SCIENCE BEHIND THE STORY

• At least one of the security problems that Sanders dealt with at the embassy in Havana is based on real world events. U.S. government personnel serving at the embassy in Cuba reported neurological symptoms in 2016 and 2017. A medical team from the University of Pennsylvania found the symptoms were caused by exposure to "direction audible and sensory phenomena" of unknown cause (*Journal of the American Medical Association, 20 March* 2018; 319 [issue 11]:1125-133). More recently, Canadian researchers have suggested a different cause for the neurological symptoms among the embassy staff in Havana—the Cuban government's use of fumigants to combat the Zika virus (*Science,* 27 November 2019; 365:1356).

All the comments made about the plague and *Yersinia pestis* in the novel are true.

• Plague (formerly called the Black Death) is an infectious disease caused by the bacterium *Yersinia pestis.* Symptoms in humans vary with the type of the infections: fever, headaches, painful swelling of lymph nodes (bubonic form), tissue blackening (septicemic form), and shortness of breath, coughing, and chest pain (pneumonic form).

The bubonic and septicemic plagues are usually spread by flea bites or by handling infected animals. The pneumonic form is spread through the air via infectious droplets. Without treatment thirty to sixty percent of bubonic-type cases and all the pneumonic-type cases are fatal in humans (WHO on Plague, 31

October 2017; http://www.who.int/news-room/fact-sheets/detail/plague). Antibiotics reduce the mortality rate to ten percent.

• A handful (usually fewer than ten) cases of plague in humans are reported most years in rural areas of the western United States. The source is wild rodents, particularly prairie dogs, and their fleas. The pathways of transmission of plague and the source of plague in these wild rodents is controversial but their effect is not. Mortality is nearly a hundred percent among wild rodents—hence the term "prairie dog die-off" (*Ecohealth*, June 2016; 12[2]:415-27 and *Emerging Infectious Diseases*, June 2008; 14[6]: 941-3).

The comments on ruminants and meat packing in the novel reflect modern veterinary and meat processing practices.

• The gastrointestinal tracts of ruminants (cattle, sheep, goats) include four stomach compartments. The first three (rumen, reticulum, and omasum) serve to predigest food. The rumen is, in essence, a fermentation vat where bacterial enzymes break down the cellulose in grasses and grains, which are not digested by mammalian enzymes. The fourth compartment (abomasum) looks and functions like the human stomach.

Adult ruminants can develop ulcers (bleeding sores) in their abomasums as occurred in sheep on the Lewises' farm. The ulcers can be caused by viruses, cancer, and anorexia due to stress, but not by *Yersinia pestis* infections. The ulcers often go undiagnosed unless perforation of the stomach lining has occurred and blood losses are large. ("Abomasal Ulcers" in *Merck Veterinary Manual*, https://www.merckvetmanual.com/digestive-system/diseases-of-the-abomasum/abomasal-ulcers).

• The U.S. meat processing industry is highly regulated. The Food Safety and Inspection Service (FSIS) of the Department of Agriculture (USDA) ensures the meat in interstate commerce is safe to eat largely through the efforts of over seven thousand certified meat inspectors in more than six thousand meat packing plants (https://www.fsis.usda.gov).

• The Occupational Safety and Health Administration (OSHA) regularly monitors safety in meat packing plants in the U.S. because the industry has been identified as one of the most dangerous for workers (https://www.osha.gov/Publications/OSHA3108/osha3108.html). Even so, workplace accidents, such as those noted in this novel occur ("The Chain Never Stops" in *Mother Jones*, July/August 2001; https://www.motherjones.com/politics/2001/07/dangerous-meatpacking-jobs-eric-schlosser).

ABOUT THE AUTHOR

J. L. Greger is a biologist and research administrator from the University of Wisconsin-Madison turned novelist. She lives in New Mexico with Bug, the prototype for the pet therapy dog who appears in her mystery/thriller novels.

She likes to include tidbits on science, the American Southwest, and international travel in the novels of her Science Traveler Series.

- ***The Flu Is Coming.*** In the first book in the series, a woman scientist traces the spread of a deadly new flu virus among the frantic residents of a quarantined New Mexico community. (Finalist for a New Mexico/Arizona Book Award)

- ***Murder…A Way to Lose Weight.*** A dean in a medical school helps police discover whether an ambitious young "diet doctor," disgruntled patients, or old-timers with buried secrets are killers. (Winner of 2016 Public Safety Writers Association [PSWA] contest and finalist for a New Mexico/Arizona Book Award)

- ***Ignore the Pain.*** A woman scientist learns too much about the coca trade and too little about a sexy new colleague while on a public health assignment in Bolivia.

- ***Malignancy.*** A woman tries to escape the clutches of a drug lord and accepts a risky assignment as science consultant in Cuba. (Winner of 2015 PSWA contest).

- ***I Saw You in Beirut.*** A woman's past provides clues for the extraction of a nuclear scientist from Iran. The author's experiences as a science and education consultant in the Untied Arab Emirates and Lebanon are featured.

- ***Riddled with Clues***. A homeless man and a woman scientist are targeted by drug gangs after she listens to the strange tale of an undercover drug agent about his war experiences. The memories of an actual CIA agent in Laos during the Vietnam War are featured. (Finalist for a New Mexico/Arizona Book Award)

- ***A Pound of Flesh, Sorta***. Police and a woman scientist can't decide whether a package of sheep guts contaminated with the bacteria that causes the plague is a plea by a whistleblower or a threat from gang leaders awaiting trial.

Learn more at: http://www.jlgreger.com